Praise for the works of M. Malone

"I am now officially in love with the Alexander family."
--*Smitten by Reading (Grade: A-) on One More Day*

"Malone has a winner with The Alexanders series! Please keep them coming!"
--*Joyfully Reviewed on One More Day*

"Malone does an exceptional job ... showcasing how two very different people can fall in love."
--- *4 stars, RT Book Reviews on The Things I Do for You*

"Nicholas is perfect leading man material..."
-- *4 stars, Romance Junkies on The Things I Do for You*

Ms. Malone does an excellent job of taking an unconventional way of coming together and developed it into a true love story. The sexual chemistry between the hero and heroine was off the charts
--*BookKraze Reviews on The Things I Do for You*

"Malone gives her reader a story full of smart dialogue, compelling characters, and a strong story-line. The Alexanders and their friends will draw you in and keep you coming back for more."
-- *4 stars, Romantic Reads on He's the Man*

Titles by M. Malone

The Alexanders

One More Day
The Things I Do for You
He's the Man
All I Need is You
Say You Will

Blue-Collar Billionaires

TANK
FINN
GABE
ZACK

Future Books
LUKE

He's the Man

the

Man

M. MALONE

CRUSHSTAR ROMANCE

CS
★

Acknowledgments

To the Alexanders super-fans!
I couldn't do this without you.
You are all honorary cousins now :)

Andre—thank you, as always, for holding
things down while I'm off in la-la-land.

Author's Note

When writing about Matt Simmons, a much-beloved character since *Teasing Trent*, I was faced with a quandary. I could do a safe, sanitized happy ending or I could tell his real story. I have such huge respect and appreciation for the members of our armed forces that I decided to write this story the way I truly see it. Your stories are not safe and sanitized, but they *deserve* to be told. To all who have served and the families that support them, thank you for your bravery. Thank you for your service. Thank you for your stories.

I wish I could give you all a happy ending in real life, but all I can do is hope to convey your struggles, fears, and triumphs as compassionately as possible. All I can do is hope to get it right.

Yours,

M. Malone

He's

the

Man

Chapter One

♥

THERE WAS NOTHING in the world Matt Simmons hated more than nagging. Which was unfortunate since his twin sister had lately turned nagging into a full-time occupation.

"No more doctors, Mara. I'm done."

He stood in the kitchen of his sister's town house and stared aimlessly out the window at the sparse patch of grass masquerading as a backyard. Not that he was particularly interested in the yard work waiting for him. It was just better than facing his sister when she was nagging him about something.

"This is important. This is your health." Mara tugged on his arm until he turned around. "I'm worried about you."

Her brown eyes were soft as she looked him over from head to toe. Despite his annoyance, he felt his resistance crumbling. His first conscious memory was of looking into Mara's eyes, so they were pretty much impossible to ignore.

"Man, you're good but you forgot to widen your eyes and look pitiful," he joked. He tugged on the ends of her long, curly dark hair. "It also worked better when you were in pigtails."

She slapped his hand away. "I'm serious. Your shoulder is still bothering you and it's been months. *Months*, Matthew. It's getting worse every day."

"Ugh, don't call me Matthew. You sound just like Mom." He covered his ears with his hands playfully.

Mara stopped in her tracks. "Okay, that was just mean."

He laughed until his sides hurt and eventually Mara joined in. Their mother was notoriously self-absorbed and critical. Usually any comparison to Carolina Simmons was enough to earn him either the silent treatment or a smack on the head.

"That probably was a little below the belt, but I have to work with what I've got over here. You're trying to force me to let a bunch of sadists poke and prod me again. There has to be something besides surgery. No more needles, thanks."

"I understand. I don't want you to go back to the hospital."

"Well, where do you want me to go then?" Matt asked.

"A physical therapist." Mara smiled triumphantly. "There's no needles involved."

"That's the same damn thing and you know it."

"No, it's really not. Plus, you know her. Remember our babysitter who used to live three streets over when we lived in

Vienna?"

"What? The pudgy girl with the glasses? Are you kidding?"

Mara made a face at him. "*Be nice.* She's a physical therapist in Northern Virginia now. Anyway, she promised to work you in on Wednesday. I've heard she's some kind of miracle worker." She turned and dug through her purse until she found her phone. "I know I put the time in my calendar."

"You actually made an appointment?" Matt shouldn't be surprised. Mara had a personality like a freight train. In her excitement to take you where she wanted you to go, she was just as likely to run you over.

Mara held up her hands. "What is the big deal? If it's really just your shoulder, why won't you go and deal with it?" She stopped suddenly, her hand suspended in midair. "It is *just* your shoulder, right?"

Matt pushed away from the counter and walked to the back door.

"Hey, where are you going?" she called.

He pushed his feet into the old pair of sneakers he always wore when he cut the grass. "To chop wood. You're almost out."

"You don't have to do that. Trent can do it—"

"I can do it," he snapped. "I might have a bum shoulder, but that doesn't make me an invalid." Then he slammed the door behind him.

He jogged down the back steps and across the grass to the small woodpile next to the storage shed. The crisp, cold air stung his nostrils with every breath. If he wanted a little peace and quiet, this was the only way he'd get it. Mara hated being cold, so as determined as she was, he doubted she'd come out to bug him while he was splitting logs.

He grabbed the small axe he'd left next to the woodpile. It

shouldn't be that hard since his injury was in his left shoulder and he was right-handed. It was mainly momentum anyway. If he aimed true, gravity would drop the axe with enough force to split the log. When he was ready to start, he took a deep breath and hoisted the axe over his right shoulder. It slipped and he instinctively reached up with his left hand to steady it. Pain lanced up his arm, radiating through his left shoulder and down his back.

"Aw, hell." He bit his lip and turned away from the house in case Mara was watching. He moved his shoulder experimentally, almost losing his breath as the pain rolled through him on a wave of nausea. The axe fell to the ground behind him with a dull thud.

It was a minor miracle that he managed to stay upright. He tried to do the breathing exercises he'd learned in the hospital. *Breathe. Just breathe.* Then he thought *to hell with it* and bent at the knees. Breathing could only do so much.

"When Mara told me I needed to talk to you, I thought she was just being her usual overprotective self."

Matt looked up to see his friend Trent Townsend standing a few feet away. Trent's blond hair had grown out some since the summer and he looked more like the surfer dude he used to be.

Matt chuckled halfheartedly. If Mara couldn't nag him herself, it didn't mean she'd given up. She'd just gotten someone else to do it for her.

Especially now that she and Trent were together.

The thought of his best friend and his sister still gave him a strange pang in his chest. He'd known how they felt about each other for years and he'd even asked Trent to watch over Mara while he was deployed in Iraq last year. In his heart, he'd known what would happen and had even been hoping for it.

Trent was a good guy, one of the best he'd ever known.

It was just that the thought of his baby sister loving someone—hell, one day soon *marrying* someone—made him feel old as hell.

And alone.

"I should have known she'd tell you." Matt stood up, stretching carefully. The nausea seemed to have passed.

"I'm glad she did. You look like shit, amigo."

Matt barked out a laugh. One of the best things about having true friends was knowing they would always tell you the truth. "I look a damn sight better than I feel, I've got to tell you." He took a deep breath. Mara was right.

It was getting worse, not better.

"I'm not going to ask you what's wrong. I'm sure Mara's been doing enough of that. I just hope you know that you can ask me for anything. Anything at all."

Matt nodded. "Yeah, I do know that. You're a great friend. The best a guy could ask for."

Trent cracked his knuckles. "Okay, so I've been sent to tell you the appointment is on Wednesday. Also, to remind you we're having dinner at the Alexanders' on Friday."

"Not on Sunday?"

"They moved dinner to Friday because Nick and Raina will find out what they're having that afternoon. Mara's betting on a little girl. She says that would be karma getting Nick back."

Matt grinned. Their good friend, Nick Alexander, had been a legendary player until hooking up with his wife. He was now totally and completely whipped. He was also totally and completely happy. It was a nice thing to see.

"Karma would be if they had twin girls that were just as gorgeous as Ridley and Raina. Then Nick could spend the next thirty years aiming a shotgun at their boyfriends."

"Even karma wouldn't be that cruel." Without another word, Trent walked over to the fallen axe and picked it up. He split a few logs and gathered them in his arms.

"I'll see you later," Trent yelled over his shoulder as he walked away.

Matt raised his chin in acknowledgment and then went back to trying not to throw up.

♥

PENELOPE LEWIS RUSHED from treatment room 1 at the Northern Virginia Rehabilitation Center. Her day had started off at full throttle and hadn't let up since. She glanced at the clock mounted on the wall of the center's waiting room and groaned under her breath when she saw it was almost noon.

It wasn't even lunchtime and she was already running behind.

She glanced over at her assistant, Georgia Thorne. "Were you able to reschedule my Wednesday afternoon appointments?"

Georgia had been working at the center longer than she had. She was a pretty, petite brunette who kept Penelope's schedule running like clockwork and was pretty much her polar opposite. Despite the fact that she made Penny feel like a galumphing Amazon most days, they had somehow become good friends.

"Yes, I did." Georgia smiled slyly. "Someone canceled that afternoon anyway, so I rearranged a few appointments to give you the entire afternoon. Who is this guy anyway? I've never known you to rearrange your schedule for anyone before. You never talk about your friends or anything other than work, actually."

"Are you trying to say I have no life?" It was hard for Penny to work up any outrage. The truth was, she didn't have much of a life outside work. Something that hadn't really bothered her until recently.

"We've been working together for two years and you know everything about me. My failed attempt to be an actress, you listen to me blabbing about the latest thing my kids are up to, and I'm sure you've gotten an earful many times when James and I are fighting."

Penny conceded the point with a nod. Georgia and her husband were the parents of three precocious little girls and with little time for romance, their marriage had definitely felt the blow. She had been more than happy to lend a sympathetic ear but hadn't wanted to share any details of her own life. What could she say? She'd feel ridiculous talking about her relatively peaceful life while her friend was dealing with so much.

"There's nothing to tell. I'm just... normal, I guess. I work. I sleep. Scott and I order Chinese and watch pay-per-view movies. Occasionally I manage to stay awake until the end. God, that sounds pathetic when I say it out loud."

"It's not pathetic. To a working mom of three what you just described sounds like paradise. James and I used to order Chinese and eat it without interruptions," she said wistfully. "Anyway, tell me about this Army Sergeant VIP we've got scheduled for Wednesday. Is he hot?"

"Um, ew? I used to babysit him, Georgia."

"So what? He could have grown up into G. I. frickin' Joe. I hope he's one of those buff, rugged-looking guys from the Army commercials."

"I seriously doubt it. I'm actually surprised he joined the military. He was a scrawny kid and kind of a brat. He didn't seem to have much respect for authority. Although to be fair, I doubt most nine-year-olds do."

"Sorry to be so nosy. I'm just trying to find out more about you. If Scott didn't drop by to see you, I probably wouldn't even know he existed."

"If it makes you feel better, I'll be sure to tell you the next time we argue about which restaurant to choose."

"Hah hah. Very funny. Well, whatever. I just want you to know you can talk to me about stuff if you need to."

Heat rose along the back of Penny's neck. It was only recently she'd started having doubts about her relationship. The uncertainty had been the cause of many a sleepless night lately. Scott was well educated, patient, and understanding of her crazy schedule. He didn't expect her to whimper or flip her hair and act like a debutante. He respected her. Which was worlds above most of the other guys she'd dated. Their relationship was exactly what she'd always wanted.

Except for the fact that she wasn't sure if she loved him.

She wondered sometimes about why Scott was so understanding of her schedule. Shouldn't he want to see more of her? Couples who were in love wanted to spend lots of time together. They felt deprived when they were separated too long, right? Only she was pretty sure Scott didn't feel desperate to see her or neglected when she worked late.

She figured that was the case because she didn't feel that way either.

Georgia was still watching her, so she shrugged. "Scott and I aren't the most exciting people, so there's really nothing to report. But I promise you'll be the first to know if anything interesting happens."

Georgia handed her a patient file and then backed away. "Okay. I'm holding you to that. I'll order you some lunch."

Penny turned to go to her office and almost smacked into her boss, Charles Winston. She dropped the file she was holding. Several sheets of loose paper slid out as it fell and fluttered to the ground.

"Penelope. Sorry about that."

She tried to mask her annoyance as she knelt and scooped up the papers, placing them carefully back into the folder. Charles didn't even attempt to kneel and assist, just stood over her with his usual pinched look.

Thanks so much for helping, Penny thought irritably.

"I've been looking for you," he said. He had a way of making it sound as if that was her fault.

"Well, you've found me." She held the file close to her chest and started walking toward her office. Charles was forced to follow.

"I was expecting an update on Chris Walters yesterday evening. When I came looking for you, you were already gone."

Penny thought of her appointment the previous day with the star of the area's pro basketball team. He'd hurt his knee at a critical point in the basketball season and many fans thought his team couldn't win the championship without him. So when he'd chosen the Northern Virginia Rehabilitation Center for his physical therapy, it had brought a lot of attention to the center.

It wasn't the first time a high-profile athlete had sought her out, either. It was all about the patient's recovery for Penny but she couldn't deny it brought her an incredible sense of pride that her unconventional methods had gotten the attention of the bigwigs in sports medicine. Enough for her to be specifically sought out by many professional athletes.

"Chris and I worked until about seven p.m. If you missed us, then you must have come pretty late."

Charles sniffed. "I do keep a late schedule. I'm fully

committed to being there for all our patients. Not just the high-profile ones."

Penny whirled around. "I already sent out the e-mail update about Chris to the team. Did you need something else?" The saccharine-sweet tone of her voice must have alerted him that she was on edge. Or maybe it was the steam coming from her ears. Either way, he smiled, or as close to smiling as Charles ever got, and then inclined his head.

"No, Penelope. Nothing else."

Penny walked into her office and closed the door behind her. After several deep breaths, she sat down behind her desk. The nerve of him suggesting that she only cared about the high-profile clients. She was the one constantly campaigning for the center to treat more patients pro bono. Charles hadn't been in favor of the idea until he'd seen how much publicity and attention they'd received as a result. Watching him smile pretty for the cameras now was borderline nauseating.

She flipped open the file for her next appointment. Her next patient had a spinal injury. These were always the trickiest and the ones with the lowest success rates. They were also some of the most determined patients she'd ever had. The ones with the most hope that they could one day walk again.

Most of the patients she treated were coming to her as a last resort. They'd already been through surgery and sometimes multiple rounds of physical therapy. These were patients who wanted more. Her patients weren't happy with just relearning how to walk. They wanted to *run*. They'd been told "no" over and over by doctors, physical therapists and even their own hearts in some cases. They came to her when they weren't sure who else would take them.

Penny was the person willing to take a chance and say "yes." She worked to push her patients past their limits. She thrived on tackling the impossible. In her opinion there was no hard-and-fast point of no return. It was just about how far you were willing to dangle over the edge before you fell.

If only she could be so sure of other areas of her life.

She shook off her lingering unease. There was no time in her life for negative thoughts. She was exactly where she wanted to be, doing exactly what she was meant to.

That was more than enough.

♥

"ARE YOU KIDDING me?" Matt gripped the steering wheel tighter and slowed down as yet another car cut him off. He didn't drive to Northern Virginia that often and each time he did, his subconscious mind blocked out all memory of how bad the traffic was until he was knee-deep in it. Naively, he hadn't thought Wednesday-morning traffic would be this bad.

A mistake he wouldn't be making again.

He let out a repressed grunt when he was forced to slam on the brakes. Again. He looked to his left and hit his horn as a car next to him tried to get in his lane.

"I'm here. There's nowhere to go." He shook his head as the driver gave him the finger.

His cell phone rang and he snatched it up. Normally he wouldn't answer the phone while driving, but it wasn't as if he was actually moving.

Over the last thirty minutes he'd managed to crawl no more than a mile on Interstate 95. He was almost to the point of pulling over and walking the rest of the way.

"It would probably be faster," he mumbled. Then he put his phone to his ear and said, "Hello?"

"Hey, Ace. It's Shep."

"Hey, man, how've you been doing?"

Shep had been in his old unit. He'd been tight with him and a few other guys. They still kept up through e-mail, but he missed hanging out with them. It had been a hard move when he'd been reassigned to a new unit after his injury. Difficult but necessary. He'd been an expert marksman before, but unless he could get his health handled, there was a chance he'd have to consider changing his specialty.

"We're going to be in your area soon, possibly. Cora wants to take a trip to see the national monuments, so I asked Tommy and his wife to come along. I'm not sure when we'll do it, though. Maybe when it's not so cold."

"That would be great. You know you're welcome anytime. Actually, just make sure you let me know first because I'm doing some physical therapy in a different city, so I might not be home."

"How is that going, by the way? I know you had a rough time last year."

After the accident, he'd been too delirious to care much about what was happening to him. He'd had the surgery to fix the tear in his shoulder, but he wasn't sure if there were other things he should have done. He'd been too lost in grief, second-guessing if he could have done more to prevent the way things had turned out. When the pain in his shoulder had started, he'd thought it was just the way it was. It had simply echoed the pain he'd been going through mentally. Pain was all he had known.

Maybe he should have done something else besides the physical therapy. Maybe it was his own fault he wasn't healed.

"Improving slowly. I'm on my way to a physical-therapy appointment now."

"Good. Maybe you'll be back with us soon. I heard we might be deployed again this year. Afghanistan this time. You know there's no one I'd love to experience the desert with more."

Matt forced himself to laugh, swallowing the bitter pill of resentment. He'd been through this once already. His old team had been deployed back to Iraq without him. Being left behind had hurt the first time, but he'd believed he'd be healed and ready to go before the next tour. Now the time was almost here, and he was no better off than he was a year ago.

"Bet on it. I'll call you later."

After they disconnected, Matt threw his phone on the passenger side seat and looked out at the traffic with disgust. He wished he could turn the car around and go home. He didn't really want to waste an hour of someone's time so they could tell him what he already knew.

Matt gritted his teeth and rested his head against the back of his seat. If he hadn't spent the past six months ignoring the increasing levels of pain, he would have already had the second surgery he needed by now. He'd likely have healed enough to be going with his unit when they deployed next week. He'd be back where he belonged instead of just taking up space.

When the next person cut him off, he leaned out the window and screamed, "Pick a lane, jackass!"

Chapter Two

♥

"SERGEANT SEXY IS here." Georgia leaned back against the door and fanned herself with her hand.

Penny sat at her desk, peering into a small handheld mirror. Eyedrops couldn't conceal the effects of exhaustion completely, but it should be enough to keep her from scaring her patients.

"I never knew you had such a fetish for military guys. Does James know about this?"

"I don't have a fetish. I just have *appreciation*. Where have you been hiding this one? No wonder you never talk about your friends. You're keeping them all to yourself."

Penny put the eyedrops back in her bag and stored it in the drawer of her desk. "What are you talking about? I told you I haven't seen either of the Simmons twins in a decade, at least."

"Oh. So you've never seen him as an adult?" Georgia touched the tip of her tongue with her finger.

"Uh no. Why?"

"Nothing. I'll let you see for yourself. It'll be more fun that way." With a wiggle of her eyebrows, she was gone.

Penny shook her head hard to clear it of any lingering fog as she walked down the hall from her office and into the waiting room. There was only a smattering of people waiting: an older woman with a lapful of knitting, a pregnant woman, and two older men chatting in the corner. She turned and called out, "Sergeant Simmons?" No one looked up. She let out a breath and then turned again, bumping into an incredibly wide and incredibly hard chest. "Oh, I'm sorry. I'm—"

The man who stood behind her looked about six feet and had dark hair and eyes. She would have known he was military even without the Army hat he was wearing. He stood too straight, his eyes darting around the room as if on alert for disturbances. That wasn't what made her lose her breath, though.

Maybe it was the muscles stretching the fabric of his cotton tee shirt. It was definitely the eyes, thickly lashed and the color of dark chocolate. Whatever it was, she shivered when his gaze roamed over her lazily. When he got back to her face, his eyes narrowed slightly. Penny shivered when she met his gaze.

He was just so unapologetically *masculine*.

"Uh, hello. You must be Sergeant Simmons." Penny automatically held out her hand.

His lips twitched. "You used to scold me for jumping out of the tree in the backyard and scaring my sister. It's weird for you to call me Sergeant. Please, call me Matt."

Penny was surprised into laughing. "Of course. Matt." Saying his name brought a curious tingle to her belly.

He stepped forward and pulled her into a hug, and she shivered as his arm made contact with her back. He hadn't shaved and the slight stubble on his face left a pleasant rasp of sensation against her cheek when she pulled back.

She swallowed and squared her shoulders, trying to get her equilibrium back. "It's been a long time. How have you been?"

A shadow crossed his face and Penny immediately wanted to kick herself. *He's an injured Army veteran. How do you think he's been? Real smooth, Penny.*

"Let's go back to my office so we can talk." She waited until he fell in step next to her. She'd never been quite so aware of her height before but standing next to Matt, she didn't feel tall and awkward at all. Her height put her at the perfect level to look directly in his eyes. It felt comfortable.

They entered her office and she motioned for him to sit down. He nodded his thanks and sat back.

"So, your sister mentioned on the phone that you've been having some problems with your shoulder."

Penny pulled out her glasses and perched them on the tip of her nose. She flipped open his medical file, which Georgia had gotten faxed from his doctor a few days ago. "I see you're recovering from a dislocated shoulder and you underwent a surgical repair to the glenoid labrum. This should have taken, at most, three months to heal."

"There were complications from the surgery." Matt lifted his arm about a foot higher than his thigh. Suddenly his face twisted. "This is about as far as I can lift my arm without pain."

Penny looked down at the file. "That wasn't documented in

the postoperative notes I see here."

"The problems didn't show up until later."

She closed the file. "So, you had more mobility after the surgery and it declined over time."

Matt looked down. "I did the exercises they gave me at the VA hospital. It just seemed to get more painful. I think it was doing more harm than good. So I just stopped."

"Your physical therapist should have adjusted your treatment. It looks like you only had a month of PT afterward."

"I was told that's all I needed."

"I disagree."

He shrugged. "Yeah, but I'm not convinced there's much to be done. I'm just here so my sister will stop bugging me about it. I don't think doing a few exercises is going to change much."

"A few exercises? Is that what you think we do here?" Penny reminded herself not to get angry. Plenty of people had misconceptions about physical therapy. Not that it didn't rankle to hear her profession dismissed as something no more important than what people did in their living rooms with a workout DVD.

Matt smirked. "No offense or anything. I just need to face reality. My shoulder probably needs more surgery."

"Oh, and you received your medical degree from what school? Because I'm pretty sure you're not a doctor."

The arrogant smile on his face showed he knew he'd gotten on her last nerve. "Right. Look, I'm not trying to put down what you do here. I'm sure this is great for little old ladies recovering from hip replacements, but I need to get back into fighting shape. I can't do my job if I can't raise my arm above shoulder level."

He sat back in his chair, tipping it back until he was balanced on two legs. Part of her hoped he fell. That would wipe the smug smile off his face. Penny pushed his file aside and stood. He let the chair drop back to four legs and stood, too.

"You know, I was completely surprised to hear you'd gone into the Army. You were something of a brat as a kid. I see that hasn't changed."

He sighed. "You're right. That was inexcusable. I got a phone call on the way here that caught me off guard, but I have no right to take it out on you. This whole situation is my fault."

"You got injured in combat, correct?"

He nodded.

"Then it's not your fault."

He looked down at her and Penny felt her resolve weaken. It didn't help that he was impossibly good-looking. Maybe she was just as weak as Georgia. Completely taken in by a handsome man with bedroom eyes. Except she was well aware that a handsome face could easily disguise a hideous soul. Being handsome didn't mean that he was a good guy.

"I want to help you, but I can only do that if you'll let me. I can't promise you a miracle, but no one else can either. All I can promise is that you'll leave here better off than when you came in. Most of my patients go on to lead happy, productive lives. You're young and you were in prime physical condition before your injury. There's no reason you can't do the same."

"Happy? Productive? Tell me this, Penny. These people you've helped, could they hold a rifle steady? Could they jump out of a moving aircraft? If I can't requalify for my unit, then my life won't be happy or productive."

"I can't tell you that you can do those things for sure, Matt.

I'm sorry. But I can promise you this. If you don't let me help you, you definitely won't get there."

"You want to help me?" Matt banged his fist on the desk between them. "Then help me get my life back! Can you do that?"

Penny froze. He looked down at the overturned items on her desk.

"I think we're done here." Penny took a step back when he moved closer. "Please leave or I'm calling security."

After a tense moment when Penny wasn't sure if he was going to leave, he spoke. "I'm sorry. I'm so incredibly sorry. It seems like that's all I feel lately."

Then he left.

Penny stood perfectly still for a moment, then collapsed into her desk chair. Her breath came in short pants until she finally felt her heartbeat begin to settle.

"Well, all right then. Great seeing you again, as well."

♥

MATT STALKED ACROSS the parking lot and stabbed the button on his keychain to unlock his truck. He swung up into the driver's seat and slammed the door, then rummaged in the pocket of his jeans until he found the pack of gum he always carried. It was stupid but the repetitive motion of chewing was strangely calming. He unwrapped a stick and popped it in his mouth. Then he dropped his head to the steering wheel with a groan.

There were a lot of things he resented about his situation. He resented being left behind while his unit was out there doing what needed to be done. He resented his own body for betraying him and not healing properly. But most of all he resented the person he'd become lately. He wasn't the guy who took his shit out on other people. Especially not people who'd gone out of their way to help him.

This is not who I am.

He raised his head and would have screamed like a girl at the face pressed against his driver-side window if his mouth wasn't full. As it was, he almost swallowed his gum.

The brunette who'd checked him in for his appointment stood next to the door, hands on her hips. After his heart settled back down in his chest, he hit the button to lower the window.

"Can I help you?"

She glared at him until he shrank back in his seat. "Come with me. There's something you need to see before you go."

"Okay." Matt got out and followed her as she led them back to the center. They reentered the waiting room and then crossed to a door on the other side of the room.

"So, what's your name?" Matt wasn't sure how to make conversation with a woman who looked like a pissed off pixie.

"I'm Georgia. I'm Penny's assistant." She held up a security badge to the gateway to the left of the door. It emitted a series of clicks before the light flashed green.

"Oh. Okay. I'm Matt—"

"I know who you are." She held the door open, her face still stony. "After you, *Sergeant.*"

Was it his imagination or did she put extra emphasis on his title? Or maybe that was just his guilty conscience. He wasn't representing his fellow soldiers well today, he knew.

They walked down a long hallway and stopped next to a door. Matt had to grab the wall to keep from slamming into her back.

"This is Mrs. Wright." Georgia gestured toward the

porthole window in the door. Matt peered through it. A middle-aged woman was using a set of metal bars to help her walk between them. When he looked again, he saw that one of her legs was shorter than the other.

"She was told that amputation was her best option after a serious skiing accident. Her right leg was completely crushed. No one believed it could be saved, but she refused to amputate. When all the other physical therapists told her a wheelchair was the best she'd ever be able to do, she came to Penny for help. She took her first steps last week."

She allowed him a few moments to observe and then started walking again. They stopped next to another door. He looked through the glass window to see a young girl, no older than nine or ten, lifting a blue ball.

"That's Daisy. She was born with cerebral palsy. It affects her ability to do all the things most children take for granted. Standing, walking, even swallowing. Her insurance only covers a certain amount of therapy. Her mom couldn't afford the additional physical therapy she needed, so Penny convinced our boss to allow the center to provide her therapy pro bono."

Matt watched, enraptured, as the little girl raised the ball slightly higher with the encouragement of the therapist who was helping her. She dropped it, but instead of getting upset, she laughed. Her eyes met his through the window and he pressed a hand against the glass. She raised a hand to wave back and then grinned, revealing a space where one of her front teeth was missing.

Matt looked back at Georgia. "Does she ever turn anyone away?"

"Of course. They call her a miracle worker, but she doesn't have a God complex. She knows that there truly are some people who can't be helped, but she's the only one willing to give people a chance even if the odds are long. Penny likes taking those cases that have a million-in-one chance of success and then making the impossible happen."

Matt followed behind her as she led him down the hall to another room. They entered a small gym area outfitted with blue floor mats, mirrored walls, and various equipment. There was a man in the corner using a machine that required him to lift and lower a weight with his leg. When he flexed his knee, he looked up.

"Is that Chris Walters? The point guard for Washington?"

Georgia folded her arms and glared at him. "He's just one of the athletes Penny has helped over the years. She's pioneered quite a few methods to help players rebound faster after knee surgery. He's recovered so fast he might even be able to play again before the season is over."

Matt glanced at Georgia from the corner of his eye. He knew what she was doing, but that didn't mean it was any less effective. He was suddenly even more ashamed he'd dismissed their work as just helping little old ladies.

"I won't ask how you know that we argued, but I am sorry. I was an idiot."

Georgia whirled around, her eyes furious. "*Damn straight you were.* She could have been at home relaxing today, but she rearranged her schedule to accommodate you."

"I want to apologize, but I'm sure she doesn't want to see me."

Georgia didn't look entirely mollified, but at least she didn't look like she was going to hit him anymore.

"Look, if you really want to apologize then come back tomorrow or Friday. I can't rearrange the schedule for you *again*," she said and cut him an evil look, "but you can slip in between appointments. Maybe if you beg, Penny will still help you. Can you come back tomorrow?"

"I'm not sure. Maybe it's better if I just don't come back. I've caused enough grief as it is."

"Okay, I can't force you into anything. I just hope you take some time and really think before you give up. Penny is your best shot at getting better."

As she walked away, Matt started to follow. What she'd shown him just now was exactly what he needed. A chance at redemption. Hell, it was the reason he'd traveled this far.

But it would take more than a pretty apology to make up for his behavior. He winced. He'd been arrogant, condescending, and worst of all, dismissive of her profession. If he went back in there now, he'd probably just make things worse. Plus, he needed to be sure he was ready for such a drastic lifestyle change. If he convinced Penny to help him and then bailed later, she'd *really* hate him. Matt stopped and then turned the other way.

He'd screwed up enough for one day.

♥

AFTER A FEW wrong turns, Matt pulled up in front of the small bungalow Elliott owned in the city of Springfield. It was small but well kept with bright blue shutters. The postage-stamp-sized lawn was perfectly manicured.

He parked the truck in the driveway and cut the engine. The street was quiet. Elliott had said it was a working-class neighborhood, so most people were gone during the day.

He reached across the seat and grabbed his duffel bag. As soon as he opened the door, icy wind brushed his cheeks. Elliott had disabled his security alarm remotely so Matt wouldn't have to worry about disarming it. He shuffled the keys on his chain until he found the slightly square one Nick had given him the prior day. It slid into the lock easily, but when he tried to turn it, it wouldn't move.

"Of course. Because I need something else to go wrong today." He dropped his duffel bag and used both hands to apply pressure. It didn't move. He took a deep breath and pulled out his cell phone. He dialed Eli's number. He answered on the first ring, his deep baritone rumbling over the line.

"Hey, Eli. I'm sorry to bother you, but I just got to your house and the key isn't working."

"You have to pull the door tight against the frame and then jiggle the key a little. Nick must have forgotten to mention that part."

"Yeah, he did. It's no problem."

Matt pulled the door toward him and then twisted the key. The lock turned easily. "That did it."

He entered the house and set his duffel bag on the floor next to the door. The entryway was narrow and a little dark. He could see the kitchen straight ahead and a small living room to his right. There was a round table next to the door with a stack of mail sitting on it.

"Since my brother obviously wasn't listening, I'll tell you again to make yourself at home. I'm rarely there anymore, so you aren't inconveniencing me at all by being there. My neighbor usually brings the mail in, but I'll tell her not to bother while you're there. I also have a cleaning service that comes every other week to keep it organized, so the sheets and towels should be clean. Feel free to use the master bedroom if you want. If it makes you uncomfortable, there are two guest bedrooms you can use."

Why would it make him uncomfortable to use the master bedroom? Matt supposed some people might feel weird about sleeping in someone else's bed but he was used to Army barracks. Anywhere with a mattress was bliss compared to some of the places he'd slept.

"Thanks. I really appreciate it." They hung up with him promising to bring Eli's mail with him when he drove back the next day.

It wasn't even four o'clock and he was contemplating going to bed. His shoulder was aching slightly and he was definitely stressed out after the day he'd had. Maybe he could order a pizza and watch some TV.

Briefly, he wondered what Penny was doing. She'd been completely different from what he'd expected. When he was a kid, she'd been a sweet, slightly overweight, quiet girl who'd spent most of her time with her nose in a book. He'd assumed she'd be easy to deal with.

You thought she'd be a total pushover.

He could admit it now that he was alone. He'd been expecting a kitten and he'd gotten a tigress. He grinned to himself, remembering the fire in her eyes as she'd faced him down. Not many people could have done that, but she'd held her own. He had a feeling if she ever took him on as a patient she wouldn't give him the gentle but dispassionate encouragement he'd gotten at the hospital. No, she'd kick his ass into shape.

Which was probably exactly what he needed.

He explored the house unashamedly, poking his head into the small guest bath off the kitchen and each of the guest bedrooms. It was a small house but well laid out. Each of the rooms had the bare minimum of furniture needed to be functional. It made him feel slightly better about his own decorating skills.

When he reached the master bedroom, he almost stepped

back out to make sure he hadn't stepped through some kind of time portal. Unlike the rest of the house, which was still plain white, the master bedroom was painted a deep navy blue. The color contrasted well with the ivory curtains at the windows and the cream-colored down comforter on the bed. A mountain of pillows covered the bed, the fussy kind women always piled all over everything. Even the carpet in this room was different—a deep, thick pile his feet sank into as he walked. He sat down on the edge of the bed and looked around again.

His phone rang and he answered before he thought about it.

"Hey, it's Nick. Did you get in okay?"

"Yeah, I'm here now. Although you forgot to tell me about the secret handshake to get past the front door."

"My fault. I thought I'd warned you. I'm convinced Eli doesn't fix it because he thinks of it as a security measure. It's probably harder for someone to break in if they can't even get the door open with a key."

Matt found himself nodding. "Eli has a nice place here. I wouldn't have thought he had it in him."

"Oh, you must be in his bedroom. Yeah I was surprised the first time I saw it, too. We used to tease Eli about not having any game but after I saw that room, I don't tease him anymore. Stay away from the closet if you don't want to lose your religion. It's always the quiet ones."

Matt's brows lowered as he looked around. "You guys just like giving each other a hard time. It's a nice room. A little over the top for my taste, but it's not that bad."

"Whatever, dude. Enjoy freak central. Call me when you get back."

Nick hung up, so Matt tossed the phone on the bed next to him and stretched out. When he was flat on his back, he opened his eyes and then barked out a laugh. His reflection laughed with him. There were mirrors hanging above the bed.

So this was what Nick meant about freak central. He stared at his reflection for a moment, observing the rise and fall of his chest as he breathed.

A second later he jumped up and headed for the closet.

Chapter Three

♥

PENNY TYPED THE last sentence of her e-mail and closed the lid of her laptop. It always took a bit of juggling when she was treating a high-profile client, but athletes took it to another level. Not only were they expecting immediate results so they could get back to playing, but she had a bevy of people interested in every aspect of their recovery, from family to coaches to the media.

"I'm heading out, Penny. Did Coach call you?" Chris Walters leaned in the open door of her office. He'd come to her after having surgery to repair a torn ACL. They hadn't had an appointment today, but he'd come in anyway because he was experiencing some pain in his knee.

"I just sent him an e-mail. We can continue with therapeutic massage for the rest of the week to aid in draining the excess fluid buildup you're experiencing."

"You think I'll be okay in time for the play-offs?"

Penny grinned at his enthusiasm. Chris was entirely different than she'd expected. He was a quiet young man who exhibited none of the arrogance she'd expected from someone considered to be the king of Washington's basketball team.

"If you keep working as hard as you have been, I don't think anything can stop you. I'll see you for your next appointment on Friday."

Matt's file was still on the edge of her desk. She picked it up and flipped through it idly.

Even if she hadn't seen him in years, there was still a lingering sense of obligation. That was it, she told herself. She felt some twisted sort of responsibility because she used to babysit him. It had nothing to do with the pain she'd glimpsed in his eyes as he'd left. He was hurting and had no idea what to do about it.

When she got to the notes about his accident, her hand stilled. It was never a good feeling when she couldn't help someone, but in this case she especially felt the loss.

Her attraction to him had nothing to do with her desire to help him. Although now that he was gone and she was done with her work for the day, she could allow her mind a few minutes to drift back to their meeting.

What the hell had that been?

She'd never been the type to go googly-eyed over a guy. Matt, however, had made her almost forget her own name. She didn't consider herself to have a "type," but if she did—he would be it. Tall, dark, and handsome was more than just a cliché in this case. It was a recipe for disaster. It was probably best that they wouldn't be working together. She'd never been tempted by a patient before.

You've also never had a patient who was six feet tall and two hundred pounds of pure masculine temptation, either.

Then she thought back to all the athletes she'd worked with. They were all tall, heavily muscled, and in peak physical condition. Georgia had panted after plenty of them. So why was she so affected by Matt in particular?

"Knock knock. Are you busy?" Georgia leaned around the door frame. "Everyone's gone now. Are you almost done?"

She closed Matt's file. "I am now. I was just daydreaming." She grabbed her coat and bag and followed Georgia to the front of the building, then waited while her friend gathered her own things and locked the outer doors. They walked out to the parking lot in companionable silence.

"This was a long day."

They stopped next to her friend's minivan and Georgia clicked her keychain so the side door opened automatically. There were two car seats in the back and a mess of books and toys on the floor.

"It'll all be better soon." There was a curiously sly note in Georgia's voice.

"What does that mean?" Penny asked. Georgia wasn't meeting her eyes all of a sudden.

"Just a hunch. That's all. Go home. Get some sleep. Wear some makeup tomorrow. And for God's sake, do something with that hair besides the prison-warden bun. A soft ponytail wouldn't kill you." Her friend gave a jaunty wave and then hopped into the driver's seat.

"What? Georgia, what did you do?" Penny rapped on the

window. For a moment she thought her friend was going to drive away without responding. Finally, the window lowered a few inches.

"I just gave Sergeant Sexy a few things to think about. He'll be back."

♥

THE NEXT AFTERNOON, Penny could barely concentrate. Her cell phone rang and she picked it up. Scott's picture flashed across the display. She ran her thumb over the screen. She really should answer. Scott didn't call during the day often. But it seemed disloyal to talk to him when she was thinking about another guy.

She ran her fingers through her hair, dislodging her ponytail. The loose hairstyle had been irritating her all day. She couldn't believe she'd dressed up for a guy. She had to get Matt Simmons out of her mind. She couldn't help someone who didn't want to be helped.

It was time to let it go.

"Um, Penny? You have some visitors." Georgia's voice crackled over the intercom system.

She snatched up her handset. "Georgia, I need a minute. Can you ask one of the other therapists to get the patient started? I'll check in on them in a few."

"I would, but these aren't patients. You have *visitors*. Scott is here."

"What? He's here? I guess that's what he was calling about."

"You have another visitor, too. Sergeant Simmons is here to speak with you as well." By the clipped tone of her assistant's voice, Penny could only assume one or both men were nearby.

"They're *both* here? Okay. I'll be there in a moment."

Penny dropped the phone in the cradle and then pushed her chair back. "*Crap.* I do not need this right now." She pulled open her desk drawer and took out her handbag. There wasn't a lot of damage control she could do in just a few minutes, but at least she could smooth her hair and make sure she didn't have anything in her teeth.

After her emergency primping session, she emerged from the patient corridor into the waiting room. Scott jumped up from his seat. He looked like he'd just come from court, his light brown hair lightly gelled back and his suit as crisp as the day he'd bought it.

"Hey, there's my girl." Scott pulled her against him and kissed her passionately.

"Whoa! Uh, hello to you, too." Penny glanced around and several of the waiting patients averted their eyes. Her face burned as she turned around. She'd never been into public displays of affection and Scott wasn't either. She put her hands on his chest to keep him at a proper distance. "What's gotten into you? You're awfully friendly."

"Just missed you. I've been calling you all morning. For a minute there, I thought you weren't going to come out. I was hoping we could do lunch."

"Sorry. I've been a little preoccupied today." Penny turned, startled to see Matt leaning against the reception desk watching her.

The same feeling she'd experienced yesterday rolled through her, forcing the heat of another blush to her cheeks, picking up her pulse, and shortening her breath.

Scott followed her line of vision. "Who is that?"

She patted Scott on the arm. "That's one of my patients.

Can you give me a few minutes?"

He nodded and wandered to one of the straight-backed chairs a few feet away. She turned back to Matt. He pushed away from the counter and walked over to her.

"Is the suit your boyfriend?" Matt glanced over her shoulder at Scott. He seemed amused. For some reason, that annoyed her. Who was he to judge her relationships? Not every man could be a pumped-up, super-alpha testosterone factory like he was.

"Why are you here, Matt?"

His dark eyes never left her face as he answered. "To apologize and beg you for another chance."

"Apology accepted. However, I don't know if we can work together."

When he opened his mouth to respond, she held up a finger. "Hang on. This isn't exactly a waiting-room conversation. Um, I have some time between appointments, so we can talk. You can wait in my office."

Matt crossed his arms, his dark eyes inscrutable. "That's okay. I'll wait right here, thanks." His lips curled up into his usual smirk.

Fantastic. Penny rolled her eyes and walked over to Scott. When he saw her coming, he jumped up. She held up a hand to keep him from grabbing her again.

"I wish I could do lunch but I have patients." Technically Matt wasn't a patient, but they still needed to talk. As excuses went, it would have to do.

His voice dropped another octave. "That's okay. I just wanted to see you since I have to work tonight and tomorrow. I have to get some work done so I can give you my undivided attention for our anniversary dinner this weekend. I'm really looking forward to it."

Penny stilled and then allowed him to pull her into another hug. "Of course. It's our anniversary. How could I forget?" She bit her lip at his knowing chuckle.

"It's okay if you forgot. I know you've been busy."

She let out a relieved breath. "I've been working too hard. It'll be nice for us to have a relaxing evening. So, where are we going?"

"Uh uh. No questions. It's a surprise. I have an entire romantic evening planned."

Penny wasn't sure how to respond to that. Scott generally had a very different idea of what was "romantic" than she did. The door to the waiting room swung open and another patient entered, which reminded Penny where they were.

"I bet. Okay, I have to run because my next patient is waiting. Where should I meet you?"

"I'll pick you up on Saturday. All you have to do is show up and look beautiful. It's going to be a night to remember."

She glanced behind her. Matt leaned casually against the counter, staring at his feet. He wasn't looking at her, but she had a feeling he was listening intently to their conversation. Just then he looked up, his black eyes fixed on hers. Her breath seized in her throat and heat rushed to her cheeks.

She wanted him, she realized with a faint sense of horror. Wanted his intense eyes on her, his muscled body over hers. He was going to be her patient and she was hot for him. Worse, judging by the faint smile on his face, he knew it.

She whirled around to face Scott. "Yes, okay. I'll see you then."

Scott kissed her again and then walked out, flicking one last uncertain glance in Matt's direction.

As soon as the door closed behind him, Matt pushed off the wall and walked toward her. "So, you never answered my question. Is he your boyfriend?"

Penny shrugged. "I don't see how that's relevant. Why are you here? I think we can both agree we aren't a good fit."

"All we agree on was that I acted like an asshole. I'm sorry."

It wasn't the most eloquent apology, but she had no doubt it was sincere.

"I understand. That still doesn't mean that we should work together. I've only had a few military patients. Most of the people who come to me are athletes or here after an accident. You have some emotional issues, understandably, that I'm not sure how to deal with. I have no problem admitting that I'm not quite sure what to do with you."

"Do whatever you have to do. I promise I'll behave." Matt spread his hands. "I'm putting myself at your mercy."

It was tempting to turn around and walk away. He was just too much. Too volatile, too arrogant and definitely too handsome for her peace of mind. The easy decision would be to turn him down. Then she could write this whole thing off and get back to her safe, ordered existence.

But in the end, it came down to the same factors she always used to make her decisions. She believed he wanted to get better. And she believed she had the tools to help him.

"Okay. I'll help you. But be warned, I'm a pretty tough taskmaster. Come on back, Sergeant. We might as well figure out your treatment schedule."

"We're back to being formal already? Do I need to remind you of the time I caught that snake and hid it in your backpack?" He stood close enough that she could feel the heat coming off his big body. "I thought we'd already established that you would call me Matt."

"Right. Sorry."

"Well? Let me hear it." He leaned over until Penny could

see the flecks of gold in his brown eyes. "Go ahead, Penny. Say my name."

"Matt," she whispered.

His eyes lit with triumph.

Penny gulped as the circus troupe in her stomach started performing again. The only thing they'd established was that Sergeant Simmons made her feel everything her boyfriend didn't.

♥

MATT FOLLOWED THE soft sway of Penny's hips as she led him down the hall to a room. There was a long table covered in the thin paper sheeting hospitals and doctors' offices used to protect plastic seats. She excused herself for a moment and then came back holding a file.

"I've been reading up on you. I want to take a look and see where you're having difficulty. Then I can devise a treatment plan." She motioned toward the patient bench with her hand and he hopped up on the table, the paper crinkling beneath his legs.

"Can you unbutton your shirt, please? I want to take a look at your scar." Penny issued the order and followed with a stern look when his lips curled up at the edges.

"Sure thing." It took everything in Matt not to make a dirty comment, but he was already on thin ice with her, so he clamped his lips shut and unbuttoned his shirt. When he was done, Penny lifted his left arm gently, then touched the thin scar beneath his collarbone. She led him through a series of movements, noting his responses. She didn't touch him any more than was necessary.

Oh yeah, he noted with satisfaction. She was feeling it, too.

After a few minutes, she walked back over to her desk. "It looks like your surgery to repair the glenoid labrum was successful, but yet you haven't fully healed."

Matt nodded even though he had no idea what she meant. "I'm up shit creek, huh?"

Penny shot him a tight grin. "I didn't say that. I can help you. Despite what you seem to think of my profession, I'm determined to use my 'little exercises' to help you build stability in the ligaments and muscles surrounding the injured area. I believe we can get you enough strength to compensate for the weak areas so they can heal. You can button your shirt now."

Matt winced. "I'm sorry about what I said. I've just been dealing with some stuff."

Penny waved off his apology. "I get that, but it doesn't change the facts. I'm going to say this once. If you are willing to work harder than you ever have, I can help you. But I am going to make you push, curse, and sweat. Before it's all over you're going to hate me."

He motioned to the dress shirt he was wearing. "I can't even wear a simple tee shirt anymore. It hurts to lift my arm that high. If you can get me back to normal, I promise I won't hate you. Hell, I'll probably get down on one knee and propose."

"That won't be necessary." The light blush that suddenly rose in her cheeks showed she wasn't as unaffected as she appeared. Matt found himself studying her more closely.

Her blond hair was lighter at the ends, like she was growing out highlights. Not that he could see much of it since she had it bundled up in some kind of knot at the back of her head. Blue eyes the color of a clear sky sparkled behind the thin frames of the glasses she'd slipped on. She looked much the same as the quiet, unassuming girl he'd known years ago except for an extra inch in height and several inches in the bustline.

He wondered if she thought the bulky white lab coat she wore hid her figure. If anything, it made her curves more pronounced because it stretched out the seams in ways that probably weren't intended.

When he looked up, she was glaring at him.

Right. Staring at her chest was probably not the best way to start off their professional relationship.

"So, what's the next step?" He sent her a tight smile before focusing on buttoning up his shirt.

"The next step is getting you on the schedule three times a week. Half the battle will be keeping you from injuring yourself further, so in the early stages I'll want to monitor you carefully. Let's start with noon next week, Monday, Wednesday, and Friday."

"Okay. That works."

"Rule number one is that you tell me what you're feeling. The truth. I know you're a big, bad soldier and you can take pain, but there's no place for machismo here. In this situation, I need to know what's really going on with your body. Your pain response gives me information. Information is how I tailor your treatment. Can you do that?"

"I can do that."

"Okay. My goal here is to get you back to one hundred percent. The tricky part is that your one hundred percent is about five times higher than the average guy's."

"I've been keeping myself in shape as much as possible. I don't have the luxury of taking time off from my workouts. My goal is to qualify for the Special Forces. I've already gone to jump school. I was scheduled to go to Ranger school after deployment, but then the accident happened. You know the rest."

"Jump school? So you jumped out of an airplane?"

Matt chuckled at her awed look. "Yeah. There are a lot of battle situations where it's difficult to bring in ground support and dropping in from above is the best option. It's important to have guys who are qualified to enter from the air and the Army always needs volunteers. So I offered to go."

"Wow. I've always wanted to do that."

At his confused look, she clarified. "Skydiving. I've always wanted to try it. I'm naturally risk averse. Everything I do, not just in my career but even in my personal life, is about minimizing risk. That probably sounds stupid to you." She looked away, a beguiling flush of pink tingeing her cheeks.

Damn, she was cute.

"No, it doesn't sound stupid at all. I can understand the fascination. There's nothing like it. Free-falling makes you feel invincible. It's one of the most incredible things I've ever done. If I can qualify to be a Ranger, then I'll do even more incredible things. It's been my dream since I joined the Army. Tell me you can give that back to me, Penny, and I'll do anything you ask of me."

Their eyes met and her lips softened and parted. It would have taken more self-control than Matt had ever possessed not to watch as her tongue darted out and traced the edge of her bottom lip. When she noticed where his attention was, she abruptly spun around and walked to the other side of the room.

"Mmm. I'm really glad you said that, because I have a feeling you're not going to like rule number two." She stood on tiptoe and pulled something down from a shelf. When she turned around she held it up so he could see it. It looked like a white bandage.

"Rule number two is you need to wear this for a few

weeks." She held up one end, then looped it over her head. She tucked her arm into the part hanging near her stomach.

"You want me to walk around wearing a sling again? I wore one when I was first injured. Shouldn't I be past that by now?"

"Your shoulder is still weaker than it should be. While I work on the surrounding areas, we need to give the muscles and tendons time to heal without being jostled too much. Wear the sling. Trust me."

He eyed the cloth she held out dubiously. It was bad enough having a bum arm without having to walk around wearing something that advertised it.

"Fine. I'll wear it. I said I would do whatever it takes."

Penny patted his arm. "Whatever it takes starts now."

Chapter Four

♥

THE DREAMS ALWAYS started the same way. The clawing fear. The panic. Everything was so clear, the image as perfectly preserved as a digital photograph.

It was pitch-black and there was nothing but the smell of burning rubber and smoke. He was on the ground, crawling, dragging his friend with him, determined not to leave him behind. He could feel the dirt and rock beneath his fingernails, the trickle of sweat running down his neck. Every few seconds the sky lit up with bursts of fire like some macabre parody of a fireworks display.

"Just leave me, Matt. Get out of here." Cy started coughing before he could even finish the sentence. His legs were twisted to the side in an unnatural position. Matt couldn't take time to dwell on what that meant. He just knew they couldn't stop moving.

"I'm not leaving you behind, man. I don't know what the hell is going on, but we're getting out of here." Matt had hooked his left arm over his friend's chest and was using his right arm to drag both of them from the wreckage of the vehicle. Cy could barely move, so he was purely dead weight. Matt's arm was screaming from the effort to pull both of them along, but he didn't let go. He couldn't let go.

The air was filled with the sounds of gunfire and screaming. Matt looked up to see the medics running toward them. They were going to be okay.

"Aah!" Matt cried out when Cy was pulled from his arm. His shoulder hurt so badly, as if he hadn't been able to register the pain until he finally let go.

"We made it." He looked to his right where the medics were packing Cy's wounds. But when he looked, his friend had no face. There was only darkness where his head should be.

"No! Cyrus, no!" Matt woke up then, the scream trapped in his throat, almost strangling him. He patted the sheets next to him frantically, his chest rising and falling with the force of his breaths. For several long moments, he was trapped on the razor's edge between nightmare and reality. Then his heartbeat slowed as he took in the familiar shapes of his room, the lamp on the nightstand, the dresser across the room. He was at Elliott's house. In bed.

Safe.

"Aw, hell." He swung his legs over the side of the bed and stood. His bare toes dug into the carpet. He'd never slept in clothes before, but he'd started wearing pajama pants since the dreams had started. He was used to getting up in the middle of the night.

He walked downstairs and flipped on the lights in the kitchen. After a glass of water and a piece of cheesecake that had been in his refrigerator long enough to be highly suspect, he trudged back up the stairs and got in bed. In therapy he'd learned to allow himself the freedom of remembering. It helped to think back on the events and remind himself that he'd done everything he could.

His friend's death was not his fault.

So as soon as his eyes closed, he allowed his thoughts to go back to that evening. He was riding shotgun in the ATV and his friend Cyrus was driving. Cy was only five years younger, but it felt like light-years. He'd looked up to Matt, even signed up for jump school when Matt explained the volunteer-only program was always in need of qualified recruits.

They'd been tasked with delivering medical supplies to a hospital in the city of Balad. Cy had been talking about what he was going to do on his leave. He had a girlfriend back home in North Carolina and he'd just found out she was expecting their first child. Matt had been teasing him about being busy at home on his last break when the first shot hit the side of their vehicle.

He turned on his side and squeezed the pillow between his arms. Cy had swerved. They'd hit something and he couldn't remember exactly what had happened after that. He just knew he'd been unwilling to leave his friend behind when he'd crawled from their overturned vehicle. It was all a blur of fire, bullets, and smoke, but he remembered that much. He'd been so determined to drag his friend out that he hadn't realized how badly his shoulder had been compromised. It wasn't until days later that the full extent of the damage was apparent.

He'd been on disability for almost six months before he'd been cleared to go back to work. He'd gone through all the requisite Army counseling, but he still couldn't pass the general physical fitness test.

He'd picked up most of his life just as it had been before, so most people thought he was okay. It was a wonder to him that he'd managed to fool as many people as he had.

It wasn't possible to ever be truly okay after watching a friend die right in front of you.

Cy would never have the chance to do all the things he'd talked about—getting married, watching his kid grow up, moving to the West Coast where, in his opinion, all the best looking women were. He'd been a fighter and Matt was suddenly ashamed that he'd been sitting around feeling sorry for himself when his friend would never again have that privilege.

More than just his ego had been bruised when he'd failed part of the fitness test. His goal of being a Ranger was now more like a distant dream. He'd joined the Army to serve and protect. It felt like he was failing at the one thing he'd been sure he was good at. But everything he'd tried so far hadn't worked, so maybe it was time to try something different. Cy would have said "If you don't like where you are, then go somewhere else."

He thought back to what Mara had said about Penny being a miracle worker.

He could only hope.

THE NEXT DAY, Matt stood on the Alexanders' front porch. He shifted the case of sodas he held so he could ring the doorbell. Before the chime even finished, the door was wrenched open and laughter and warmth spilled over him.

"Hey! Look who's here," Elliott Alexander yelled over his shoulder. "Come on in, man. Everyone else is already here."

Matt accepted a handshake from his friend's older brother and allowed himself to be pulled into the warm, welcoming interior of the Alexanders' ranch-style home. Mark Alexander stood next to the window, looking out. When he saw Matt, he ambled over with his hand outstretched.

"Hey there, son. I'm glad you were able to come out. It's always good to see you."

"Thank you, sir. It's good to see you, too." He followed Mark and Eli toward the source of the noise, the kitchen. Matt loved spending time with the Alexanders. There was always tons of food and just good people having a good time.

Julia Alexander walked out from the kitchen carrying a platter. She stopped short when she saw her husband and son.

"What are you two doing out here? It's almost time." When she caught sight of Matt, she let out a little squeal. "Matt! I didn't think you were going to make it. Come on in, honey. Everyone else is in the kitchen."

He put the drinks he was still carrying down on the table and followed them all into the next room. A chorus of "hellos" rang out. His friend Jackson Alexander stood next to his wife, Ridley, as she stirred a bowl of something. Nick Alexander stood across the counter from them holding a plate of oranges while his wife, Raina, ate the pieces one by one.

"Matt's here!" Mara raced over and gave him a quick hug.

"That's everyone. Now that we're all here, you can tell us. Is it a boy or a girl?"

Trent chuckled and just shook his head. "Mara, we're still missing one. I'm sure Raina and Nick want to wait for Bennett."

Matt looked at his sister in disbelief. "Have you been badgering her the entire time you've been here?"

Raina answered for her. "Yes, she has, but it's okay. She's not the only one." She glanced at Mrs. Alexander from the corner of her eye. Matt laughed along with everyone else when Julia crossed her arms in mock outrage.

He thought back on the stilted Christmas dinner he and Mara had spent with their parents in Florida. He loved his folks, honestly, but spending time with his parents couldn't be called relaxing. His father usually spent their time together rehashing his glory days as a lieutenant or badgering him about when he was going back on active duty. He sighed. It wasn't as if Mara had it any easier. His mother had always been extremely critical of his sister until recently. Once she'd gotten wind that Trent had proposed, she was obsessed with planning a big society wedding.

Even though that wasn't what his sister wanted.

Then he looked around at the crazy, loud bustle of people in the Alexanders' kitchen. Everyone was accepted exactly as they came, no criticism about what they were wearing or where they'd been. No nosy questions or pressure.

When he was here, he could just be himself.

"So, how did things go with Penny?" Mara whispered.

"Fine. It was okay." He flinched internally. A weak answer was a surefire way to get his sister interested.

Mara narrowed her eyes. "So, she's going to help you? Does she think you'll get better?"

"I don't know, Mara. It's too soon to tell. Stop worrying."

Mara crossed her arms and probably would have given him an earful if Raina hadn't cleared her throat just then.

"Okay, I know you guys are all dying to know what we're having, so we won't keep you in suspense. Bennett tends to lose track of time when he's working on something, so we might as well just go ahead." Raina ate the last orange slice and delicately wiped her fingers on the napkin her husband held out. She turned to her sister, who was spreading icing on a small cake. "Ri, is it done?"

"Almost... Okay, now it's done." Ridley lifted the cake and winked.

Raina grinned. "I decided to use my newfound ninja baking skills to make a pink or blue cake. So, you won't know until we cut the first piece. Who wants to cut the first piece? Mark, would you like to?"

He took a step forward, but then glanced back at Julia. "I'd better let Mama Bear do the honors."

Julia rubbed her hands together and stepped forward. "I'd love to. I wasn't blessed with any baby girls, but a granddaughter would be just as good."

Mark rolled his eyes fondly behind her back.

"Okay, here's the knife. Let's do this. Drumroll, please!" Ridley motioned to Elliott, who banged a loud staccato rhythm on the table.

Looking back, Matt couldn't be sure what had triggered him. Perhaps it was because the room was so quiet before the loud sound or because his shoulder was still aching from earlier. He was always on edge when he was in pain. Either way, the sudden loud sound hit his eardrums like a bomb going off. Matt dropped to the floor and rolled. He hit the leg of the table. A second later, something shattered. Instinctively, he covered his head with his arms.

Everyone went silent. Then there was a sudden cacophony of voices.

"What the hell?"

"Did he fall?"

Mara kneeled next to the table. He looked up from the cradle of his arms and their eyes met. Her face fell.

"Oh, my god. *Matt.*" She stopped, obviously overcome. "It's okay. It's all going to be okay."

Adrenaline was still flowing through his bloodstream so strongly that Matt started shaking. As much as he wished he could just sink into the floor, the best he could do was wrap his arms around himself and hold on.

Once his heartbeat slowed a little, he turned and looked at the shards of glass on the floor next to him. He could hear his friends whispering back and forth. Probably trying to figure out how long he was going to be under their table. The first wash of shame settled in the pit of his stomach.

"I'm going to ask everybody to take a step back and give Matt some space."

Elliott's deep voice cut through the chaos until everyone fell silent. All Matt could hear was the steady whoosh of his own breath sawing in and out of his chest. There was a soft crunch and he flinched. Eli knelt next to him but didn't touch him.

"You want to take a minute outside, buddy?"

Matt nodded quickly, hating the desperate relief that flowed through him when he realized that Eli wasn't asking any questions. He climbed from beneath the table and stood slowly. There were pieces of broken crockery near his foot.

Eli nudged it aside. "Don't worry about that. You just go on out and get some fresh air. No one will bother you." His words held both comfort and a promise. Matt looked up, stunned to see no pity reflected in Eli's gaze.

He walked to the back door, not meeting anyone's eyes. As soon as the cold, fresh air hit his face, he gasped, taking in a lungful of freezing air.

Breathe. Just breathe.

♥

"YOUR LAST APPOINTMENT is here. Also, you might want to check your messages." It was Friday evening, and Georgia handed her the file for her next patient.

Penny groaned when she saw the name. She was not in the mood to deal with Mr. Grabby-hands Eisenberg today.

"You might need this." Georgia held out her hand. Penny's cell phone sat on her palm.

"You found it! I've been looking for that all day." Penny snatched up her phone and let out a sigh of relief. She wasn't sure how people had survived before technology. Her entire life was in her phone. She hadn't been looking forward to having to buy another one.

"It was in the garbage can next to your desk. You must have knocked it off when you were eating lunch."

Penny pulled up the call log on her phone, shocked to see two missed calls. Scott wouldn't call her during the work day unless it was important. He was an assistant district attorney, so he understood her crazy schedule. Plus, he'd already told her he'd be too busy catching up with work to see her tonight.

"Okay, I need to listen to my voicemail. Can you go check in with Mr. Eisenberg? I'll be right there."

Georgia grimaced. "Do I have to?" At Penny's pleading look, she crossed her arms. "If he tries to cop a feel again, I'm holding you personally responsible."

"I'll owe you one. Thank you, Georgia." She laughed as her assistant shot her a withering look before turning the corner toward the waiting room.

Penny walked into her office and dropped down wearily into her desk chair as she pressed the button to listen to her first message.

--Hey Penny. I guess you're with a patient. I'm really looking forward to tomorrow and I hope you are, too. I'll pick you up at eight o'clock sharp. I bet you're wondering where we're going, but I'm not going to tell you. I have the perfect surprise planned for you. It's going to be a night to remember. See you tomorrow, babe.

She looked out the window aimlessly as Scott's voice rumbled over her phone's speaker. He sounded as harried as she felt. She rewound the message and listened again, noting the time he'd said he was picking her up.

Georgia stuck her head in. "Mr. Eisenberg's all set. Anna is getting him started."

Penny stowed her phone in her desk drawer and grabbed the patient file on her desk. Georgia followed her into the hall.

"Scott was calling to remind me about dinner. He keeps saying it's going to be *a night to remember*." They walked down the hallway toward the treatment rooms. "You remember the last time he tried to plan a romantic evening? We spent three hours listening to opera in some language that I couldn't even identify. And then—"

"You got stuck talking to that anti-women's-rights senator." Georgia erupted into giggles. "I remember. God, you were pissed. I'm sure he was just as pained trying to talk to you. Imagine his horror at being forced into conversation with a professional woman. One who's happily single at that. I'm surprised he didn't keel over dead from the shock. I'm more surprised you didn't say something outrageous just to get a rise out of that old fart."

"Well, I was surprised he didn't ask me to make him a sandwich. I was tempted to say something outrageous, believe me. The problem is that Scott's idea of a good time is cocktails with the Washingtonian in-crowd, whereas I just want a dinner that isn't so fancy I can't pronounce it. Who knows what he'll plan this time? Especially since it's our anniversary."

"It's your anniversary? That's so nice. How long have you guys been dating?"

"Three years. It's hard to believe it's been that long."

They reached the door to treatment room 5. Penny peeked in through the glass square on the door. Mr. Eisenberg saw her and wiggled his thick, bushy eyebrows and leered back. Penny sighed. It was going to be a long hour of trying to avoid him pinching her on the bottom. She knew he wasn't really aware of what he was doing half the time, but it made for an extremely uncomfortable session.

"Three years. Wait, he said it was going to be a special night? Whoa." Georgia slapped a hand in front of her to prevent Penny from entering the treatment room. Her brown eyes widened and her eyebrows shot up so high they almost disappeared into her hairline.

"What? Is there something special about three years? You know I'm oblivious about this kind of thing, so you'll have to enlighten me."

"Are you serious?" She held out her left hand and waved her wedding ring in front of Penny's face.

Penny couldn't help but snort. "Oh no. There is no way."

"Helloooo. Did you think you'd just be dating forever? Three years is generally considered *shit or get off the pot* time."

Her first instinct was to laugh again but then she thought back to how strange Scott had been acting lately. He'd been talking about how nice it would be to have a bigger place since her house only had two bedrooms and he lived in a condo. He'd also asked if she wanted to take a vacation that summer. They'd never made plans that far in advance before. Ever.

Penny's stomach dropped until it felt like it was dragging on the linoleum floor.

Georgia nodded, knowingly.

"He's going to ask you to marry him."

♥

"WE SHOULD GO after him." Nick paced back and forth while his mother silently swept the pieces of broken pottery into a pile. They'd eventually cut the cake, revealing the bright pink center. The mood was still somber, however. The cake sat forgotten on the table next to Eli.

Julia shook her head, sadly. "Someone needs to talk to him. It's obvious he's hurting, poor thing."

Nick didn't disagree, but he was pretty sure his friend's wounds went a lot deeper than a hand-holding session and a heart-to-heart chat. Matt likely needed help that none of them were qualified to give.

"We've been talking to him. We just haven't been listening." He'd been completely wrapped up in his own problems between convincing Raina to marry him and worrying about her pregnancy. He hadn't given his friend's strange behavior a second thought. Nick clenched his fists at his sides. When Matt had needed him, he'd been too busy.

"He's right," Jackson added. "After Divine's first album came out, that's all I've been thinking about. We've all been so wrapped up in our own worlds that we couldn't see he's self-destructing right in front of us."

"He joined the Reserves in college, but last year was his first year being on active duty. He's up for reenrollment this year. I've tried talking to him about it but I just don't know what to say." Mara's voice broke and she turned and rested her head against Trent's chest. "He knows I want him to get out, but I don't know if that's what he really wants. Plus, if he does get out, what would he do? I'm sure just the thought of it is overwhelming."

Elliott had been quiet up until now. "I have a lot of ex-military guys on my team. If Matt's interested, he could always come work for me. With all the extra work Raina has thrown my way to protect her when her normal guy is off duty combined with guarding Ridley and the Divine girls, my team is about stretched to capacity. I'll need to hire more local guys soon, anyway."

"Wait, guarding me?" Ridley sat up and glared at Eli. "Since when have you been guarding me?"

"Um." Eli looked over at Jackson and shrugged. His brother shook his head slightly, then smiled sheepishly when Ridley turned and caught him.

Ridley crossed her arms. "I knew it couldn't be coincidence seeing you at the grocery store that many times!"

Elliott looked like he was trying to smother a laugh. "Right. *Anyway*, I'm sure between my team and Raina's we can find a job for Matt if he wants it. Right, Raina?" He looked around the room and then looked behind him.

"Where's Raina?"

Nick glanced behind him where he'd last seen his wife. It was as natural as breathing for him to be around the people who loved him; however, Raina still wasn't completely comfortable at family gatherings. She had a habit of sneaking off in the middle and then suddenly reappearing when it was time to leave. For someone who'd grown up mainly on her own, it was overwhelming to be in the midst of so much chaos. He understood and respected that.

"I'm sure she's around. Probably looking for something else to eat since we ran out of oranges."

Eli looked confused. "We ran out of oranges? I thought there was a whole bowl in the kitchen."

"Well, there was a whole bowl when we arrived. Not anymore." Nick walked down the hall and peeked in his old bedroom to see if she was hiding out in there. Nothing.

As he turned to leave, he heard muffled voices outside the window. He crossed the room and pulled back the curtain slightly. The second story had been added years after the house was built, so it sat at a slight angle to the back porch. He could see Matt standing at the railing. Raina stood next to him. Raina wasn't usually the social sort, but apparently she'd found a way to get through to his friend.

Matt looked tense, but he was listening.

Chapter Five

♥

THE SUN HUNG low in the sky, bathing the barren landscape with a golden haze. There was no furniture on the porch since it was too cold to sit out, so Matt leaned his hip against the railing. He could see the barn in the distance, the faded red like a beacon amongst the icy gray landscape. It was so calm out here. The perfect stillness curled through him until the ball of tension in the middle of his chest began to loosen up.

He wasn't sure how long he'd been standing there before he realized he wasn't alone. Raina stood at the railing next to him, looking out to the distance. She wore a long tunic sweater and leggings, a little bump at her waist the only evidence of her pregnancy.

She'd lost her summer tan, so her skin was a very light brown and her long curly hair swirled around her face in the cold wind. He looked down at his own skin, which was also considerably lighter than it had been in the summer. Mara always joked that he'd sucked up all of their mother's Columbian heritage in the womb since he tanned so well and she didn't. At the thought of his sister, he glanced behind him at the house. He'd have to go back inside eventually. The thought of it, of all the pitying looks, was exhausting.

"I don't mean to bother you," Raina stated. She exhaled, her breath forming an icy cloud in front of her face. "We don't have to talk if you don't want to."

He marveled, as he did every time he saw her, at not only how beautiful she was but also at how different she seemed from when he'd first met her. Gone were the designer clothes and the heavy makeup. She looked like a person now instead of a fashion icon. She looked real.

"You know, you and I have never actually been introduced."

If she was perplexed by that sudden strange statement, she didn't show it. She stuck out her arm and he saw she held his leather jacket. He accepted it gratefully and pulled it on. She still carried a long black cape that she now swung over her shoulders.

"No, I suppose we haven't. But then again, we didn't need to be. Some things don't need to be stated to be understood. You're one of my husband's best friends. I don't need an introduction to *know* you, Matt."

He wasn't sure how to respond to that, so he just tucked his hands in his pockets. "I'm sorry about—"

"Don't apologize. You don't have to apologize to me for anything." Tears sprang to her eyes and she shook her head hard.

"Christ, I made you cry."

"It's not you. It's these damn pregnancy hormones. I'm either starving, throwing up, or sniffling at some sappy commercial on TV." She swiped her hand under her eye quickly, almost as if pissed off at the inconvenience.

"So, did you draw the short straw to see who'd come check on me?"

"Hell, no. Do I look like the intervention type?"

It was such a blunt, politically incorrect thing to say that it immediately made Matt feel better.

"But that is why you're here, isn't it? To tell me it'll all be okay, so I should come back inside with everyone."

She shook her head. "When I'm dealing with crap, I don't want an audience. I brought your coat and car keys so you can get out of here. I understand not wanting company. Especially mine, since I'm hardly the warm and fuzzy type."

He closed his eyes. "It's not that I don't want your company. I'm just dealing with some stuff."

"Matt, you have no idea how much your friends admire you. How much they care about you and *worry* about you." She looked back at the screen door. "None of us can even pretend to understand what you're going through, but we just want to help. You picked me up when I was too sick to walk and got me to the hospital. I owe you for that. Mara told us about your shoulder. I'm sure carrying around pregnant women is not helpful when you're dealing with an injury."

"Raina, my shoulder was messed up before that happened. This is not your fault."

She shrugged. "Maybe. Or maybe it wouldn't be this bad if you hadn't had to do that. Either way, I want to do whatever I can to help you."

A slow creep of guilt grabbed Matt by the throat. Raina had been dealing with some pretty serious health issues during her pregnancy. The last thing she needed was to feel stressed and guilty about his injury.

"Seriously, my shoulder isn't that bad. It just needs physical therapy. Mara already got me an appointment with a new therapist who's supposed to be really great," he assured her.

His thoughts drifted to the suspicious expression in Penny's eyes when he'd left the center Thursday. She wasn't a typical bombshell by any means, but there was something about the way she looked when she got all worked up. She looked like she could take a bite out of him and for some reason, he wanted her to.

There was no denying he was attracted to her. Not that she'd done anything to encourage his attention. He almost laughed out loud. She definitely wasn't trying to throw his libido into overdrive. The woman couldn't have been any pricklier if she'd had a porcupine stuck on her head.

Matt would have his work cut out for him since he was pretty sure Penny wasn't going to give him any slack. Any goodwill he might have had with her had been destroyed when he'd lost his temper. He was going to have to work twice as hard to get back in her good graces. He couldn't have her mad at him. Penny represented everything he needed.

Everything he needed for his *health*, he amended. He couldn't afford to think of his physical therapist with her severe demeanor and devil's-playground body as anything other than the woman who could help him get back his life.

Raina brightened. "So you're going back to physical

therapy?"

"Yes. As a matter of fact, I'm going back next week. You don't have to worry. I'll be fine."

"*Great!* Well, I'll distract everyone so you can sneak around front and leave. Oh and by the way, the cake was pink. It's a girl." She turned and walked back to the house, incredibly buoyant for someone who had just been in tears.

"Hey! Did you—" Matt crossed his arms, stuck between outrage and amusement. "You just played me, didn't you? Did Mara send you out here to find out about my therapy since I wouldn't tell her?"

Raina rested a hand on her belly and blinked at him, her brown eyes perfectly innocent. "I have no idea what you mean." Then she walked in the house and closed the door behind her.

♥

"ARE YOU READY to go?" Ridley stood at the entrance to the nursery the next day, holding a small arrangement of wildflowers. Even though none of the flowers were the same type, somehow the whole bouquet made sense.

More of her sister's magic, Raina thought.

"I'm waiting on Nick. I told him we were just dropping off flowers at The Rush, but he insisted on coming with us." Raina ran a finger over the edge of the crib and straightened the comforter hanging over the side. It was surreal that by summertime the crib would be in use. She'd be up to her neck in diapers and bottles and totally sleep deprived.

She couldn't wait.

"Why? He thinks we need an escort just to go into town? Hah, he probably just wants to hit Miss Doris up for some of those sweet-potato fries. I already promised Jackson I'd bring some back for him."

Raina shook her head. "He's afraid to let me out of his sight. A girl can't have a fainting spell without everyone getting all crazy."

"I heard that." Nick poked his head around the doorway and Raina made a face, but secretly, she was thrilled. A husband who adored her and a healthy baby on the way were things she'd always dreamed of but never actually thought she'd have.

Nick pulled the car out of the garage and shuffled a few things around the backseat before finally declaring it safe for Raina to get in the car. Ridley smiled at her behind his back and then climbed in the front, holding her flower arrangement in her lap. As they passed through town, Raina observed all the minute changes from the summertime.

The peninsula was at its best in the warmer months when the boardwalk was open and the air was filled with the squawks of seagulls and the excited chatter of children at play. In the winter, most of the businesses took in their outdoor seating and everything looked slightly shuttered. Still, it was one of the only places she'd ever felt at home.

When they pulled up to The Rush, Ridley climbed out, balancing her flower arrangement carefully. She'd just started supplying bouquets to some of the local businesses and Raina hoped it worked out. It was what Ridley loved to do. Dealing with all the people in town was Raina's worst nightmare, but it made her sister happy. Ridley had always been the social butterfly.

Nick opened the door for Raina and they followed Ridley at a slower pace. He pulled out a chair for her at the counter and she sat gratefully. An older woman came out from the back and gave a *whoop* when she spotted them.

"Nick Alexander! Come here, you rascal." Miss Doris hugged him so hard she almost lifted him off his feet. Then she turned to Raina, who braced herself for the effusive brand of welcome she'd come to expect from everyone in New Haven. But to her surprise, Miss Doris just put a gentle arm around her shoulders and squeezed.

"I'll bring you out some oranges, dear. Your mother-in-law mentioned in church that you've got the Alexander cravings. I remember when she was pregnant if you can believe it. Feels like forever and a day."

"You don't have to do that," Raina said. When Miss Doris's face fell slightly, she added, "but I am kind of hungry, now that you mention it."

"Of course! Don't you worry. We'll fix you up." With a wide smile and another squeeze to her shoulder, she was gone, back through the swinging doors leading to the restaurant's tiny kitchen.

"What did you say to Matt last night?" Raina turned at the sound of Nick's voice. He sat on the stool next to hers and moved it close enough that he could pull her into his arms. She leaned against him and allowed him to take her weight.

"I just told him that we're all worried about him but I understand why he doesn't want to talk yet."

Nick wrapped his arms around her, resting the palm of his right hand on the top of her belly. It warmed her through and through every time he did it. He hadn't been able to keep his hands off her belly ever since she'd started showing. Not that she was very big yet, but still. After how hard they'd worked to get her pregnant and after being hospitalized due to her extreme morning sickness, every pound she gained felt like a gift.

"Thanks for doing that. I feel guilty that he's been helping me out and I never realized how much he's going through."

"He doesn't want a lot of people asking him about his feelings. I haven't been to war and that would drive me batty."

Nick sighed, the soft huff of his breath tickling her neck. "I know. I don't want to be nosy either. I just want him to know we're there if he needs us."

Raina squeezed his hands. "He knows that, baby."

"I also wanted to thank you for suggesting that Eli offer him his house key. If Matt has to be in Northern Virginia for all those appointments, it's got to be better for him to crash at a friend's house instead of staying at a hotel."

"It's all going to work out. You'll see. I have a good feeling about it."

♥

BY SATURDAY EVENING, Penny had managed to work herself into a near frenzy. Georgia's words had been banging around in her head for the past twenty-four hours.

She wasn't entirely sure why the whole thing was so shocking. They had been dating for three years. Realistically, what had she thought would happen? That they would just continue eating Chinese and hanging out forever? That one day she would wake up with absolute certainty that Scott was "the one" and be swept off her feet? She wasn't that naive.

There was nothing magical about sexual attraction. It was called "chemistry" for a reason. It was the end result of an eager adrenal system pumping dopamine to the brain.

Like the way you respond to a certain sexy army sergeant?

Penny groaned and fell back on the bed. There was no denying it. Chemistry was a pretty powerful force and when it came to Matt, she felt it. She felt a lot of things around him that she should not be feeling about a patient. She was supposed to feel that way about her boyfriend. He was the one she should have been daydreaming and fantasizing about. But she hadn't. Instead she'd been imagining the look on Matt's face when he'd leaned close and told her to say his name.

God, she wanted to say his name, all right. He'd probably planted the idea in her head on purpose, the arrogant jerk. He knew he was sexy. Probably used the fact to play with women's heads all the time.

But if you know it's just a chemical reaction, why does it matter so much? Why does it bother you that Scott doesn't make your heart race or your palms sweat?

She grabbed yet another dress from a hanger in her closet and held it up in front of her body. Her mirror hadn't magically morphed in the last ten minutes, so her reflection was still the same. A tall, dishwater blonde in white lace underwear holding up a dress that did nothing for her figure.

"Why is everything I own either casual or a business suit?" She sat down on the edge of her bed. It was at times like these she missed her sisters. Gabby would have come over and found a way to turn the contents of her closet into the perfect date outfit. Elisa was no better with fashion than Penny was, but she would have held her hand and calmed her down. But both of her sisters were happily married and living in different states now. She only saw them on holidays and over the webcam on her computer.

Even though she'd hated moving around as a kid, she'd at least always had the love of her parents and her two older sisters. They'd been a close-knit family and she'd always known she wanted kids of her own. She just wanted to stay in the same place after having them.

Her eyes landed on the picture of her parents she kept tacked to her dresser mirror. That was all she wanted for herself. Her parents were a great team. Just like she and Scott were a great team.

Countless nights she'd come home late to find Scott waiting for her with takeout and a movie. She didn't have a lot of time to spend at home, so they had to make their time together count. He understood her drive to succeed and supported it. Lots of men would be intimidated by a woman who was as driven and committed to her career as she was.

So why does the idea of getting married leave you completely cold?

Penny stood and yanked the first black dress she saw out of the pile of clothes on her bed.

She was half in and half out of the dress when the doorbell rang, causing her to jump. "Crap. He's early for once." She quickly finished dressing, rushing to put on her heels and earrings before racing down the stairs. He'd used his key and stood in the foyer, adjusting his tie in the hall mirror.

"You look beautiful," he commented without turning around. Their eyes met in the mirror. "But then again, you look lovely in a pair of scrubs, too."

There it was. That was the guy she cared about. The one who went out of his way to make her feel good about herself. Just because they didn't have the kind of passionate relationship portrayed in books and movies didn't mean their marriage wasn't going to be awesome. Everything in life wasn't going to be exciting. Some things were just steady and reliable and good. Scott was a good guy. Getting married was the sensible next step.

"Thanks. I'd say the same to you, but you always look perfectly polished."

He kissed her cheek lightly and then opened the door for her. "It's just part of the job. After you, my lady."

They rode through downtown Alexandria until they turned into a parking garage. As they walked out of the parking structure and onto King Street, she turned suspicious eyes to Scott.

"I'm guessing we're close. Do I get a hint?"

He didn't respond, just tugged on her hand until they stopped in front of a small awning. Penny turned to Scott in surprise when she saw the name written across the fabric in fancy lettering.

"The Tasting Room? How did you get reservations? I'm pretty sure they're wait-listed into next year!" She didn't add that she also knew he didn't care for seafood, which was the main thing on the menu. Now she really felt guilty for her earlier thoughts. The guy was willing to eat seafood just to make her happy. That ought to carry more weight than sizzle and excitement.

"I know a guy who knows a guy who took pity on me. That's all I'll admit to." He held the door for her again and then gave his name to the hostess.

Within minutes they were seated and she almost bounced in her seat looking at the menu. She'd been reading raves about their crab cakes ever since the restaurant had opened a year ago. They placed their orders with an extremely bored-looking waitress and then Scott surprised her by ordering a bottle of champagne.

He winked at her. "Let's go all out."

The champagne was brought by a different waiter and presented and poured with more pomp and circumstance than she could have imagined. Once they were alone again, she raised her glass of the bubbling golden liquid. "Here's to a night to remember."

"I'll toast to that." Scott tapped his glass against hers.

Their food was brought ten minutes later and Penny grinned at Scott over the plate. "This is amazing. Thank you." She took her first bite and hummed with pleasure. She was so absorbed in her food that she didn't look up until Scott reached across the table and took her hand.

"I brought you here to celebrate more than just our anniversary, babe." Scott leaned closer. "I've been thinking a lot about the future lately."

Oh my god, this is it.

Penny took a long, bracing gulp of her champagne, then moved her chair slightly closer. "I have, too. Just today I was thinking how well we get on together."

"Yes, we do. You complement me perfectly. I need a partner I can rely on. One who'll understand and support my goals. You've always pushed me to reach the next level. To be a crusader for justice."

Her brow furrowed at the last part. *Crusader for justice?*

"I suppose so. Of course, I'm all for… justice." She could only hope her face didn't look as awkward as it felt.

"Well, I did it. Babe, I'm going to be the district attorney in Atlanta. I always thought I'd be district attorney already so I could be running for office soon, but this is exactly the kind of step up I've been working toward. It's a little late, but I'll take it." He chuckled at his own joke.

She hesitated a beat too long before her manners kicked in. "Congratulations. Scott, that's wonderful." She meant it. Scott was a brilliant attorney and he deserved a promotion. Although, considering that she'd been expecting a heartfelt declaration of love, she wasn't sure if she was insulted or relieved that he was only thinking about work.

"Wait, you're *going* to be the new district attorney? Not, they offered you the job or you're thinking about it, but you're *going* to be." She sat back in her seat, the champagne turning a little sour in her stomach. Scott wouldn't meet her eyes and without a word she knew. "You've already accepted it, haven't you?"

He finally lifted his eyes to hers. "Well, yes. This is my dream job! It's a huge step up for me."

"It's in Atlanta. It's a big move," Penny added.

"I know. I do know that." Scott looked contrite. "I want to marry you, Penny. Let's be crazy and just do it. I know it's a big move, but coming from a military family I figured you'd be up for the challenge. We make a great team."

Hearing her own thoughts echoed back to her was like a glass of ice water to the face. She smiled automatically, but it felt like it was pasted on her face. It must have looked normal though, because Scott's shoulders dropped and he let out a sudden breath, his easy smile back in place.

Despite their many conversations about family and her experiences growing up, it hadn't occurred to him that she might not want to move. Or worse, it had occurred to him and he hadn't cared. In essence, he hadn't said *would you consider moving to Atlanta with me* at all. It was *I'm moving to Atlanta with or without you.*

How was it possible to spend so much time with someone and not have them *see* you at all? She was one more box to check off on his list of things to take care of before the move. She might as well have been a piece of furniture he was deciding whether to take with him or put into storage.

What to toss and what to keep.

"You're right, Scott. These past few years we've been a great team." She let out a breath and took another gulp of her champagne. "Just not so much a great couple."

The waitress came back then. "Would you like to see our

dessert menu?"

Scott held up a hand. "No, we need a few—"

"Actually, could you bring a box for these crab cakes, please? They're too good to waste. I'll also have the double-decker chocolate cake." She looked over at Scott before turning back to the waitress. "I'll have that to go, please."

Chapter Six

♥

THE NEXT MORNING, Penny woke up feeling like a tiny man was playing the drums behind her eyelids. She also had a serious case of dry mouth. She rolled her tongue around experimentally and opened her mouth gingerly. She caught a whiff of her breath and it was so bad it made her eyes water.

"Ugh. You know it's bad when you're grossed out by your own morning breath."

That was what she deserved after finishing the entire bottle of champagne at dinner last night. Scott had just watched, quietly, as she'd poured herself glass after glass. She'd never been much of a drinker, but she didn't think he had room to judge her after his half-assed proposal.

After he'd dropped her off at home, she'd closed the door in his face, put her food in the refrigerator, and gone straight to bed. She had barely managed to get her dress and bra off before she passed out.

She walked down the stairs and stumbled through the kitchen to turn on the coffee maker. Her phone rang and she grabbed it from her bag, which she'd dropped in the middle of the living room floor. She had several missed calls from Scott and one from Georgia.

She wasn't ready to face Scott for sure or Georgia and all her questions about the proposal. Her friend was going to be expecting something romantic and exciting. All she had was a halfhearted "let's go be crazy and do it." Which he hadn't even mentioned until after his big news about the job in Atlanta.

Which kind of told her where she ranked on his priority list, didn't it?

"Oh, it was a night to remember, all right."

Now that her initial anger had passed she was more pissed at herself than Scott. He was oblivious, of course, but she shouldn't have been so harsh. Was her reaction any better than the way he'd gone about things?

He should have told her about the job offer before accepting it, that was true. However, ignoring him all through dinner and then leaving him on the doorstep without so much as a farewell wasn't earning her any maturity points either. They needed to talk. They really did.

It was just going to be a little while before she could deal with talking to him in a calm and rational manner.

The phone rang again in her hand and she recognized Georgia's number. She silenced the call and went back to the kitchen to get her cup of coffee. She couldn't hide forever, but she needed caffeine and a shower before she could be expected to deal with the real world.

♥

PENNY KNEW SHE should be thinking about what she was going to say to Scott tonight. She'd agreed to meet him at the bar across the street after work to talk. They'd been together for three years. That wasn't something you just threw away because you were angry.

However, when she looked up to see Matt standing in the doorway to her office Monday afternoon, the frantic beat of her heart told her several things she'd been trying to deny since she'd watched him walk away the prior week. *One*, he truly was as gorgeous as she'd remembered. *Two*, her body responded to him in ways that were both exhilarating and embarrassing. And *three*, she was happy to see him. Purely, simply happy.

Which made absolutely *no* sense.

They weren't friends. She wasn't even sure she liked him. He was definitely going to be a challenging patient. By all accounts, she should be dreading this.

But her heart rapped a steady beat that to her ears sounded nothing like dread. It sounded like excitement. It sounded like anticipation. It sounded like trouble with a capital T.

"Are you ready to get started?" She rose and came from behind her desk. As soon as she got close, his scent reached her nose. It was subtly masculine, like wood smoke and evergreens.

Matt shrugged. "I hope so. Do I need to undress again?"

"Uh, no. Not exactly." Her eyes traveled over the loose

sweatpants and tee shirt he was wearing.

"How'd you get the tee shirt on?"

He shrugged again. "Very carefully. I figured I'd better dress to sweat."

"You were right. Come on, then." She led him down the hall to one of the treatment rooms. "First thing I want to do is get a baseline on you. I'm going to lead you through a series of motions. All you have to do is move your arm and tell me what hurts."

"That doesn't sound so bad."

"You might not say that by the time we're through." It sent a little pang to her heart. Despite his behavior that first day, she didn't relish the thought of causing him any pain, but Penny knew from experience that what followed likely wouldn't be pleasant.

They spent the next twenty minutes going through a range of movement. She had him hold his arm out as high as he could, lift it and rotate his thumb up and down. She noted where he grimaced and where he physically couldn't move his arm anymore. By the time they were done, Matt had a fine sheen of sweat on his brow and his eyes were pinched with pain.

"You can rest back against the wall now. You must be exhausted."

Matt let out a disgusted sound and leaned back. "I shouldn't be this tired from doing nothing."

"You weren't doing nothing. Every motion requires the use of not only the active muscles but also the rest of your body. I suspect you've been compensating for the injured areas so long, you don't even realize how much of a strain it's putting on your other muscles."

"That's why I need to get this figured out. I should have

been healed long before now."

Penny glanced up from her notes. "I know it's really important to you that you stay in shape. I'm curious how you've managed to do that while compensating for your injury. You're in near-perfect physical condition."

"You think so?" He turned to look at her, his dark eyes holding hers. The tips of her ears felt like they were on fire, so she knew her face was probably red, too.

"The musculature on the uninjured shoulder doesn't seem to have been impacted in any way." She ignored his smirk when she didn't respond to his innuendo. "How long did you wait after your surgery before you resumed working out?"

Suddenly he didn't look so smug. Matt glanced at her and then down at the floor. "A few weeks, I guess. I'm not exactly sure. I didn't do anything with that arm for a long time, though."

Exactly as she'd suspected. He'd probably been working out all along. That would explain why he'd never healed properly after the first surgery and also why he was still experiencing pain almost a year later. He could have easily caused new injuries to himself in the months since without even realizing it.

Penny picked up one of the stress balls on the table and wrapped his right hand around it. "Lift this. Higher."

He complied and she put her hand on his injured arm. "See that, right there? Even though you're using your uninjured hand, you can feel it in your injured shoulder, right?"

"Yes. It's tensing when I move."

"Exactly. I don't want you doing any other upper-body work right now. It might feel like you're losing ground, but it's worth it so you can heal overall."

She took the ball back and placed it on the table next to him. "Now you can just lie back and relax because we're going to do some heat therapy. The hard part is over."

Matt reclined on the table and let out a heavy sigh. "You promise?"

There was something inexplicably vulnerable about the way he looked up at her just then. For the first time, he looked like a shadow of his old self, the playful and mischievous boy who'd lived to play tricks on his sister and cause trouble, but who'd looked as innocent as an angel when it was bedtime. It made Penny feel good to see that part of him hadn't been buried completely.

Penny couldn't resist stroking her hand over his brow. "I promise. Now close your eyes."

Although he looked surprised at the gesture, he closed his eyes obediently and let out another heavy sigh. The stress lines on his forehead flattened out after a few moments.

"The hard part is over," he whispered.

Penny wished she could make the same promise to herself.

♥

AFTER HER LAST patient of the day left on Monday evening, Penny leaned her head on the reception desk where Georgia was sorting a stack of patient files.

"Are you okay?" Georgia poked at her arm. "You've been mopey like this all day."

"Can you blame me? First, there's the situation with Matt. I really want to help him, but what if I can't? Then there's Scott. I told him I'd meet him at the bar after work. I know we need to talk, but part of me wishes I could avoid it for a while."

Honestly, it was probably a mistake to meet at a place where so many of her coworkers liked to hang out, but Penny would have agreed to just about anything to get him off the phone before Matt's appointment. It shouldn't be weird talking to him in front of Matt. He was her boyfriend, even if they were fighting.

"You need to just put that man out of his misery. I know the proposal was not exactly ideal, but this is bordering on cruel and unusual punishment," Georgia said.

"I know. It's just that I know this is going to be a difficult conversation. I envy you sometimes," Penny admitted. "You've been married to James since college, so you got to skip the whole dating rat race. No matter what happens, you know he's there for you. You guys may fight, but at the end of the day, you're still a team."

"We work well together and that's important, but that's not why I married him, Penny. If all I needed was a teammate, I could have married one of my girlfriends and gotten sex on the side."

Penny shook her head. "I didn't mean to imply you're like roommates. I know you love him."

"I'm not offended. I just want you to understand. I'm not with him because he's great at handling money and keeps my shopping binges in line. I'm not with him because I need help. I'm with him because I *want* to be. I want to snuggle with him after a hard day and wake up each day with him. I'm happier when we're together. I'd still be married to him even if he wasn't so organized and smart."

"You make it sound so easy. That connection is what I was hoping I'd one day feel for Scott. I thought it would come with time, but it didn't."

"It's not easy, but it is simple. Love isn't complicated, Pen. It's all the other stuff that's complicated. Money, careers, in-laws. The love is the easy part. Do you love Scott?"

Penny looked down at her hands. She'd twisted the rubber

band she was holding into a knot. "I guess the fact that I even have to think about it says it all."

Georgia patted her shoulder. "You know what you need to do. Go talk to him."

Penny went back to her office to gather her things. She took a minute to brush out her hair and wind it back up into a neat bun. She left her white coat hanging over the back of her chair. Georgia waved as Penny left the building.

The bar across the street had an official name, but no one ever used it that she knew of. It had always just been "the bar." When she walked in she immediately spotted Scott sitting at one of the tables on the far right. It was good that he'd gotten a table. Their sure-to-be-awkward conversation wasn't one she wanted overheard.

He stood when she approached. "Hey, I already ordered you a beer."

"Thanks. I need it."

He slid the bottle across the table and she took a sip. The cold liquid sliding down her throat shouldn't have felt so good after being out in the icy wind, but it cooled the blush in her cheeks.

Breaking up with someone was never easy.

"I'm sorry about dinner." Scott grimaced. "I went about that entirely the wrong way. What woman wants her marriage proposal announced at the same time as a job transfer? I didn't even get down on one knee."

Penny took another sip of her beer. "It's okay. I apologize for being so cold afterward. I was upset, but I could have handled it better, too."

He smiled at her across the table and she wondered why he couldn't be the one. Why couldn't she go all mushy when he smiled at her? Why didn't she want to go to sleep with him every night and wake with him in the morning? It would be so much easier if she did.

"You don't want to marry me, do you?" It wasn't so much a question as a statement.

Penny didn't look up as she answered. She couldn't meet his eyes. "No. I don't. I'm sorry."

He let out a breath and drummed his knuckles against the table. "I know. But I'd rather hear it straight out than always wonder."

They sat in silence for a while, each taking sips from their beers. The music changed from the latest country hit to a dance tune and the lights dimmed. The bar was filling up with a much younger crowd. Penny couldn't remember what it felt like to be that young and carefree anymore.

A young guy who didn't even look old enough to drink legally asked to borrow a chair from their table. Scott pushed it toward him.

"It's starting to get crowded. That's my cue to leave." He waited until she looked up. "I'll come by to get my stuff this weekend."

"Of course. There's no rush." They sat in uncomfortable silence before she blurted out, "This is your dream job, right?"

He grinned for the first time since she'd sat down. "Yeah, it is."

"It's what you dream about at night. It's what you want to do when you wake up in the morning. Just the thought of it makes you happy."

"It does," he admitted.

"Have you ever felt that way about me?"

His smile dimmed.

"It's okay. I didn't feel that either. That's why I know it's not right." She leaned across the table and looked him directly in the eyes. "Either way, I'm really proud of you, Scott. Not that it matters now, but I am."

Scott stood and left a few bills on the table. Then he leaned down and kissed her cheek. "It matters to me. A lot. Thank you."

He brushed the back of his hand against her cheek. "Goodbye, Penny."

Chapter Seven

♥

MATT SPENT MOST of Tuesday running errands, picking up groceries, and getting a feel for the neighborhood. If he was going to stay for a few months, he didn't want to have to call Eli for every little thing. It made sense for him to learn his way around his temporary home.

When he walked into the waiting room at Penny's office for their Wednesday appointment, it was empty. He stood at the reception desk and peered around. After a few minutes, he rapped his knuckles on the counter impatiently.

The door next to the reception area opened and an older

man walked out. Matt watched the door slowly close. At the last second, he sprang forward and caught the handle. He glanced behind him before slipping through the doorway.

"Penny? Are you here?" He waited a moment, expecting a nurse or the receptionist to come out at any moment. He walked down the hallway they'd gone down last time. Maybe she was still in her office. Then he heard her voice. He stopped outside one of the treatment rooms and peered through the door. Penny was standing in front of a patient, counting out reps as a man lifted one of his legs off the table and lowered it.

"I must be early," Matt muttered. He might as well just hang in the waiting room until she was done.

Just before he turned around, the man reached a hand down and patted Penny on the behind. She grabbed his hand and placed it back on the table. Her movement was so quick that if he hadn't been watching all along, he would have missed it. It was also automatic, like she was used to it happening.

Rage rose up in Matt's chest. He slapped a hand on the door and shoved it open. Penny turned.

"Matt! What are you doing here?" She glanced at the clock on the wall. "Oh, it's almost time for your appointment."

When she moved closer to him, she stepped slightly to the side and he was able to see the patient's face. The old man on the table behind her looked between them uncertainly. Then, seeing that Penny's attention was diverted, he reached out and patted her on the bottom again. Penny jumped and then whipped around.

"Okay, Mr. Eisenberg. We're done for today. Your daughter will be here any moment to take you back home."

Matt stood staring for a second before a laugh bubbled up and out of his throat. He clamped his lips shut when Penny turned to him with narrowed eyes.

"What is so funny?"

I'm not going to ask. I am not going to ask.

"Nothing. I'll be in the waiting room." He turned and walked back to the lobby before she could say anything else. The receptionist was back at the desk, so he signed the appointment list, grabbed a magazine, and settled in one of the chairs in the far corner of the room. He was halfway through an article about offshore drilling when his name was called. He looked up to see Penny standing in front of him.

"Hello, Sergeant."

Matt tossed the magazine on the table next to his seat and stood. "Hey. Are you ready for me?"

Her eyes narrowed again, as if she wasn't sure if he was making fun of her. "Yes. Glad you made it back. Were you sore after Monday's workout?"

He followed her back down the hallway into a different treatment room than they'd used the last time. "Surprisingly, I was. A little. I have to admit I wasn't expecting to be."

"I know you're in excellent shape, but the exercises we'll be doing are going to target areas you've never had to worry about before. It's normal to be a little sore." Penny turned and looked at him directly. "If your pain rises above mild soreness or irritation then you need to call me. Immediately. Okay?"

"Okay. Will do." He fought to keep his amusement hidden since he knew it would only piss her off. He wondered if she was aware of how her chest heaved when she got all worked up and bossy. He doubted it. She wouldn't wear that prim hairstyle if she was the type to flaunt herself. No, he'd wager money she had no idea just how hot she was.

Matt sat on the end of the long plastic exam table and watched as Penny bustled around the room. She gathered a small red ball, a couple of weights, and what looked like a belt.

As she moved, her scrubs bunched and tightened over her behind. Her incredibly toned, perfectly round behind. No wonder the old guy couldn't keep his hands to himself.

I'm not going to ask. I am not going to ask.

He lasted about forty-five seconds before he blurted, "So, did that old guy just grab your ass?"

Penny stopped moving abruptly. Then her lips stretched into a big smile. Matt had to stare. Her entire face changed when she smiled. She went from pretty to radiant.

"Mr. Eisenberg? Oh, yeah. We have a nickname for him around here. Grabby-hands. The assistants all pick straws to see who'll deal with him at check-in. Luckily, he only needs therapy twice a week now."

"I know the guy is older than dirt, but that's harassment. And it's gross."

Penny looked over her shoulder at him. "He has Alzheimer's."

"So you feel sorry for him? I don't get it. I guess I'm not that nice, but I'd still kick him to the curb. It's not like he'll remember, right?"

"Matt!" Her mouth fell open. "Not okay!" She stared at him in shocked silence for a moment. Then he saw it. Her lips twitched like she was trying not to laugh. It seemed to make her angrier because she crossed her arms and glared at him. "That is... I can't even state how many ways that is *not* okay."

He held up his hands. "Sorry. I'm not making light of his condition. I'm just saying."

Penny narrowed her eyes at him. "And I don't feel sorry for him. As you so elegantly stated, it's not like he's aware of what's happening to him most of the time. But his family is. He has children and grandchildren. They deserve to have a grandpa who has enough mobility to give them a hug when they come visit."

Matt sat back and observed her. "I'm starting to understand you a little better. You like to fight for the underdog."

"I like to help people. Everyone deserves a little help, right?"

"Yeah. I'm just not as selfless as you are."

"I wouldn't say that. You jump out of airplanes to keep the rest of us safe. I'd say that's pretty selfless."

Matt looked down at his hands. "I don't do it because I want thanks."

"Heroes are never asking for thanks, but that doesn't mean they don't deserve it."

Heat rushed to his cheeks. Many people expressed their appreciation for his military service and he'd learned to accept the praise with some grace. With Penny, it was different though. It made him feel like a little kid being praised by his favorite teacher in front of the class.

Because you're trying to impress her. You care a little too much what she thinks.

"I guess. So, you've been putting up with Mr. Grabby-hands for how long now?"

"It's been about a year since he started coming here. His mind is usually back in the seventies, so he still thinks it's okay to call women "sweetheart" and pinch our bottoms as a form of affection. It's gross but he's harmless."

"So does that mean I'd get the same treatment if I had wandering hands?"

Penny pushed a stray lock of hair behind her ear and got busy lining up the items she'd collected on the table next to him. "That's different. You're different."

"Am I? Why? Maybe I temporarily forget my manners and reach out when I see a pair of soft, perfectly round—"

"Matt!" Her head snapped up.

"I was going to say '*stress balls.*' Why, Penelope, what did you think I was going to say?"

It was an unexpected pleasure to watch her blush and stumble over her words. Teasing her was just too easy.

"Nothing. You're not pulling me into your perverted games." She sniffed and picked up a clipboard from the table.

She didn't look at him as she made a few notations on the sheet. He leaned over and tried to read it but when she saw him looking, she pulled it away and flipped the top page down. He could only imagine what she'd written about him in her small, neat handwriting. *Patient is being difficult,* probably.

The thought made him smile.

"There's nothing perverted about it. I assure you, it's completely natural for a straight man to lose most of the blood circulation to his brain when he sees a woman like you."

"A woman in scrubs and who wears her hair in a bun? You really are a charmer if you expect me to believe that." Penny scoffed.

Matt leaned forward. "Trust me, I'm not worried about how you wear your hair. And as for the scrubs…" Something in his voice or maybe his facial expression must have conveyed how serious he was because she suddenly stood ramrod straight.

"Enough talking. We have work to do." She didn't meet his eyes as she motioned for him to raise his arm.

Matt complied, more than eager to get started. As she led him through a series of exercises, Penny was tough but encouraging. When he did something wrong, she corrected him. When he did something right, she praised him.

No pushover, she didn't hesitate to yank him back in line if he got out of order. She didn't respond to any of his suggestive comments, just gave him a stern look that was quickly becoming his favorite on her. By the time his hour was up, he was sure he'd never been so rebuffed by a woman.

He'd also never smiled as much.

♥

FRIDAY AFTERNOON, PENNY got her first glimpse of Matt's determination. Most patients needed a break by the second or third appointment. This was when it sank in how much hard work was ahead if they wanted to reach their goals. This was often when self-doubt made them want to reconsider.

Matt's features were pinched and strained ten minutes into the appointment, but he never balked, no matter what she asked him to do. He didn't ask for a break or back down. His ego probably wouldn't allow it, she realized.

Ego could get a patient in trouble just as quickly as giving up. She didn't want him to push himself too hard this early. After the first half an hour, she let go of his arm and stepped back. "Time for a break."

Matt glanced at her in surprise. "No, I'm good. Let's keep going."

She pinched his triceps when he didn't lower his arm. "Pushing too hard this soon can do more harm than good. I want to do some massage now."

He lowered his arm reluctantly. She motioned for him to turn so she could reach his back. After one last suspicious glance, he turned to face the wall. When she placed her hands on his shoulders, he jumped.

"Just relax, Matt. I'm not going to do anything painful. So, how are your parents doing?" She figured it couldn't hurt to distract him with small talk.

Matt grimaced as she pressed gently on the top of his

trapezius muscle. "They're great. My dad retired a few years ago, so they moved to Florida to be near his family. We see them a few times a year at holidays. Which is about all we can stand, honestly."

"What? Your parents are awesome. I remember being completely in awe the first time I met your mom. She had the best clothes, and the way your dad looked at her..." She sighed. "I'd never seen anyone so glamorous."

Matt acknowledged her comment with a slight grunt. "What about your folks? The Colonel should be retired by now too, right?"

"Yeah, although my mom had to bribe him to go through with it. I'm sure if he had his way, he'd work until the day he dies. He's taken up playing checkers and reading biographies. Mom's happy to have him home, even though she complains he's driving her crazy." Penny chuckled thinking about her parents.

"I bet they're really proud of you. All that studying paid off."

"Yeah, they are. My dad wanted me to go to medical school at first. He couldn't understand why I chose physical therapy specifically. But even though he didn't exactly get it, he was cheering the loudest when I graduated with a doctorate in physical therapy. Every article that mentions my name, he has it saved in a scrapbook somewhere."

"That's as it should be," Matt said. He glanced at her as she massaged down the muscles of his back. "You know, I used to envy your family."

Penny was so shocked that her hands stopped moving. "Why would you envy us? Your parents were so in love."

He shrugged, his muscles bunching beneath her hands. "My parents' brand of love didn't leave much room for us kids. I always felt like they were waiting for us to grow up so they could be alone again. We were more like cute toys they could play with and show off to their friends. Until we got too big to be cute anymore."

"Oh. I see." Penny hoped her voice didn't convey the sorrow she felt. He'd balk if she showed any pity. So she tried to sound unaffected when really she just wanted to hug him.

"It's not that big of a deal. I'm not the sensitive type, so I didn't really care."

He hesitated just long enough for Penny to get the sense that it *had* mattered, even though he hadn't wanted it to.

Matt glanced over his shoulder again and this time he raised his eyebrows. He sent a pointed look at her fingers until she started massaging again. She rolled her eyes. He grinned at her before turning back around.

"I didn't care, but Mara did. She used to follow my mom around, trying to act like her and do her hair the same way. They had a decent relationship until we were teenagers. When Mara didn't want to compete in beauty pageants the way my mom used to, that strained things a lot. They haven't been close since."

"That's hard," Penny said when he didn't offer anything else. She was surprised by the swell of anger she felt on his behalf. "No child should be made to feel like their presence isn't wanted. I'm sorry you were ever made to feel that way. You've done pretty well for yourself, Matt Simmons. I'm sure you'll do even better things in the future."

"You haven't changed a bit," he whispered. "You were always softhearted."

He turned to look at her and she realized how close they were. Close enough that she could see the faint shadow of his beard where it was starting to grow in. Close enough that she could smell the scent of his skin.

See the look in his eyes.

He was staring at her mouth. She momentarily stopped breathing. When he looked up, he didn't even try to pretend he wasn't looking. She could read the question in his eyes as clearly as if it was written on his forehead in magic marker.

"We can't," she blurted. "I can't get involved with a patient."

"Just tell me you're not interested. Look at me, Penelope." His voice was soft, but she flinched at the sound of her name. Finally, she looked at him. His dark eyes focused on her face with laser-like intensity.

"Tell me you don't feel anything when you look at me, and I'll never bring it up again," Matt offered.

After an interminably long time in which she contemplated lying, she finally whispered, "I can't."

He didn't argue, just leaned back against the wall and said, "So, I guess we're at an impasse. For now."

♥

THAT SUNDAY WHEN Matt arrived at the Alexanders' for dinner, he was braced for a round of questions. Showing up around all his friends wearing a sling was just asking for it, but when Ridley answered the door, she didn't even bat an eyelash.

She merely said hello and directed him inside.

When Jackson had followed a few minutes later, he'd gone straight to the kitchen and emerged with trays of food. He'd then started talking about basketball. Before long he'd been engrossed in the conversation and had forgotten to be self-conscious.

After Jackson went back to the kitchen to help his mom bring out the rest of the food, Matt remembered that his friend didn't even watch basketball that often. He was more into football. He'd successfully taken Matt's mind off things though. It hit Matt then just how much he appreciated his friends.

Matt pulled out the paper plates and bowls and arranged them on one of the folding tables in the family room. He was glad now that he'd changed his mind and decided to wear the sling. He hadn't even planned on wearing it at first, but a promise made was a promise kept in his book. Penny had said he'd be back in fighting shape if he could follow her rules and he wanted that more than anything.

A sudden round of feminine squeals erupted behind him. He turned to see one of Jackson's singers, Kaylee Wilhelm, struggle through the door juggling a baby carrier and a bright pink baby bag. She was immediately surrounded by cooing, squealing women.

Trent met his eyes over the clamor of the girls and they shared a sympathetic look. His sister was right in the middle of the throng.

"Oh my gosh. Look at those tiny toes." Mara glanced back at him. Matt just shook his head. He liked kids as much as the next guy, but he didn't envy his friend right then. Mara had always loved babies and no doubt Trent was in for a load of baby talk when they got home.

Eli walked up next to him and handed him a beer. He observed the squalling pack of women with interest. "This is going to take a while."

Matt took a swig of his beer and nodded in agreement. His sister and all the other women were cooing at the baby and fighting good-naturedly over whose turn it was to hold her next.

"Thanks again for letting me crash at your place. I would have been exhausted if I'd been driving back and forth all week. In fact, I wanted to talk to you about renting more long-term. A couple of months, maybe."

The thought of spending months away from home suddenly didn't seem so bad. Working with Penny had given him new hope for the future. If he could stay the course, there was a good chance he could get back everything he'd lost.

He thought of Penny, the way she'd so naturally given him the strong encouragement he'd clearly been lacking all along. She was going to get him where he needed to be. He could feel it.

Eli took a long sip of his beer. "No need. You're one of my brother's best friends. I know you aren't going to trash the place. Just keep the key and use it as long as you need. I'm planning on staying down here through the summer. Maybe even for good."

"Wow. Does everyone else know that?"

"Not yet, so I'd appreciate you keeping that quiet for a little while. I've missed being home and I've been thinking about coming back for a while." Eli looked behind him at the cluster of people around Kay and the baby. His brothers stood off to the side, watching their wives indulgently. "I've got two nephews and a niece on the way. It's finally time. The business is thriving and I can run things from anywhere at this point."

"I understand. I've been thinking about making some changes myself," Matt admitted.

It wasn't often he talked about his parents, but Penny's words had stayed with him. He didn't need anyone to approve of the way he lived his life; he'd learned that a long time ago.

However, Penny hadn't sounded like she was just stroking his ego or placating him. She'd sounded like she was proud of him. As someone who'd known him when he was a kid, that counted for a hell of a lot.

Maybe he wasn't as immune to needing validation as he liked to believe.

"Actually I wanted to mention to you that we have openings if you're ever looking to get into a new line of work. Security is a natural fit for someone with your training." Eli took another long swig of his beer, finishing it off.

"I might just take you up on the offer once I'm back to one hundred percent."

"I can give you the names and numbers of some of my employees. A few of them are ex-Army. They can give you the no-bullshit lowdown on what it's like to work for me if you're interested."

The offer made Matt smile. If he'd ever wondered if Eli was a stand-up kind of guy, he'd have his answer now.

"Thanks, but that won't be necessary." Matt gestured with his chin toward the crowd in the center of the room.

"You've got all the recommendations I need right here."

Chapter Eight

♥

OVER THE NEXT few weeks, Matt worked harder than he ever had before. He was grateful that Eli had offered the use of his house because he wasn't sure he could have handled driving such a long distance three times a week. Penny had him on an aggressive treatment plan. She'd explained everything she was doing, but most of it went over his head. In the end, the only thing he cared about was that his shoulder hurt less and less each day. He didn't feel like he was getting stronger yet, but at least he wasn't in as much pain. That was something.

Matt decided to drive home in mid-February and check on

his house. His sister had been checking on it for him, collecting his mail and watering the few scraggly plants he had. She and Trent were there currently to keep him company his first weekend back in town.

"So, tell us about therapy. How is Penny doing?"

Matt froze, his beer halfway to his mouth. "She's great. Things are going well so far. I'm still supposed to wear the sling when I'm hanging at home, but she said I can take it off when I go out now."

"That's great, Matt. See? I was right. Penny was exactly what you needed."

Matt made a noncommittal sound. "How are things with you? Do you still hate your job?"

He was eager to turn the conversation to his sister. She was relentless when she caught wind of something to do with his love life. He'd been mostly successful at keeping her away from the few girls he'd dated the past year. The last thing he needed was for Mara to dig her heels in and pester him about Penny. Especially since he wasn't even sure how he felt about Penny.

"I got a promotion and I'm assisting one of the top executives now. He's slightly less annoying than my previous manager, so that's a plus. It also means a good pay raise."

"That's great, right?"

"Yeah, it is. I can finally stop worrying about money so much. I can start paying you back, too."

"You don't need to, I already told you that. It's not a big deal. It was a gift."

"I know." Mara hooked an arm around his neck and pulled him into a quick hug. "I just feel bad taking so much money from you. What if you need it?"

Trent rapped on the table to get Mara's attention. "If your brother is in a generous mood, just say thank you."

"Okay, okay. I'm not trying to be ungrateful. I've just never had someone give me ten thousand dollars before."

Trent spit out the sip of soda he'd just taken. "Wait, how much?"

Mara looked between the two of them uncertainly. "Ten thousand dollars. He gave me part of my down payment for the town house. I never would have been able to afford to buy it if he hadn't done that."

Matt shook his head. "That's not true. I was living with you off and on for years so I wouldn't have to pay for my own place. I appreciated you letting me crash with you. It was more like paying you back."

Trent stood so suddenly that his chair teetered on two legs before crashing to the ground behind him. "Mara, can I talk to you?"

Mara glanced at Matt. "Sure, okay. Matt, I got those pretzel things you like. They're in the kitchen." She walked with Trent back toward the bedroom.

Matt got up too and wandered into the kitchen. He found the jumbo pretzel sticks and stuck two in his mouth. There probably wasn't much on television, but if nothing else, he could turn to sports. When he sat on the couch, the voices floating back from the bedroom got progressively louder.

"I'm not comfortable with owing Matt that kind of money."

Matt turned up the volume, hoping it would drown them out. It was embarrassing enough to be caught in the middle of an argument between his sister and one of his best friends. Having to pretend not to hear it was just icing on the cake. He couldn't even sneak out since they were at his house.

"He's my brother. He's just looking out for me. It's not like I got the money from some pimp on the streets or something."

"Your brother is always there to save the day, isn't he?"

"What the hell does that mean?"

"It means I'm starting to wonder if there's any room left for me to help you, Mara. Seems like you never really need my help. The role of protector has already been taken."

After an uncomfortably long minute, Matt was starting to wonder if he should get up and check on them. Another minute passed and finally he couldn't take it anymore. He rounded the corner and stopped short. Mara was leaning against the wall, the faint black trails on her cheeks evidence that she'd been crying.

Matt had been working to tamp down his overprotective-big-brother instincts for the past year, but the sight of his sister in tears gave him the immediate urge to hunt his friend down and beat his ass. Just for the hell of it.

"Are you okay?"

Mara wiped at the wet tracks on her cheeks. "I'm fine. Trent left. He had some stuff to do."

It was a little ridiculous to pretend he hadn't overheard their conversation, but Matt was tempted to. Partially because he was afraid talking about it would make her break down in tears again. "Look, I can take the money back if it's going to cause a problem between you and Trent. You can pay me back whenever you get the money."

"Can I hang out for a while?" Mara spoke as if she hadn't heard him. He figured that was her way of saying she didn't want to talk about it.

"Of course. You can stay as long as you want. Anytime."

Mara wiped her cheeks with the edge of her sleeve. "I'll put on a movie. No chick flicks, I promise."

Matt loved Trent like a brother but he'd better fix things and soon. He'd never liked to see his sister cry, especially not when it was his fault.

"Go ahead and put on one of those sappy movies you like so much. I'm man enough to take it."

Mara smiled tremulously through her tears. "I know you are."

♥

THE FIRST WEEK that Matt showed up for therapy looking like someone kicked his dog, Penny let it go. He had to be getting run-down driving back and forth so much. He was probably just tired. She could use a weekend to relax, herself.

When he showed up the next Monday looking just as dejected, she tried to pry it out of him subtly. He answered all her questions and was perfectly polite, but there were no jokes or inappropriate comments. He was like a robot. He did his therapy, followed all her directions without complaint, and then left.

Something was *definitely* wrong.

By Wednesday afternoon, she decided to just ambush him. Before he even sat down on the table, she turned to him and said, "What's wrong with you?"

Matt shook his head. "Nothing. Wait, you mean with my shoulder?"

"No, not your shoulder. Your shoulder is great. But *you* aren't. You've been in a funk for the past week and a half. It's depressing and completely unlike you. I can't believe I'm saying this, but I liked you better when you were a smartass."

A hint of his trademark smirk appeared. "I'm sorry. I'm just tired."

This was what she'd wanted, she reminded herself. He was probably just trying to respect her wishes. She couldn't get involved with a patient and wasn't looking to get involved with anyone, actually. If they were going to keep their distance, this was how it had to be. Unless he was unhappy with her for some reason. The thought made her feel a little sick. Was that what it was?

Was Matt *angry* with her?

She ran through everything they'd covered the past four weeks. Other than small talk about their parents and catching up on what they'd been doing the past few years, they'd been completely focused. They hadn't discussed anything that deep or controversial. Nothing that would cause him to give her the cold shoulder. His therapy was going well. He was gaining strength and flexibility at astounding rates.

It couldn't be about his treatment, she assured herself.

"You know, we could restrict your appointments to Tuesday through Thursday or even just go to twice a week if you want. It would keep your driving to a minimum."

Matt leaned back against the wall and rolled his head to look at her. "Actually, I've been staying at a friend's house in Springfield. It's about fifteen minutes away."

Penny sat in the plastic chair next to the treatment table. "If driving isn't what's putting those circles under your eyes, what is?"

"It's nothing. I'll be fine. I just need to relax." He must have realized his explanation was pretty weak because he added, "I'll be fine after I get a good night's sleep."

"Right. Insomnia is what makes you look like someone just stole all your toys from the sandbox." Penny pursed her lips and stood. "Look, since you're in town we should hang out. I feel bad. If I'd known you were in town all this time, I would have invited you out before. Georgia loves to plan happy hours."

"You want to hang out with me?" Disbelief dripped from every word. "What happened to keeping our distance?"

"Surely we can have a drink in a public place without incident. Besides, we'll have a whole group of people with us. Meet me back here at five o'clock. No excuses."

Matt stood slowly, stretching his arms overhead. His shirt rose up, flashing an irresistible patch of bronze skin. "Fine. I'll see you at five."

Penny let out a soft sigh of appreciation as soon as he left. After making a few notes in his file, she walked down the hallway to the reception desk. Georgia looked up when she leaned over the counter.

"Could you work your magic and plan a happy hour? Get some people together and I'll actually go this time."

"What's got you interested in happy hour all of a sudden? You've never attended any of the ones I've organized before now."

"It's for Matt. He doesn't know anyone in town. We should take him out."

Georgia narrowed her eyes. "*Penelope Lewis.* Are you trying to seduce Sergeant Sexy?"

Penny gasped and glanced around them. "Would you be quiet? What if he were to walk up and hear you call him that?"

"He'd probably be flattered. He doesn't have a stick up his butt like some people I know. And I say that as your friend."

"Hah. Some friend," Penny muttered.

Georgia just grinned back at her and then bent down to rummage in her handbag. When she straightened, she held her cell phone. "Give me a few minutes and we'll have a group for happy hour. But you will owe me. I will want details. Lots of dirty, kinky details."

Penny let her head drop into her hands. She'd been trying so hard to keep things platonic and casual between her and Matt.

How could she do that when everything around them seemed determined to throw them together? There was only so much a girl could take.

"Oh, yeah, and you'll probably need this later." Georgia pressed something into her hand and then walked away, whistling. Penny uncurled her fingers and stared, slack-jawed, at the foil square in her palm.

"I am going to kill her."

♥

"SO, ARE YOU finally going to tell me what's wrong?" Penny ordered them both beers and then leaned her elbows on the bar. At first she'd been on her way to the back, but then her eyes had strayed over to the table where she'd sat the last time she'd been here. No, they were definitely staying at the bar.

No intimate discussions in dark corners. Especially not with the condom Georgia had given her burning a hole in her pocket.

It was bad enough that Georgia had totally set her up. She'd arrived at the bar at five o'clock with Matt in tow, only to find no one else was there. They'd waited half an hour before Penny had finally figured it out. This was a classic Georgia move and she knew her friend wouldn't deny it. She'd been hinting that she should make a move on her sexy patient since day one.

"I've been staying in Northern Virginia the last few weeks to avoid my sister. I wanted to give her space to fix things with her fiancé." Matt finally answered her.

"This is about Mara?" Penny knew it was silly, but she'd been desperately worried he was dissatisfied with his treatment. "Why do you have to stay away for her to fix her relationship? You don't get along with the guy?"

"It's not that. We're friends. Good friends. At least I thought we were. I've been wrong about a lot of things lately." He turned toward her, resting his hand on her knee. Her skin ignited beneath her slacks, goose bumps springing up beneath the gentle press of his fingers. She was so distracted by the sensual slide of his hand that she almost missed what he was saying.

"Here's the thing. I've been friends with Trent for a long time. He's a great guy. But even great guys do stupid shit when they're young. And I'm not holding it against him because hell, I was right there next to him for most of it."

"So what's the problem?"

"The problem is *I was right there for most of it.* I know some stuff about him that I should not know about the guy who's sleeping next to my sister. I know about the chick he used as a booty call for three straight semesters. I know about the threesome he and his ex-girlfriend were planning senior year. I know too much. I wish I could scrub it all from my brain."

Penny took a deep pull on her beer. "Wow. So you feel like you're keeping stuff from your sister that she needs to know. I get it. I wouldn't want to know that kind of stuff about my sisters' husbands. At all."

He glanced at her. "Men are dogs. Most of us conceal it well, but we're all animals when it comes to women. My job was always to keep the other dogs away from Mara. Now I'm supposed to just step back. It's not that easy to do."

Penny stood and waved a finger at the bartender. He came right over and leaned against the bar, grinning a little too intimately for her taste. Matt scooted his barstool a little closer to Penny's and gave the guy a hard look. Penny couldn't suppress a little shiver of pleasure when his arm came to rest on the back of her seat.

"Another round for me and my friend." She looked at Matt. "Are you staying with beer or you want something a little stronger? I don't mind driving."

"What the hell. Glenlivet, neat."

Penny raised her eyebrows. "A scotch man, huh? My dad keeps a bottle in his office. I can't stand the stuff, but hey."

She turned back to the bartender. "I'm switching to water."

"Don't worry. You won't have to carry me home."

Penny crossed her legs and experienced a uniquely feminine thrill when Matt's eyes followed the motion. She'd left her sweater back at the office, so once she shrugged out of her coat, her arms were bare and brushed up against him enticingly when she moved.

"How did you know about the threesome? Do guys really talk about that kind of stuff?"

He gave her a look. "We don't have sleepovers and braid each other's hair if that's what you mean, but yeah, we talk." He faced forward. "Plus, who do you think they asked to be their third?"

Penny swallowed wrong and then dissolved into a coughing fit that drew the attention of the entire bar. She held a napkin over her mouth, trying to muffle the sounds of her hacking while Matt watched her with knowing eyes.

She couldn't even imagine being in bed with Matt and someone else. Matt was enough to have her synapses misfiring all by himself.

"So what did you fight with your sister about?" It was a struggle to feign nonchalance after her humiliating fit of spluttering, but she was determined to try.

"Before my first deployment, I gave my sister some money. Okay, it was a lot of money."

"Well, that was generous of you."

"Her fiancé, Trent, doesn't agree. He thinks she should pay me back. He doesn't want them to owe me so much. But I don't see it as a debt. It's a gift. I just wanted to give my sister a gift and make her life a little easier. It doesn't come with strings attached."

"I know that. If it was anyone else, I wouldn't believe that, but it's you. Taking care of people is what you do. It's who you are."

Matt accepted his drink with a nod for the bartender. He took a sip and regarded Penny over the glass. "Sometimes I feel like you can see straight through me. That may not always be a good thing."

"You're like a relic from another era, Matt Simmons. A time when people meant what they said, did what they should, and people looked out for each other. That's nothing to be ashamed of."

"You'd be surprised."

"Well, you know how some people feel about relics. They either want to collect them and put them on a shelf or they stick them in a museum. I just want to make sure neither happens to you. That's why I've been pushing you so hard."

"Am I going to recover? Really?" He put his glass down and looked at her until she met his eyes. "If I'm always going to have weakness in my shoulder, I'd rather just hear it straight. You can tell me the truth. I can take it."

"I believe you can take just about anything, Sergeant." Her lips tipped up at the corners at his glower. "It's my professional opinion that you're going to be just fine. I wasn't sure about you in the beginning, but your healing has been amazing these past few weeks. You're very lucky."

"I am." Matt leaned close enough so that she couldn't mistake his meaning. "Very lucky."

Penny blushed and choked on the sip of water she'd just taken. "So, we should probably get out of here. Are you ready?"

"For anything."

Chapter Nine

♥

MATT HELD THE door for Penny and then held out his arm to escort her across the street. She glanced behind her once and then tucked her hand into the crook of his elbow. Most of the other homes had a light burning out front. Eli's house was the only one that was completely dark. He'd forgotten to leave the front light on.

"Nice place."

"Wish I could take the credit. This is my friend's house. I'm just staying here until I'm done with therapy."

"Oh right. I forgot." Penny laughed softly.

They climbed the steps to the porch. Matt paused in front of the closed front door. "I had fun tonight."

"Me too. I had a good time, too." Penny looked up at him from beneath her lashes. She hopped from one foot to the other, then glanced at the front door. "I guess I should go. It's pretty late. I'll be a zombie tomorrow."

"Right. Thanks for hanging out with me for a few hours. I hope I didn't keep you from anything important."

Penny fiddled with her keys, swinging them around on the keychain a few times. "No, you didn't. There's nothing waiting for me at home. *No one* waiting for me."

If she hadn't looked so dejected then maybe he could have let her walk away. But when she looked at him like that, her gorgeous blue eyes swimming with sadness and vulnerability, he was powerless to stop himself for reaching out for her.

Matt slid a hand under her hair and pulled her forward slowly. When they were only a breath apart, he rested his forehead against hers. They stood like that for a few moments, their breath mingling in the cold air.

"*I've been waiting for you.* It's been driving me insane," he whispered, the words lingering between them.

She made a soft sound that traveled directly down his spine and hit him right in the gut. "Matt." His name was no more than a puff of air from her lips.

"If you don't want me, you have to tell me now," he gasped. "I don't know if I can keep from touching you, Penny." He tugged her up until she was on her toes, using the opportunity to feast on the soft skin of her throat. She whimpered, a soft helpless sound in the back of her throat.

"I can't think when you do that. Well, I can, but all I'm thinking is don't stop." The tortured tone of her voice was the last straw. Matt pulled out his keys and went through a furious tussling match with the door until he finally managed to get it open. He grabbed her arm and pulled her across the threshold, kicking the door closed behind them with his foot.

Before the door was even shut, he had her in his arms. She arched against him and then made a strangled sound and pushed back.

"Oh no, Matt. Your shoulder—"

"Is fine." It touched him that even now she was worried about him but he didn't want her thinking about his therapy. Hell, he didn't want her *thinking* at all. He nipped at her earlobe, pulling the skin between his teeth until she melted against him. "I have this awesome physical therapist, so it's much better now. I can even lift things. You want to see?"

Wordlessly, she nodded. He lifted her carefully and leaned against her, fitting himself directly between her thighs. She cried out at the contact, her muscles going rigid. He didn't release her, just used the opportunity to hold her captive for another kiss. Her mouth opened under his, their tongues meeting and sliding over each other. It was like he was consuming her whole until the taste of her meshed into him, a permanent tattoo on his soul.

Her long legs wrapped around his waist and held him to her as they kissed. The woman was nothing but legs and curves. He'd been pathetically grateful when she'd left that awful white coat at work so he could see the intriguing dips and valleys of her figure. She did interesting things to her simple navy blue blouse and gray slacks.

She tilted her head back, presenting Matt with the perfect line of her throat. He kissed the soft skin, loving it when she shuddered and clutched his shoulders. Then she took his hand and pressed it between her legs. Her blue eyes held his for minutes, hours, days, as his hand slipped beneath the waistband of her slacks. When he encountered the soft cotton between her thighs, the noticeably damp cotton, he lost all semblance of his finesse.

He moved her panties aside easily and pressed against her, two fingers sliding deep. That was almost enough to make him lose it right there, the sensation of his fingers being sucked into warm, velvety heat. But if that wasn't enough to knock him flat on his ass, Penny went rigid and her head fell back, thumping against the wall. The look of tortured satisfaction on her face...

Penny pushed against his shoulder gently until he put her down. Her eyes stood out against her pale skin, looking even bluer than before if that was possible. She wore very little makeup and with her hair pulled back so severely, it was clear she wasn't trying to attract anyone's attention.

Well, she had his whether she was trying for it or not.

Without losing eye contact, she popped the first button on her blouse. Then another. His blood pressure jacked higher with every inch of skin revealed. Matt was a slave at that moment because a nuclear explosion could have occurred behind him and he wouldn't have been able to turn away.

Her eyes shifted behind him and she suddenly went rigid. Her fingers shook as she re-buttoned her blouse. "I have to go. I'm really sorry, I just... have to go."

"It's okay. Do you need me to come with you?"

"No. I'm sorry. I just need to get home." She didn't look at him as she straightened her clothes. Matt touched her back gently and she froze.

"Penny, what's wrong?"

"Nothing. This is just not a good idea. I shouldn't have let things go as far as they did." She finally looked up at him. The apology in her blue eyes softened the blow to his ego slightly.

"I'll see you next week."

Matt watched, dumbfounded, as she yanked the door open. He stood in the doorway until she was safely in her car. It wasn't until she drove away that he remembered he'd left his truck at the bar.

He closed the door and leaned against the wood. "What the hell happened?" She'd been right there with him right up until the end. She'd been like fire in his arms, hot and just as dangerous to his control. Until she'd suddenly gone cold. It just didn't make any sense.

He lifted his eyes and his gaze landed on his Army hat sitting on the hall table. He reached out and picked it up.

Then he let out a harsh curse.

♥

THE NEXT DAY, Matt decided it was time to stop winging it. Penny writhing in his arms had been an unexpected pleasure. One he wouldn't mind repeating.

He'd suspected they'd be good together, but he'd had no idea just *how* good it would be. He hadn't gotten any sleep the prior night with her taste still on his tongue and the memory of her rubbing herself against his leg. She'd worked him up good and then left him hard up.

Literally.

He'd never had this much trouble convincing a woman to go out with him before. He wasn't exactly a ladies' man—he was far too blunt to be smooth—but he'd never had anyone run away from him either. Matt scowled. It was probably time to admit he was striking out.

He needed help.

Normally, he'd call Jackson or Nick for advice. The

Alexander brothers could probably give him an entire seduction plan, complete with date ideas and a list of things to talk about. Too bad he probably couldn't pull off anything they'd suggest.

Matt pulled out his phone and looked at his recent calls. Eli's name was at the top. He'd been in contact with him a lot lately and even though he didn't know Elliott that well, he felt a connection with him. He was a gruff kind of guy and definitely not a smooth talker either. Yet, looking at his bedroom, he apparently didn't have any trouble in the seduction department. Before he could talk himself out of it, he hit the number.

"Yeah." Eli answered on the first ring.

"Hey, it's Matt. Sorry to bother you, but I was wondering if I could get your advice on something. The thing is... I was hoping you could tell me what there is to do in the area. You know, places you could take a date."

There was a smile in Eli's voice when he responded. "I see you've found time for something other than physical therapy. Good for you."

"Well, actually I haven't."

Eli was quiet, then he broke out into chuckles. "Your therapist must be a pretty girl then."

Matt leaned back and kicked his feet up on the bed. "Look, here's the deal. I really like this girl. It would be nice to spend a little time with a woman that's about more than just sex. I don't want to take her to some club where everyone there is drunk and trying to pick up on each other. But at the same time, going out to dinner doesn't seem all that original either."

"All right, I can send you the names of a few local places with decent food and live music. I've always found them good for a casual date. If you want something fancier, you'll probably need to drive into D.C."

"Thanks. I'm trying to find something a little different. She's not exactly the easiest person to impress. Normally I'd ask Jackson or Nick, but their brand of flattery won't work on this girl. And I'm pretty sure any ideas they gave me would be stuff I couldn't pull off anyway."

"I understand where you're coming from. Jackson and Nick operate on an entirely different wavelength. I've never had the patience for the types of games they play. My advice is to let her tell you what she likes to do."

"Let her tell me," Matt mused. "So I should ask her?"

"No, definitely don't do that. Women never say what they mean anyway. Just *listen* to her. If she mentions something that she likes, see if you can make it happen. Even if it's Argentinian flamenco dancing or something you really don't want to do."

"I really hope she doesn't want to see me dance. I definitely won't have any chance with her then."

Eli's laugh rumbled over the line. "Just trust me. No matter what it is, if you can give her an experience she'll remember, then you have a chance."

♥

WHEN MATT ARRIVED for his therapy appointment Friday morning, Penny was wearing her strictly business face. He would have laughed if he hadn't been so frustrated. Every step forward he made with her seemed to be followed by two steps backward.

"Good morning, Matt. Are you ready to try something new?"

Matt clapped his hands. "I'm ready for anything. What have

you got for me?"

Penny motioned for him to follow her. They walked down the hall and ended up in the gym. She crossed to the equipment rack in the corner and picked up a small white ball.

"You're progressing well with the exercises we've done so far. So I thought we'd start some plyometric drills today. We'll do some wall dribbles and some overhead throws." She handed him the ball. "Let's take it slowly."

Matt dropped the ball and tried to bounce it back with his left hand. He frowned when his arm wouldn't cooperate and the ball hit his hand and rolled to the side. Penny retrieved it and handed it back.

"You can do it at your own pace. It's going to take a while to regain the flexibility you once had."

Matt finally got his arm in a good position and was able to dribble the ball against the wall a few times. It was a challenge to catch it and hold it at chest level. It was still hard for him to believe just how many muscle groups were used in everyday activities such as reaching overhead or picking up a grocery bag. Things most people did and took for granted until they suddenly couldn't do them anymore. He had a new appreciation for the human body.

He thought back to the little girl he'd seen the first day he'd come to the center. He had it easy compared to someone who'd been born with a disability. Someone like that little girl would probably give anything to be able to do the things he could do. It made him ashamed of the times he wanted to slack off and galvanized him to work twice as hard. There was no excuse for complaining when you had the chance to get better.

He looked up at Penny. When their eyes met she glanced away. He sighed. If her plan was to keep them from having time to talk about the weekend, it was working. He couldn't talk and concentrate on the ball at the same time.

He waited until the ball bounced back and then grabbed it. "It doesn't have to be awkward, you know."

Penny's mouth dropped slightly. "It's not awkward, is it?"

"Yeah, kind of."

She looked at the floor. "Sorry. I told you I'm not good at this."

"How about we just rewind and go back to the way it was? I'll make off-color jokes and you'll give me that side-eye you're so good at. Then we'll get back to work."

Penny shook her head. "I don't know how you do that."

"What?"

"Make me feel better."

Warmth spread through him at her words. "Let's try this. We'll be all business when we're here, and then in the evenings we can enjoy each other's company as friends."

"Just friends." Penny narrowed her eyes. It was clear she didn't believe him.

"I'm more than happy to make myself available for whatever you want to do. But there's no pressure. However, if you can't stop yourself, I promise I won't be offended if you take advantage of me."

A laugh escaped before she could stop it. Matt grinned unrepentantly when she tried to regain her stern expression.

"I think I can control myself."

"Well, then, you have nothing to worry about. Right?" Matt stared at her until she acknowledged the point with a small nod.

Penny crossed her arms. "What did you have in mind?"

"Nothing special. Just meeting up after you get off. I don't know anyone else up here and I hate eating alone. You have to eat dinner anyway, so does it really matter if you eat it with me?"

"I guess not."

"Okay, so I'll see you tonight. I'll meet you at your house. I'd invite you over, but I still feel weird about entertaining in my buddy's house. I'm sure he wouldn't care, but still."

Matt doubted Eli would care one way or the other, but this was a great opportunity to see where she lived. Eli said he should pay attention to her to find out what she liked. Her house was probably full of clues.

"No! I mean, my house is a wreck." She flushed a second later when Matt raised his eyebrows. "Let's meet at the Italian restaurant across the street. I should be done around seven. Is that too late?"

Matt decided not to push. If she didn't want to invite him to her house then he could wait. "Okay. I'm always in the mood for Italian food."

Penny smiled. "Me, too. Italian is one of my favorites other than seafood."

Listen to her.

Matt bounced the ball a few times. "Great. So why don't you distract me while I practice by telling me what else you like to do in your spare time besides check out new restaurants."

♥

DINNER WITH MATT that first night was a surprisingly easy affair. He had a refreshingly honest perspective that Penny could appreciate. Matt didn't know how to be anything other than Matt. When he gave his opinion on something, she knew it was the unvarnished truth, free of guile or agenda.

He met her after work again Monday night and they went to a local pizza place that Penny had been addicted to ever since she'd found it. They'd talked and laughed over huge slices of pizza dripping with cheese. Just a few weeks prior, she wouldn't have believed she could be so comfortable with him, but the entire night she hadn't felt self-conscious about how much she was eating or worried whether she had food on her face. Unbelievably, he was keeping to his "just friends" promise. He hadn't done anything or said anything suggestive. Well, not too suggestive anyway.

It was still Matt, after all.

Tuesday evening when his truck pulled into the lot of the center, she was already waiting outside. She skipped over to his truck and climbed up to the passenger side.

"Am I late?" Matt regarded her with amusement as she dropped her bag on the floor and buckled her seatbelt.

"No, I was just ready. So, where are we going?"

"I heard about this great seafood restaurant that's near my buddy's house. Are you up for trying a new place?"

"Yeah. Sounds like fun." Penny rubbed her hands together and they pulled out of the lot.

The radio blared a country song Penny didn't recognize. She glanced at his profile as he drove. Everything about him fascinated her. He was so rough around the edges but had so many moments of unexpected sweetness. Such as his fondness for sad country songs and his devotion to his family and friends. He'd told her about his friend Nick who was expecting his first child with his wife. She could hear his excitement and happiness on their behalf. It was an unexpected thing to see this side of him.

Part of her had to wonder if he was just doing all this to impress her. Pretending to want to be her friend as a way to soften her up. It was hard to gauge what was sincere and what was flattery.

They pulled up in front of a small building with a painted sign out front that read "Selma's Crab Shack." Penny followed Matt to the front door and a bell tinkled merrily overhead as they entered.

"I heard about this place from my buddy, the one who's letting me crash at his place. He said it's small but the food is great."

Penny looked around, already enchanted by the atmosphere. It was a small, cramped space with walls painted lobster red. Each table was covered in old-fashioned brown paper and the chairs looked like they'd been salvaged from a junkyard. Scott wouldn't have been caught dead in a place like this.

She instantly loved it.

"I bet it is. I can't wait."

He looked at her in disbelief. Then a smile broke out on his face. "Good, I'm glad. It's a little rustic, so I wasn't sure if you'd be up for it."

They followed their waitress, a petite redhead who looked like a teenager. Penny picked up the menu. It was only one page.

"It looks like we have a choice of fish, shrimp, or scallops. All fried." Matt put the menu down. "Well, that was easy."

Penny shook her head. "I'm definitely going to have to make up for this later, but I don't even care. I have a feeling this place will be worth it."

She put her menu down and noticed Matt was still watching her. "What?"

"Nothing. I'm having a good time." He sat back in his chair and regarded her openly. The blatantly appraising look in his eyes gave her a thrill.

"We aren't even doing anything yet." Penny fidgeted with her menu. It was hard to sit still when he was staring at her like he was trying to see through her clothes.

"I know. I'm still having a good time."

She tucked a stray lock of hair behind her ear, hating how self-conscious she felt under the weight of his sexually charged stare. He'd kept to their bargain and hadn't made any moves on her but man, *those eyes*. It was almost like being touched when he looked at her like that.

"So, tell me more about you." Matt sat forward, fixing his entire attention on her. "Who do you normally hang out with when you aren't tempting me?"

She laughed at his insinuation that she was tempting him. If anything, he was the one causing her to experience severe lust overload.

"I don't really hang out with anyone. I'm too busy with work. Georgia has been trying to get me to do happy hour for ages. I won't be trusting her to set up happy hours for me again anytime soon."

Matt's deep laugh echoed throughout the restaurant. "Oh yes, I still need to thank her for that. I'm surprised you don't go out. I still remember how tight you were with that dark-haired skinny girl that summer. You two were always together. Whatever happened to her, I wonder?"

Penny fought to keep the smile on her face. "Rachel Addams. Yeah, we were best friends. I haven't seen her in years." She threw a napkin across the table at him. "What about you? What would you be doing on a Wednesday evening normally?"

"I'd be out with my friend Nick, hanging with Trent and Mara, or we'd all be over at our friend Jackson's house. We're a pretty tight group. Since our parents live in Florida and

Trent's folks live in the Midwest, when we got homesick freshman year of college there was nowhere for us to go. Luckily, Trent and I lived across the hall from Jackson. Nick was two years older, but he was always in Jackson's dorm room. They used to go home every weekend so they could sweet talk their mom into doing their laundry. They'd invite us all to come along and hang out. Nick and Jackson's parents sort of adopted Trent, Mara, and me after that."

"I love what I do, but I've been pursuing my goals so long that I haven't left much time for anything else. Including friends. It's one of the only things I regret about being so focused on work."

"Well, you're changing that now." He reached across the table and offered his hand.

Penny stared at his outstretched hand for a moment. He watched her, his dark eyes never leaving her face. Finally, she clasped his hand atop the table.

"I'm definitely changing that now."

Chapter Ten

♥

THAT WEEKEND, MATT decided to stay in town. Mara had called and they'd talked for a long time. It was difficult to take a step back and let her solve her own problems, but he was determined to do it. She and Trent were working it out in their own time and nothing he could do would hasten the process.

It was time for him to focus on getting the things he wanted. Penny was at the top of the list. He couldn't figure out why he was so fascinated by her, but he couldn't stop thinking about her. Wondering what she was doing. Who she was doing it with…

Eli had a wraparound couch and a pretty impressive sound system, so he'd suggested they do a movie marathon. Considering that her last visit had been a train wreck, Matt had been hesitant to suggest that they stay in for the night.

They'd been eating dinner together after she got off work each day, but they'd always gone home separately afterward. This would be the first time they were really alone together since the kiss. That was how he thought of it.

The kiss.

Matt opened the door around six o'clock that evening to see Penny standing on the step holding a handful of movies and a grocery bag.

"I hope you don't mind, but I brought a few of my favorites." She came in and slipped out of her coat. He hung it on one of the pegs by the door.

"But I also brought ice cream." She held up the grocery bag.

"I hope it doesn't have nuts." He rummaged through the bag to find one Rocky Road flavor and one that was plain chocolate and plain vanilla. "You remembered?" Matt looked up in surprise.

Penny rolled her eyes. "You used to make such a fuss as a kid whenever we got ice cream cones, how could I forget? You never wanted anything but plain flavors. Personally I want as much junk in mine as possible. Chocolate fudge, sprinkles, marshmallows, peanuts. Bring it all on!"

She sucked on the tip of her finger playfully and then took the ice cream into the kitchen. Matt followed a few steps behind, trying to give his overworked libido a chance to cool down.

He'd never been this desperate for a woman, and he hadn't even seen her naked yet. Thousands of fantasies bombarded him every night, but the scary part was he wasn't just fantasizing about the abundant curves she kept hidden under her lab coat. He kept replaying the moment when she'd run her fingers over his hair and told him the hard part was over. She'd looked at him so tenderly then. He wanted to know what it was like to have a woman like her worrying about him. Waiting for him.

Loving him.

His thoughts came to a screeching halt. It was hard enough to get her to take him seriously as a potential friend. There was no way she'd consider him for anything serious. Not that he was ready for serious. Was he? When had he gone from thinking of this as a little fun and games to potentially falling in love?

He walked into the kitchen and stopped short at the sight of Penny wiping down the counters.

"Here, let me do that." Matt placed his hand over hers on the sponge, secretly gratified when she sucked in a sudden, shocked breath. He wiped the counter quickly and put the sponge back on the sink.

"It's nothing. I just spilled a little ice cream." She smiled brightly and picked up one of the ice cream containers. The ice cream was so thick it took her several tries before she was able to dig out a scoop and stick it in her mouth.

"Are you sure you don't want any of my mixed up, totally delicious ice cream?" She teased him, scooping up another bite and waving it in front of his face. Then she popped it in her mouth, her lashes lowering as she savored the taste.

A second later her eyes opened and she stilled. Matt gripped the edge of the counter as he leaned closer. "I need you to do me a favor, Penelope."

She gulped. "Sure. What is it?"

He looked down at the ice cream, then leaned a little closer. Her pupils dilated as he got closer still, until their mouths were only a breath apart. Her blue eyes went soft. "Let me choose the first movie." Then he pushed back and walked into the living room.

If he was going to be horny as hell and suffering the whole time, he might as well give her something to think about, too.

The living room couch was nice and deep, so Matt put on the movie and then settled himself into the corner. Penny poked her head in from the kitchen. "You want ice cream now?"

He nodded. She came over and sat next to him on the couch and handed him the pint of ice cream and a spoon. "Where's yours?" he asked.

She didn't look at him as she replied, "I already had a few spoonfuls of mine, so I figured I'd share some of yours."

Matt's body tightened when she looked up at him and then snuggled against his side. It was going to be really hard to keep his "hands-off" promise when she was rubbing up against his chest like that. After a few more minutes, she finally settled down and they watched the first movie. He'd chosen an action flick that he hadn't seen yet, hoping it would force him to pay attention. Instead, he spent half the movie staring down at the top of Penny's head. At one point he was sure she fell asleep because her hand dropped into his lap and she didn't move it. He'd finally picked up her hand and shifted it to his thigh.

The last thing he wanted was for her to wake up with her hand on his massive boner and think he'd done it on purpose.

She woke a little while later during a particularly loud fight sequence. He could tell she was awake because she went stiff. She glanced up at him sheepishly. "Sorry. I have a horrible time staying awake during movies."

"I'm glad you feel comfortable enough with me to sleep. That's a compliment."

"It is. I don't trust that easily."

Matt picked up the remote and lowered the sound on the movie. "I've noticed. I've been trying to figure out why that is."

"It's really hard to put your faith in someone, you know? When you spend a lot of time with a person and then they're suddenly just gone from your life, it leaves a hole. It hurts."

It sounded like she'd experienced true heartbreak.

"Who broke your heart? Let me at him. I'll beat him up for you," he said, only half joking. It was startling to realize that he'd do things for Penny that he wouldn't do for anyone else.

He was in a lot deeper with this girl than he'd realized.

"It wasn't a guy."

Matt's head swung toward her so fast he almost gave himself whiplash. Penny scowled at him.

"It's not what you're thinking either. You're so predictable."

Matt shrugged. "Most guys are. So who was it?"

She looked down at her hands. She did that a lot, he'd noticed. When the conversation turned to something personal, she'd either brush it off or give him only half an answer. Matt figured she was still deciding whether she could trust him. Finally, she glanced up at him.

"It was Rachel. It wasn't a romantic relationship but my heart *was* broken. I didn't see her again until I was an adult."

Matt sank back into the cushions of the couch, pulling Penny with him. With a soft sigh, she relaxed into his chest, her head nestling in the cradle of his arm. "You lost your best friend."

"I'd never had a friend like her before. Rachel and I just

connected. I could talk to her about anything. I adore my sisters, but they're very different from me. Luckily they didn't tease me for being the geeky one, but they still didn't share any of my interests. Rachel did."

Matt pulled back slightly so he could see her face. "I remember how close you two were that summer. It was rare to see one of you without the other."

Penny's eyes danced as she remembered. "We spent more time at each other's houses than we did alone. She'd read all the same books and she was fluent in several languages. She seemed so worldly and sophisticated, but she liked me. She didn't think I was geeky at all. Rachel made being smart seem cool. I'd never had a friend that I loved like a sister before."

"What happened to her?"

"Nothing. My dad got reassigned after that year. I cried until I had nothing left. We wrote letters for a while, but like all things, it wasn't the same. After that, I was too afraid to get close to anyone again. I spent more and more time studying. Then I was in college, then graduate school, and then I came here. Georgia is the only person I've let in since. And that's mainly because she didn't really leave me much choice."

They laughed together. Matt decided he owed a debt to Georgia not just for pushing him to come back and apologize that day, but also for being such a good friend to Penny.

"Thank you, Matt."

"For what?"

She shrugged, not meeting his eyes. "For asking. For actually wanting to know the answer. It's been a while since I had someone I could confide in." She pushed her hair back self-consciously and picked up the ice cream melting on the coffee table. "I'd better go put this away."

Matt watched as she shuffled to the kitchen, but she

couldn't hide the slight redness to her eyes. The sight made him feel unsettled. He wasn't surprised that he was so protective of her already. They were friends, at the least, although that felt like a monumental understatement considering how stirred up he always was around her. But he *was* surprised at the longing that had taken root lately. The desire to give her everything she needed.

Everyone thought she was so no-nonsense, but he was starting to see through the mask. She was a secret romantic. Deep down, she wanted to believe in the magic.

And he wanted to be the one to give it to her.

♥

THE NEXT WEEK was a lesson in patience for Penny. It was important to her that when Matt came to the center, he was her patient only. She wouldn't jeopardize his recovery by going easy on him. She had to treat him just like anyone else. She'd thought it would keep the situation under control if she only agreed to see Matt after work.

Except all she could think of during the day was how considerate he'd been by looking up local seafood restaurants. Then there was the movie marathon. He'd obviously been listening closely when he'd asked her what she liked to do in her spare time. A man who listened was surprisingly hard to resist. Especially one who listened while you spilled your guts. She hadn't told any of her boyfriends about Rachel. None of them had ever asked the right questions or cared enough to wonder about her past.

Wednesday afternoon, Matt sat in her office. They'd finished early, so he'd made himself completely at home in the chair in front of her desk while she updated the notes in his file. He looked good. Really good, she admitted.

"Aren't you going to get that?" Matt asked.

It was difficult to keep her mind on what she was supposed to be doing when he was sitting in front of her desk looking like chocolate-dipped temptation. His brown hair had grown out some so the ends were just starting to curl over. He seemed to have stopped bothering with shaving lately, too, so there was an appealing layer of masculine scruff on his cheeks.

Simply put, he looked *hot.*

"Get what?" Penny asked absently, trying to keep her attention on her notes.

Matt picked up the cell phone sitting on the desk between them. "Your phone. The screen just flashed."

"Oh, yes. Thanks. I had the ringer off earlier because I was in a staff meeting." When she took the phone, Scott's picture and the words "missed call" were displayed. She looked up to meet Matt's eyes.

"I'm not going to ask," he muttered.

"It's just my ex-boyfriend. He probably lost something and wants to know if he left it at my house."

"Yes. The suit. I remember. Is he trying to get you to come back to him?"

"The suit is in Atlanta with his dream job, so I doubt he much cares what I'm doing anymore." It was a small triumph that she could think of Scott without any bitterness over the way things had ended.

"He moved to Atlanta? Why didn't you go with him?" Matt leaned forward, resting his elbows on the edge of her desk.

"Because I have a life here."

"You wouldn't change your life for the right guy?" He wasn't looking at her, but there was a muscle in his jaw that seemed to be going crazy.

"I don't think he was the right guy." That one statement summed up their entire relationship. It was nice to be able to look back and see things clearly now. As hard as it had been to admit it, things had never been right with her and Scott. Kind of like two puzzle pieces that almost fit together.

Almost but not quite.

"So, what are we doing tonight?" Matt must have been satisfied with her answer because he was looking at her now.

"Um, I actually have a couple of things to do after work." They needed to take some time apart. If she was ever going to get this obsession with him under control, she had to stop spending so much time with him.

"Things?" Judging by the incredulous look on his face, he didn't believe her. The fact that she was a horrible liar probably didn't help her case. But still, why was it so hard for him to believe that she had other things to do with her time? Did everyone think she had no life?

"Yes, *things*. I have a life, you know?"

"Okay, fine. I was just thinking that we'll both be at home and bored. We might as well be bored together."

"As tempting as that sounds, it's probably not a good idea."

Matt sat back in his seat casually. "I guess I can understand your position. You're a respected medical professional. It wouldn't be good for your career if word got out that you couldn't keep your hands off me."

The papers she was holding slipped from her fingers and dropped to the desk. "Excuse me? You think I would have trouble keeping my hands to myself?"

"Yes. I can understand you wanting to keep your distance."

Penny knew he was goading her, but it was still a struggle to keep the grin from her face. "You are unbelievable. Well, I should say your ego is unbelievable."

"At least let me take you to lunch." Matt flipped his wrist to look at his watch. "Since we finished early, you should have time, right?"

Penny shook her head. "No need. I'll just grab something really quickly before my next appointment."

"When is your lunch break usually?"

Penny froze and then turned, pretending to rearrange something on one of the shelves behind her. "In about ten minutes, actually. Come on, I'll walk you out."

Matt followed her down the hallway. A hand brushed against her backside and she jumped. Matt appeared at her side, looking forward innocently.

"No funny business, remember?" Penny glanced around, worried that someone else in the hallway might have seen. Luckily, no one else was walking behind them. It would be just her luck for Charles to be right behind them.

"What? If you don't want me noticing your ass, you need to wear different pants. Something baggy. Actually that probably won't help since I'll know what you're hiding under there. The memory alone will be enough to drive me crazy."

Face burning, Penny pushed him through the doors into the waiting room. "It's definitely time for you to go."

"So, you're not really brushing me off tonight, are you?" Matt leaned on the doorframe, blocking her from closing the door.

"Can we discuss this later?" Penny whispered.

"Tell me you're coming and I'll go away." His eyes glittered as he leaned closer, his dark eyes fixed on her mouth. There was something about the way he looked at her. His eyes didn't hide anything that he was thinking, so she could see his every dirty thought written all over his face.

"Oh geez, you have to get out of here. You can't look at me

like that in public."

Heat rushed to her face again as his trademark smirk appeared. "You're blushing, Miss Lewis."

"Okay, okay. I'll be there," Penny muttered, glancing around to see if anyone had noticed them. "Now I need to go before my next patient gets here."

"See you tonight." Then with a wink, he was gone.

♥

THAT NIGHT, MATT thought Penny should direct their date. He'd strong-armed his way into seeing her, but he needed her to come the rest of the way on her own. He'd let her choose the restaurant. It soon became clear it was the right decision because everything she suggested was loud and crazy. She clearly wasn't angling for an intimate dinner where they could talk.

She needed distance.

"I could go for Italian food again. What do you think?" Penny smiled at him and he thought he'd be willing to eat almost anything if it kept that look on her face.

"Okay by me."

They walked from the parking lot of the center down the street to the restaurant. Matt held the door open for her, and Penny walked up to the platinum-blond girl at the hostess stand.

"Two for nonsmoking please."

"Sure, but it's at least an hour wait. Is that okay?" The girl looked over at Matt and wet her lips. "You could wait at the bar. I'm sure we can provide something to distract you."

Matt groaned internally as Penny turned to look at him. He really didn't want to get caught at the bar, fending off advances from this barracuda.

"Actually, I think we'll try the place next door. Thanks." He grabbed Penny's hand and pulled her outside into the cool air.

"Everywhere we go is probably going to be crowded," Penny said finally.

"Probably, but at least they might not be staffed with man-eaters. She was looking at me like I was a steak and it was time for her last meal. No thanks."

Penny shook her head but at least she smiled, finally. "You don't have to pretend not to look. I'm not one of those insecure girls who expects you to develop temporary blindness just because we're together. She was stunning."

Matt pulled her against him. "She was *obvious*. Hair color from a bottle, boobs from a surgeon, and a face covered in paint. There wasn't a real thing about her. Considering how hot I am for you, you should know by now that's not my type."

"What is your type, then?"

"Stern, bossy blondes who yell at me when I slack off."

"Shut up. I'm encouraging you."

"I know," Matt replied. "It's a little scary sometimes, but always hot. I keep having these fantasies of you hitting me with a ruler."

Penny giggled. The sound did funny things to his chest. What he wouldn't give for her to be this happy all the time. "That's a hot-for-teacher fantasy. I think you're confused."

"It's your fault. You've warped me so now I can only get hot for female authority figures. In fact, you might need to take me home and spank me right now."

"Oh, no you don't, buster. I'm starving and I need food. Come on." Penny dragged him into two more places. They were all crowded.

"Let's try this one." Penny pulled open the door to the fourth restaurant they'd tried. It was almost eight o'clock and they hadn't found a place yet with anything less than a forty-five-minute wait. He hung back near the doors while Penny walked up to the hostess stand. When the dark-haired girl shook her head, he groaned. By the time Penny walked back over to him, he couldn't take it anymore.

"You know what? Why don't we just keep it simple? Let's go to the grocery store. I can cook. Some stuff, anyway." Matt hoped he could find the ingredients to make either spaghetti or pizza since those were the only two things he knew how to make.

"You want to go to the grocery store with me?"

"Yeah. It'll be fun. I can't guarantee the results will be edible though."

Penny didn't say anything, just stood watching him with those impossibly blue eyes. He had a feeling she was coming to a decision about something. Courting her was like teasing a skittish animal out when it had been backed into a corner. He was scared to say anything or make any moves that would send her scampering in the other direction.

"We could go to my house. I mean, I have food." Penny glanced down at her hands, then back up at him.

Matt recognized the gesture for what it was. An offering of trust. She was letting him into her life as more than just a temporary, casual thing. She was allowing him into her personal space.

"Sounds good to me."

As soon as her back was turned, he pumped his fist in the air. Finally. Now he just had to show her how good things could be between them.

Chapter Eleven

♥

THE RIDE TO Penny's house was made in silence. In fact, she hadn't said much since she'd extended the invitation. As much as he hated to do it, Matt had to give her an out. He wasn't exactly a ladies' man, but he'd never had to force a woman to spend time with him.

He wasn't going to start now.

"We don't have to do this, Penny. We can just grab some burgers or something and then head home. I'm sure you're tired. You don't have to entertain me."

"No, I want to. It's just been a long time since I've had a guy in my house other than Scott. It feels weird. Is it wrong that I feel that way?"

"The psychologist I saw after I got home from overseas always said that feelings aren't wrong, only actions. We all have the right to however we feel. We should examine our feelings to see what they tell us."

"I'm not sure what it says about me that I feel guilty for moving on with my life. Maybe it's my subconscious telling me I'm an insecure twit."

"It's your mind telling you to be cautious. Which is not a bad thing. I know we jumped the gun a little bit. I can't apologize for it because I'm honestly enjoying it too much. But you were right when you said we should take things a little slower this time. So that's what we're doing. We're going to cook and talk. That's it."

Penny shot him an incredulous look. "That's it? No funny business?"

"I've never understood that expression," Matt mused. "If you're doing it right, there's nothing funny about it."

"Matt," Penny said warningly.

He held up two fingers. "I promise I won't kiss you again unless you kiss me first. Scout's honor. And I was actually a scout, so that's not a line."

Once they were inside, Penny took his coat and hung it up in a small closet near the front door. He walked into the living room and looked around. It was decorated in warm greens, reds, and golds. The color palette was as warm as Penny was. It reflected her style perfectly. He sat down on the sofa, feeling completely at home already.

Penny perched on the seat cushion next to him. "So, I have some chicken breasts already defrosted. I could cook those and we could eat them with a salad. Or I could do a quick teriyaki stir fry. Or maybe you want pasta?"

Matt covered her hand with his. She instantly stopped chattering. "I just want to spend time with you. The food doesn't matter. You have to know that if I was willing to eat my own craptastic cooking to spend time with you."

"So, you were lying about being able to cook? Well, I guess it's a good thing we didn't go to your place," Penny joked.

He'd never seen her quite so flustered. It was different talking to her outside of therapy. When they were in her territory, she was confident and bossy as hell. He was man enough to admit it turned him on a little. Now he was seeing a different side to her. She was fidgeting, picking at a loose piece of lint on the edge of the couch. It was strange to see her nervous. He wanted his brazen, ballsy Penny back.

"What's the easiest thing to make?"

She shrugged. "Chicken doesn't take long to grill."

"Let's do that. Then we'll talk. In the meantime, I almost forgot to ask about the most important ingredient."

"What's that?"

He got to his feet and headed for the kitchen. "What do you have to drink?"

♥

THE AROMA OF grilled chicken soon filled the kitchen. Penny stirred the sliced-up chicken breasts in the skillet with one hand and took a nervous gulp of her wine with the other.

It was a lot easier to be "just friends" with Matt when they were out doing things in public places. Now she had him here in her kitchen, looking so good that she wanted to put him on her plate instead of the chicken.

How was she supposed to entertain a man who made her want to tear her clothes off when she'd resolved *not* to tear her clothes off?

Stop thinking about tearing stuff off. There will be no tearing around Matt Simmons.

Her libido didn't seem impressed with the warning. Her temperature was rising with every minute they were alone together.

She turned down the heat on the chicken and pulled out the ingredients for a salad. Crisp lettuce greens were tossed in a bowl, followed by sliced tomatoes and cucumbers. She layered the salad on plates and then scooped the chicken slices on top. Last, she mixed oil and vinegar in a jar as a quick dressing and dashed a little on each plate.

"Here you go. It's not gourmet, but it's fast."

"Thank you. I'm starving." Matt accepted the plate and fork and shoveled a big bite into his mouth. They ate in silence for a while until Matt finished. Penny was only halfway through with her own salad when he got up to refill their wine glasses.

Her eyes followed him as he reached into the refrigerator. The move only emphasized his long, lean body and amazing ass. He turned and caught her staring. She choked on the piece of chicken she'd just taken a bite of.

Dammit. The man couldn't even bend over to look in the refrigerator without her molesting him with her eyes. Sexual desperation was turning her into a pervert.

"So, how are things with your sister?" She thought dimly after the fact that she probably shouldn't have asked that. It was obviously a delicate subject and she wasn't trying to pry into his business, just distract herself. Luckily, he didn't seem to mind.

"Things are good. She and Trent made up. It was just a

shock for him because he hadn't realized how much money I'd given her."

He poured a generous amount of wine in both of their glasses before pushing the cork back into the bottle.

"I'm glad. It sounds like they have a solid relationship. Too many people give up too easily. If you're lucky enough to have that special connection, you have to be willing to work things out. To compromise. That's a lot more realistic than all the soul mate crap we're spoon-fed from the cradle."

Matt raised his eyebrows. "Wow. That wasn't what I expected. I thought all women went in for the love at first sight, romantic stuff."

"I know I sound like a brat. It's just that girls are conditioned from a young age to expect the fairy tale. The handsome prince who saves you from whatever. A great and grand love."

Penny shrugged and concentrated on the last remaining lettuce leaf on her plate. She pushed it back and forth with her fork, trying to find the right words.

"There is no *great* love. There's just love. It's toxic to pretend otherwise. If people are expecting a fairy tale, then they aren't expecting to have to work at it. The fairy tale conditions us to expect something that doesn't exist. It makes us think it should be easy. It's hard enough to deal with reality without having your expectations built up to expect something that will never happen."

"I'm not sure I agree." Matt calmly took a sip of wine as she gaped at him.

"You're not seriously telling me you believe in all that fairy tale nonsense, do you?" Penny barely recognized that she was holding her breath waiting for his answer. He trailed a long finger down the stem of his wineglass and her eyes followed the motion.

"I agree that all relationships take work, but I also I believe when we meet the person best suited to us, we feel it. I'm not sure if I'd call it love at first sight, but there's definitely *something.*"

Penny let out her breath in a soft huff. "Have you ever felt like that?" She wasn't entirely sure what she wanted him to say. The thought of Matt being in love with some nameless woman left her with a desperate sense of loss. A loss she had no right to claim. He wasn't hers.

His finger stopped moving on the glass. "Yeah. I have."

When she looked up, his eyes were focused on hers. He moved closer so he was sitting in the chair right next to hers. Penny's heart sped up as their thighs brushed. She jumped when his arm landed on the back of her chair.

"Penelope," he whispered. His firm lips moved sensually just pronouncing her name.

It was a struggle to get her mouth to cooperate, but she finally answered. "Yes?"

"I need you to kiss me now."

Penny didn't even answer him. She just jumped out of her seat and into his lap.

♥

THE FIRST BRUSH of his lips against Penny's was so soft it almost didn't register. Just a whisper of a touch. Then he pressed his lips to hers again. Harder this time, until she melted under his touch and opened her mouth.

Then it was all heat.

His hand left the back of her chair and slipped under her

shoulders to hold her against him as he devoured her mouth. She fit perfectly in his arms, her height aligning their bodies in just the right ways. She gripped the front of his shirt and held him to her, keeping him anchored in place as their mouths mated.

They finally broke apart to take desperate, greedy breaths. Penny gazed up at him with her impossibly blue eyes. "I have no idea what we're doing, but I don't care anymore. I want you, Matt."

Matt stood and helped her pull her top over her head. It fell to the floor in a heap. Next, he slowly pulled his shirt off and then threw it behind him. Her eyes roamed over his naked chest with obvious appreciation.

"You are perfect. I could just stare at you all day."

He looked down to where her breasts threatened to spill over the edges of her bra. "Believe me, the feeling is mutual."

Placing a hand in the center of his chest, she bit her lip just to tease him. It had the desired effect, because he groaned at his body's immediate response, then unbuttoned and unzipped his jeans to relieve the pressure. She giggled as she observed his discomfort.

"Your fault," he growled, nuzzling behind her ear.

"Definitely my fault," she whispered back. She skipped down the hall, glancing back to make sure he was following before she ducked into a room at the end. It would have been funny under any other circumstances. Where did she think he was going to go?

When he pushed the door open a few seconds later, his heart almost stopped at the sight waiting for him. Penny lay sprawled across the bed. She'd shucked her jeans so she only wore her underwear.

It wasn't fancy, just plain white cotton underwear and a

beige bra. But in that moment, it was the sexiest thing he'd ever seen. Penny lived up to every fantasy he'd had about her over the past month. Her waist dipped in enticingly and flared out to full hips. She crossed her legs and his gaze trailed appreciatively over the long length of her toned limbs.

Those were going around his waist. *ASAP.*

"I'm feeling distinctly overdressed." He yanked off the rest of his clothes and then crawled onto the bed, lowering himself gently on top of her. She pushed at him until he rolled so she was straddling him. She reached behind her and unhooked her bra.

"Sweet Jesus, you're beautiful." He cupped her full breasts in his palms, brushing the tips gently with his thumbs.

"Mmm." Penny's eyes drifted closed as he caressed her. She rolled off him long enough to ditch her panties. Then she climbed back on top of him. The first brush of her wet sex against the skin of his stomach lit a fire within him. Penny leaned over him, her long blond waves trailing over the skin of his chest.

Matt sucked in a breath as she trailed kisses down his abdomen. When she circled the indentation of his navel, he reached out and grabbed her hair, holding it gently to prevent her from going farther. "Wait a minute. I'm too on edge for that. I've been wanting you for too long."

She crawled back up his chest with a satisfied smile. "You have?"

"You know I have. You knew I wanted you the whole time. Every time you touched me it was a struggle not to drag you into my arms."

Penny settled until her wet heat hovered directly over his erection. He could smell her arousal and it was doing crazy things to his head. It made him want to pin her to the bed and thrust into her until she screamed his name. Only his name, so many times she'd never forget who owned her. He hadn't felt like this in so long. Out of control. Possessive.

Primal.

"What I said before about leaving you alone, that's over. There's no way I can leave you alone now."

She seemed determined to avoid any serious entanglements with him. But now that she was here in his arms, he couldn't just let her walk away without a fight. She had to know how good they'd be together.

"So, you'll give me a chance? You're all in on this, right?"

Penny's hands tightened on his shoulders, but she didn't look afraid. Her pupils dilated slightly, making her eyes look dark. Hungry. "All in? What does that mean?"

"It means I get to do this."

Then he drove into her, her soft flesh enveloping him in a fist-tight grip, his mouth swallowing her frenzied cry.

"All mine."

♥

PENNY CURLED INTO the cradle of Matt's body, her bottom snugged up against his incredible washboard abs. Matt rolled over so he was propped on his right arm. Now that she had free rein to touch him, the first thing she'd done was trail her fingers over the ridges under his bronze skin. He was like one of those perfectly carved marble statues in museums.

Except for one thing. She glanced down and then back up at him in surprise. He was erect again.

"Do you want to come home with me next weekend? I'm leaving on Saturday. I know Mara would love to see you again."

Penny rolled away to face the wall. "I don't know if that's such a good idea. Won't she get the wrong idea about us?"

She could feel him tense behind her. *This is why you don't bring guys home, Penny. People have expectations that sex leads to more sex or a relationship. Neither of which you are ready for.*

"I guess I have the wrong idea about us myself." Matt rolled over and sat up, the bed sinking beneath his weight.

"Matt, I just don't think we should get too deep here. This is already stretching the boundaries of ethics. You're my patient."

Penny turned her head to see him stepping into his boxers. He dropped out of view and then stood, holding his tee shirt. When he turned toward her, she almost sighed at the sight of his bare chest. The man was perfectly chiseled. He yanked the shirt over his head, knocking his hair askew.

"Oh, bullshit. We've known each other for years. Your co-workers never treat their friends or family?"

"Well, yes. They do, but not people they—"

"What? People they what?"

Penny closed her eyes. "You know what I mean. People they've slept with. I seriously doubt my boss has ever brought a one-night stand into the office for treatment."

"Is that what I am? A one-night stand?"

Penny wasn't sure how to answer. The term didn't sit right with her. It made it sound like she'd picked up a guy she didn't know in a bar. Well, she'd picked up Matt and they had been to a bar before, but she knew him. He definitely knew her.

"Don't answer that. The look on your face says it all." He bent to pull on his jeans. "I should have known you didn't go for the dumb-jock type."

Stunned by the quiet vitriol in his voice, Penny got up on her knees. "Matt, what are you talking about?"

He continued speaking as if he hadn't heard her. "Even when we were younger, you were smart. You always had your nose in a book."

She put her hand on his arm and squeezed. "You are smart and you're any girl's type. I just don't date military guys. I'm not made for that life. I did it growing up and promised myself that as soon as I had a choice, I was putting down roots somewhere. No more moving around. It's not a good idea for us to spend too much time together because we'll start to get attached. What would be the point? You'll finish therapy and be going back home soon."

"I understand. So, what happens now? We just chalk this up to a mistake?"

"It's not a mistake unless we make it one. We're both adults. We have amazing chemistry, and it was probably inevitable that we'd give in to it eventually. It doesn't have to be any more complicated than that. We can enjoy a fun night without it getting serious, right? Let's just enjoy it. We can go back to being all business tomorrow."

"A fun night. That's all you want?" Matt asked skeptically.

"Yeah. And the night's not over." She trailed a finger down his chest until it snagged on the top of his jeans. "It was definitely fun. Okay, I'm lying. It was mind-blowing."

He stared at her for a long time before his lips curled up at the edges. "Mind-blowing, huh? I can do better than that."

♥

THERE WASN'T A single man alive who hadn't found himself naked, in bed with a woman, and trying to figure out how to get rid of her. So it was a surprise to Matt to find himself on the receiving end.

"I have a really early day tomorrow, so I'd better start getting ready for bed." Penny yawned and stretched her arms overhead. The sheet slipped, revealing the tip of one plump breast. Matt's attention remained fixed there until she got up.

"Wait, what? Where are you going?" He reached across the bed and grabbed her wrist, pulling her back into the bed. With a laugh, she tumbled on top of him. Her curves pressed against him and he filled his hands with warm, soft, curvy woman.

"I need to start getting myself ready for tomorrow. I think I'm going to turn in early."

Awkward silence descended between them when Matt finally understood what she was saying. She wanted to get ready for bed.

Without him.

"Oh right. I'll get out of your way." He pulled on his clothes, keeping his back to her. As he dressed, his mind raced back over the past several hours. He'd had the best time and he'd been sure she felt the same way even though she'd only allowed him to cuddle her for a few minutes before she hustled into the bathroom and showered alone.

They dressed in silence, maneuvering around each other as they scooped up clothes and Penny pulled her hair up into its usual neat bun. Less than ten minutes later, he'd driven her back to the center to pick up her car.

With a jaunty wave and a smile she'd driven off, leaving him in the empty parking lot, standing next to his truck.

He stood there for a full ten minutes trying to figure out what the hell had just happened.

He'd never had a woman seem so anxious to get rid of him after sex. If he didn't still have the memory of her soft, aroused little moans echoing in his ears, he might have wondered if she hadn't enjoyed it as much as he had.

No, she'd definitely enjoyed herself. Multiple times, in fact. However, it seemed that enjoyment had been all she'd wanted, because she hadn't been able to get away from him fast enough.

He pressed a hand over his heart. He was as guilty as the next guy of taking women to bed just for fun and not wanting anything more. He'd never understood before what it felt like for women. It was a kick in the gut to spend time with someone and enjoy their company, only to realize they didn't want anything from you but sex. It was a rejection of the worst kind.

For all her talk about them being adults and not letting it interfere with their work relationship, he wondered how much of that she'd even meant. After everything they'd talked about and shared, it felt like he'd been spurned when she'd acted as though she couldn't even share a bed overnight with him.

He wished he'd planned his trip home for the coming weekend. A little distance was exactly what he needed.

Chapter Twelve

♥

PENNY WAS ALMOST done for the day when the door to her office opened and Charles stepped through. It was a struggle to keep her eyes in place when they wanted to roll all over the place. It had been an exhausting week. The last thing she needed was a confrontation with her boss.

Matt had skipped his Friday appointment the previous week and she really couldn't blame him. She'd been on edge all that morning, wondering how to act when he came in. It was almost a relief when he didn't show. Then she started to feel guilty.

He'd shown up on Monday morning with his usual smirk in

place. That had made her feel a little better. She'd decided to just pretend like nothing had changed. It had worked, for the most part. But touching him and smelling his scent had her nerves stretched to the breaking point. It had been her decision to keep things professional between them from here on out, but she hadn't counted on how hard it would be.

"Hi, Charles. I was just about done for the day. Did you need something?"

He had never been her biggest fan and never seemed to have much positive to say to her. She was not in the mood to deal with any of his nitpicking about the amount of pro bono work she did or how many vacation days she took to do it. It still chapped her ass that she had to take vacation to do her unapproved pro bono work in the first place. It wouldn't kill the center to allow her to do it while she was attending to her paying patients.

"Yes, I wanted to talk to you." He pushed the door partially closed behind him and Penny's heart sank. Her dreams of getting home at a decent hour and taking a hot bath were looking more and more unlikely.

"Of course. What's on your mind?"

Charles threw the folded up newspaper he held on the desk in front of her. She leaned over to read the article on the front page.

"Oh, it's the article about Chris Walters's recovery. We made the front page. That's exciting."

Charles leaned down and tapped the headline. "Except they didn't mention the name of the center. They also didn't ask anyone else here for a quote. You aren't the only one he's been working with here."

"I know that, Charles. I told the reporter about his full treatment plan, and I even took him on a tour of the whole facility. He had a photographer with him who took pictures of all the new equipment."

He scowled. "Yet somehow the only picture they printed was one of you and Chris. How convenient for you."

"What exactly are you implying? I have no control over what some reporter chooses to write!"

"Of course you don't. Nothing is ever your fault. You know, I may be older and I don't have all these fancy new techniques you seem to invent each week, but I've been in this game a long time. I know bullshit when I hear it. This is not the Penny Lewis show. Although you seem to be doing everything in your power to make sure it is."

"You're going to want to walk away now."

They both turned at the low, gravelly voice. Matt stood directly behind Charles and somehow managed to look menacing without moving a muscle.

"Who the hell are you?"

Penny stood, sensing that the situation could easily go nuclear. "It's okay, Matt. Charles was just leaving anyway."

Charles peered at Matt. "I've seen you around here before." He turned back to Penny with a nasty gleam in his eyes. "A patient, Penny? Really?"

Penny glanced at Matt. This was exactly what she'd been afraid of. Charles would be all too happy to have this to hold over her head.

Before she could speak, Matt stepped closer. "I'm her boyfriend. And yes, I'm also her patient. Why would I go to someone else for physical therapy when Penny is the best in her field? *The best.* You've never treated a family member, Charles, was it?"

Suddenly Charles didn't look so sure of himself. "Well, yes I have, but—"

146

Matt leaned forward and nailed Charles with a hard stare. "Because I'm sure you're not suggesting that Penny should have turned away her boyfriend, an injured Army veteran. I bet that newspaper reporter would love to hear your views on that."

Charles turned toward Matt. "I beg your pardon? How dare you?"

He looked like he was going to say something else, but Matt stepped closer and growled. "Walk away. Now."

He glared at Charles until the man picked up the newspaper and backed toward the door. Charles gave Penny a hard look as he left. "This isn't over. We'll talk again later."

Once the door closed behind him, Penny let out a breath. "Matt, what the hell? You can't just come in while I'm talking to my boss and threaten him."

Matt closed the door and turned back to her. He didn't look at all sorry as he leaned against the wall and crossed his arms. It gave her a small thrill of triumph to see him do that. He couldn't have done that a month ago.

"I didn't threaten him. I made a suggestion. One he was wise to take."

Penny stood and grabbed her handbag. She was more than ready to go home and escape the stink of male aggression.

"Matt, I don't want you to take this the wrong way. You stood up for me and that feels nice. I wish I had done a better job of that myself. He's been a nightmare ever since I've been working here. I really appreciate what you were trying to do. I'm just worried about what's fueling this anger. I thought you'd been doing better lately."

"Some guy standing over you and speaking to you like that is reason enough for me to get angry."

"Did you ever call that therapist I recommended?"

Matt didn't look at her. "I've already had a psych eval. I'm fine."

"Just like you'd already had physical therapy?"

He conceded the point with a small nod. "I'm fine, Penny."

When she opened her mouth to respond, he held up a hand. "I'm sorry if I got you into trouble. That wasn't my intention. I just stopped by to let you know I'll be gone for the weekend and might not make it back in time for our appointment Monday."

"Are you running away?" Penny tried not to let her hurt creep into her voice. Even though she didn't want things to get too serious, the thought of never seeing him again made her heart stop. What if he didn't come back?

"Honestly? I don't know."

"This is exactly what I was afraid of. If you quit at the most critical phase of your treatment just because you don't want to see me, I'll never forgive myself. I want so much more for you than that." Penny had never spoken truer words. It had been inevitable that she'd succumb to the attraction between them at some point, but she wished she'd been able to hold out until he was completely healed.

"You want better for me?" Matt turned to leave and then stopped to look back. "You know, you're the one who didn't want to care about a military guy. You can't pick and choose when you care and when you don't."

♥

MATT WOKE THE next morning, and after wolfing down a quick breakfast of a bagel and coffee, he got on the road. He'd learned from experience that the traffic in the area was unpredictable and Mara would never let him forget it if he missed her party.

He guessed it was his party as well since they were twins, but his sister and friends knew how he felt about birthday parties. He'd rather be deployed on a mission than have to stand at the front of a room while people sang to him. After everything that had happened with Penny he'd been tempted to skip it, but Trent was planning to formally propose to Mara. Despite their argument, he couldn't miss that. He was one of the main people who'd teased his friend about his sister's bare finger.

A part of him suspected that his sister had also left more than a few hints about wanting a real proposal. He'd overheard her complain she didn't want to tell their children their father had proposed while the two of them were in bed.

He could understand that because he'd immediately wanted to bleach his brain when he'd heard it.

To his surprise, traffic was light and he was driving into New Haven roughly three hours later. He pulled out his cell phone and dialed Jackson's number.

"Hey, man, I just got back into town. The party is at your house, right?"

"Yeah, it's here but it's not starting until four o'clock. Ridley is already driving me crazy obsessing over the details. Was there anything you needed to tell her?"

"No, I was just checking to make sure I had the right location. I'll be there in a few hours. See you later."

He glanced at the clock on the dashboard of his truck. It was barely noon, so he decided to go straight to his house and wait until a little later to announce his presence. If his sister found out he was back in town already, she'd expect him to come over and hang out with her and Trent.

He'd accepted Trent's apology and understood where his

friend was coming from, but it didn't mean he was comfortable hanging out just yet. It was going to take him a little while before he could recapture the carefree, easy rapport they'd had before.

He pulled into his driveway and turned off the engine. The tension between him and Trent was a sober reminder of the power of words spoken in haste. He thought back to how he'd brushed off Penny's concerns. She was only worried about him and he'd thrown her words back in her face.

Their rapport was undoubtedly ruined as well.

He turned on the lights as he stepped over the threshold into his house. He could tell his sister had been here keeping things clean because there wasn't a speck of dust in sight. His mail was stacked on the counter in the kitchen. He dropped his duffel bag on the floor by his feet.

After standing in front of the refrigerator for a few minutes, he finally pulled out a canned soda. He sat on the couch in the living room and drank it while watching the sports channel. He should be happy to be back in his own space. It felt like ages since he'd been here, surrounded by his own stuff. He was just going to kick his feet up and relax.

It wasn't even ten minutes before he got up. At least at Jackson's house he could help set up for the party and distract himself with small talk.

Anything was better than torturing himself with thoughts of everything he'd done wrong lately.

♥

PENNY WONDERED FOR the hundredth time that morning what the hell she was doing. She should have been spending her morning working out, cleaning her house, or doing some shopping. Anything but chasing a man a couple of hundred miles away. A man who was probably not going to be all that happy to see her when she showed up on his doorstep.

At least the drive itself was worth the trouble. She leaned forward to get a better view as she drove over yet another bridge that crossed a sparkling river. She was well acquainted with the Chesapeake Bay since it stretched all the way up through Northern Virginia and Maryland, but there were quite a few smaller rivers that she'd never heard of documented on the signs she drove past. She exited the highway and tried to pay attention to the directions coming from her GPS system.

"*Turn left onto New Haven Drive in 1.4 miles,*" the electronic voice said.

Penny followed the instructions and was sure to slow down when she noted the speed limit was only twenty-five miles per hour. The town wasn't as small as she'd thought. There were several major chain stores in a shopping center she passed and the roads were wide and recently paved. However, there was a small-town feel to many of the businesses. The smaller shops lining the road all sported distinctive bright red awnings and the people on the sidewalks nodded to each other as they walked, enjoying the sunny day.

She passed a sign for a boardwalk and realized it must be the entrance to the beach. There were people walking that way even though it was only March. Matt had mentioned the town had a small local beach that was less commercial than the neighboring one in Virginia Beach.

"*Turn right on Shoreline Avenue. You have reached your destination.*"

Penny turned into the driveway of a cheerful one-story house with a small porch. The grass was slightly wild and there were no flowers in the tiny bed in the front. The driveway was empty.

"Great. He's not even here." She got out and knocked on the door anyway. She hadn't wanted to call him because she suspected he wouldn't answer, but she finally gave in and dialed his number. When it went straight to voicemail, she texted Mara. After a few minutes, she put her phone away. It looked like her grand plan to surprise Matt was a bust.

Then her phone rang. She snatched it up without even looking to see who it was. "Matt?"

"No, it's me. Mara. I got your message."

"Hi, Mara. I know this is weird, me showing up out of the blue like this. I was hoping to surprise Matt, but he isn't even home."

"He's not at home but he's in town. We're at our friend Jackson's house. It's not far from where you are. I'll text you the directions, okay? See you soon!"

After they hung up, Penny programmed the address Mara sent into her GPS. It took only ten minutes for her to reach the swanky community called Havensbrooke. She drove past the towering houses and pulled up to the white brick colonial that Mara had said belonged to Jackson Alexander.

She'd thought the name sounded familiar but hadn't thought Mara's friend could be *the* Jackson Alexander, the music producer. But judging by the size of the house, it must be.

There was no answer when she knocked, but she could hear music and laughter inside. Could they even hear her knocking? She twisted the doorknob and it turned easily under her hand. When she opened the door, she was stopped by two burly-looking men in black.

"Name, please."

Taken aback, Penny stammered. "Penelope Lewis. I'm looking for Matt Simmons."

They glanced at each other and then waved her in. "Go ahead."

Penny scampered into the room, then stopped short at the huge collection of balloons and the massive "Happy Birthday, Mara" banner stretched across the wall.

It was Matt and Mara's birthday?

He hadn't mentioned it before leaving, and Mara hadn't said anything on the phone. Typical. Now she was here at a birthday party empty-handed. Although there were so many people here it was unlikely anyone would care.

Penny walked around for a few minutes. There was no sign of Matt or Mara. She decided to ask the next person she saw. A curvy girl with brown skin and long, dark, twisted hair stood at the buffet table staring at the food with a mournful expression.

"Trying to decide between the mini egg rolls and the artichoke dip?"

The girl whirled around with a guilty look on her face that turned to surprise when she spotted Penny standing next to her. "Oh, hello. I was just wondering what I could eat that wouldn't instantly add five pounds."

"You and me, both. I'm looking for Matt Simmons. Have you seen him?"

The girl jerked her head toward the other side of the room. "He's with the beautiful people. It might take a while."

Penny looked in the direction the girl had indicated until she found him. He was in the middle of a group, holding a beer and looking supremely uncomfortable. Mara stood next to him, holding hands with an attractive blond man. She recognized Jackson Alexander, whom she'd seen on TV a lot recently, and his brother, the finance guru. There was also a pair of twin girls so beautiful it instantly made Penny wish she'd changed clothes into something a little nicer than her jeans and button-down white shirt.

She was supposed to go over there and interrupt them? No way. "Geez. I haven't felt like this since high school," she mumbled.

"Welcome to my life, sister." The girl at the buffet picked up one of the mini egg rolls and bit the edge of it delicately. "Those are the cool kids and the rest of us mere mortals are just caught in their orbit. Luckily, they're all really nice, but the Wonder Twins are so perfect they cause an instant inferiority complex, so you're not alone. I'm Kay, by the way. Nice to meet you."

Penny grinned, liking the girl more and more. "I'm Penny. So, the Wonder Twins, huh? Which ones are you talking about? The girls, or Matt and Mara?"

Kay stopped chewing and tilted her head. "Does it matter?"

"I guess not."

"Don't worry, though. The girl twins are both attached, so they aren't hitting on Matt if that's what you're worried about. Are you his girlfriend or something?" Kay swallowed her food with a loud gulp, looking suddenly worried.

"Not exactly. It's kind of complicated. So what about you? Which one are you attached to?"

Kay looked behind her. A stocky, dark-skinned man stood a few feet behind her. When he caught Penny's eye, he nodded. He was handsome and completely focused on Kay. Penny wasn't sure she could handle being at the receiving end of that kind of intensity.

"What about that guy? He's been staring at you this entire time."

Kay whipped around and snatched another egg roll from the table. "That's Elliott Alexander. But we are not attached by my choice. Trust me."

"Never mind. I have a feeling that's complicated, too." Penny picked up a plastic cup and poured herself a drink. At least she wasn't the only one having trouble understanding the opposite sex.

"Penny? What are you doing here?"

Matt appeared at her elbow. He didn't exactly look happy to see her. She lifted her arms and said, "Surprise. Happy Birthday."

He met her eyes. "I was under the impression that you wanted us to spend less time together, not more."

Penny's stomach clenched. He looked so cold. He'd always looked at her so warmly before. Now it was like they were strangers. "I was wrong. That's what I came to tell you."

His eyes narrowed.

"I also wanted to apologize. It's not fair to assume that you're reacting inappropriately every time you get angry. You have a right to your anger just like everyone else."

Matt's scowl softened. "Thank you for that. I don't like it when we fight."

"I don't either," Penny admitted. "So let's not fight anymore. Let's dance and eat some birthday cake and then..." She leaned closer so only he could hear her. "I can give you your present when we get back to your house."

The fire she was used to sparked in his eyes. He smirked, the trademark smartass grin she loved so much. "Am I going to like it?" His hand trailed down her back and rested on her hip.

She had to clamp her thighs together against a sudden ache of desire. The man could arouse her with nothing more than a grin and a hand on her hip. "I hope so, because it sure likes you."

♥

IT SHOULDN'T BE this hard to follow one person, Eli thought. But yet when Kaylee walked through to the kitchen, she looked up and saw him and walked back out. She snuck out to the back porch when his back was turned. No matter what he did or when he did it, somehow she could anticipate his plans and blow them all to hell. Guarding one small girl shouldn't take this much of his mental energy. It was maddening and annoying and *exhausting*.

The bathroom was probably the only place he could be sure she'd be safe.

When she walked across the room to use the powder room next to the kitchen, she glanced behind her and then spun around. Startled, Eli stopped dead in his tracks.

She jabbed a finger at his chest. "What are you doing? Stop following me!"

"It's my job." Eli made sure his voice held no emotion. It probably didn't matter to her that she was driving him crazy, but he definitely didn't want to hand her that kind of ammunition. Most women loved the power they held over men.

"Surely you don't think there are armed assassins lying in wait for me somewhere in your brother's house?" She looked at him like he was an idiot. Even when she was angry, she tempted him. Her smooth brown skin was completely free of makeup and her dark hair was twisted and pulled back into a long ponytail. There was nothing about her that said *seductress* but she was fatal to his control anyway.

Eli took a deep breath and resolved not to take his bad mood out on her. It wasn't her fault that she was exactly his type physically. Mentally, she was far too young for him, but that didn't stop his dick from reacting like he was a teenage boy with his first dirty magazine whenever she was near.

156

"It's my job to assume there are armed assassins waiting for you everywhere. In my brother's house. In your house. In the supermarket. In the goddamned bathroom."

"You're going to follow me into the bathroom now?" Kay's mouth fell open.

For a hyper-charged moment, Eli couldn't stop his gaze from dropping to her lips, then down to the generous cleavage concealed beneath her fuzzy pink sweater. She had the kind of shape that women bemoaned and men celebrated. After having a baby, she was even more round and soft. A pinup girl in the flesh.

A baby pinup girl, he reminded himself. One who was far too young and sweet for him to be lusting after.

"When Jackson made the decision for you to go solo, things changed in that moment. There's going to be even more intense media scrutiny on you now, and that level of coverage brings out the whack jobs. You don't think you need protection, but you do. You have no idea how much." He added the last part under his breath.

"Ugh! You are impossible!" Kay stomped into the bathroom and closed the door firmly behind her. The loud punch of her turning the lock made him smile. His girl had spunk.

Except she's not your girl. She's your charge. *You're only relation to her is to keep her alive.*

Eli hoped she never figured out exactly why he was keeping her so close. Plenty of his clients had received death threats that didn't amount to anything. But this one had been very specific and chillingly calm. Jackson had wanted to tell her immediately, but Eli wouldn't allow it. Kay was a sweet girl and she wasn't prepared for that kind of stress. He'd shield her from it as long as he could.

It was his job to do the worrying.

Chapter Thirteen

♥

MATT WAS REALLY happy to see his friends. After being gone for the better part of the past two months, it was nice to see everyone was thriving and happy. Raina had popped out a few more inches and for the first time actually looked pregnant. There was no lingering tension between Trent and Mara. They were back to their sickeningly sweet lovey-dovey mode. Eli was following Kaylee around like a guard dog, and he wasn't exactly sure he even wanted to know what was up with that. But for the most part everyone was great.

Now he just wished they'd all go away.

"Stop fidgeting. And stop doing that," Penny said through gritted teeth while simultaneously moving her bottom away from his hand.

"This is the longest party ever. How many ways can you say happy birthday?"

"It's nice your friends wanted to throw you a party."

"It is nice. It's also incredibly *long*."

He couldn't think past dragging Penny home and making love to her. Standing next to her with her baby-powder scent tickling his nose was pure torture. The only reason he'd been so determined to come in the first place was because Trent had told him he was planning to propose here. Now it had been almost three hours and he hadn't done it yet and Matt couldn't get him alone to ask him about it. Maybe he'd decided to do it later in private.

"We need to sneak out a little early."

As soon as he spoke, the music stopped and he heard a gasp. He pushed forward a little to see Trent on bended knee while Mara stood with her hands over her mouth.

"Will you marry me, Mara?" Trent's voice carried across the room, loud and clear.

Matt grinned. It was hard to shock his sister, but she looked really surprised. Her eyes lifted and met his across the crowd. She stood there, her eyes darting around wildly for a few moments.

"Mara?" Trent prompted.

"Yes. Yes, of course!" Mara said finally. Trent slid the ring on her finger and then stood to pull her into a passionate kiss. A cheer arose from the crowd. They broke apart and were immediately surrounded by people, Trent getting slapped on the back while the women clustered around Mara to admire her ring. The music started again and Penny leaned against his shoulder.

"Did you know he was going to propose today?"

Mara met his eyes over the crowd. After a second, she smiled at him, but it didn't quite reach her eyes. Matt's heart clenched and he took an instinctive step forward. Then his eyes landed on Trent. His friend raised his hand in a wave and Matt nodded back. When he looked back at Mara, she was surrounded by chattering women.

"Yeah, he told me last week. That's why I wanted to be here. Except she doesn't look... I don't know. Something doesn't look right."

"She's smiling, but she doesn't look happy," Penny murmured. "There's a certain look a woman has when she's putting on a good face."

"You sound like you know from experience." Matt knew she'd had a boyfriend when they'd met, but he hadn't known she was thinking about marrying the guy. He clamped his lips together, trying to stem the questions that wanted to spill from his lips. Questions that he was sure he didn't actually want the answers to.

"I do. I know exactly how it feels to get a proposal from a man you think you should love."

Matt felt the tidal wave of irrational jealousy recede a little bit. She hadn't loved the suit. "That's not the case here. Mara loves Trent."

"Does she?" Penny asked softly, turning her head to look at his sister.

Matt turned to look, too. Trent and Mara stood surrounded by friends and family. His sister was smiling, but her arms were behind her back and her smile was a little too wide.

♥

PENNY DIDN'T HAVE much of a voice, but she sang happy birthday enthusiastically as Matt and Mara leaned close to their cake. As soon as they blew out the candles, he was taking her home. The look in his eyes had her worried. Knowing Matt, he might blow out the candles before they even finished singing.

"Happy Birthday, Matt and Mara. Happy Birthday to you!" Penny sang and clapped along with everyone else as the song finally drew to a close.

A few minutes later, the candles were extinguished and Matt had smiled his way through the crowd back to where she stood.

"What'd you wish for, Mara?" someone called out from the crowd.

Mara smiled tightly, then glanced behind her at Trent. "I don't need wishes. I already have everything I need."

"How come no one asked what you wished for?" Penny turned to Matt and raised her eyebrows.

Matt grabbed her arm and steered her through the crowd toward the front door. "Every guy in here already knows what I'm wishing for. It's not the kind of thing you announce in front of friends and your surrogate parents."

"Matt!" It should be impossible for her to be shocked by anything he said at this point, but he could still take her off guard with his naked, undiluted passion for her. She'd never dreamed that a man would look at *her* that way. Plain, ordinary Penny. Matt made her feel like she was wearing skimpy lingerie and come-get-me heels even when she was just wearing jeans and a worn-in tee shirt.

"We can leave now. No one will notice."

"Yes, they will."

"Okay, they will notice and they'll definitely tease me about it later, but I don't care." He steered her through the crowd until they were finally out on the front porch. Penny giggled as Matt dragged her down the driveway to where his truck was parked on the street.

"By the way, I'm really glad you're here." Matt pushed a tendril of hair behind her ear.

Penny wasn't sure what to say to that. Things were still so up in the air. However, whenever she wasn't sure what she was doing, she remembered Matt standing up for her to Charles. She remembered the way he'd looked in her eyes and put her pleasure first. She wasn't entirely sure she could give him what he wanted, but she was definitely sure it was worth trying.

♥

"SO, I ASKED Eli to look into Penny or to drop in on Matt's next appointment and meet her," Mara announced. She spoke in a hushed whisper so they wouldn't be overheard.

Kaylee stood with Mara, Ridley, and Raina after most of the guests had left for the night. The guys were across the room playing cards, but Kay had no doubt they were paying attention to their women. Jackson looked at Ridley like he wanted to gobble her up, and Nick always followed his wife around the room with his eyes and not just because she was a supermodel.

The pure love and joy reflected in his gaze when he looked at her was reason enough.

"You want him to spy on your brother's new sort-of-girlfriend? Why? I only talked to her for a little while, but she seemed really nice," Kay whispered.

"I know. It's just that, did you see the way Matt looked at her? He's never looked at anyone like that. What if she's not the nice, sweet girl I remember? Penny might have changed in the last decade. What if she's crazy and evil now? Matt's been through a lot in the past year. I just don't want him getting blindsided. Either way, Eli won't do it. He turned me down flat. I need you guys to help me change his mind."

"Good luck with that," Kay drawled. "Eli doesn't change his mind. He thinks his way is best all the time. Plus, he's too busy stalking my every move just in case there's a crazed fan in the bushes outside my condo."

Eli had been a nightmare the past few weeks. He acted like she was some dim-witted twit who couldn't be left alone to do much besides shower and sleep.

Mara tilted her head and regarded Kaylee through narrowed eyes. "Eli's been following you for a while now. Maybe you should ask him."

"What? No. I'm not getting in the middle of this. Besides, he follows me because he has to, not because he wants to. He's barely said two words to me all day."

Except for when I yelled at him, she thought.

Ridley picked at the food left over from the party. "It wouldn't be that hard for Jackson to book you a gig in D.C. Then you'd have a perfectly good reason for going that way. Eli would have to follow and keep you safe."

Everyone turned to look at Ridley. Raina snorted out a laugh. "And you all thought she was so innocent."

"I'm starting to realize I've grossly underestimated you," Mara said with a note of respect in her voice.

Kay turned to Ridley. "This is crazy. What would I say when I got there? I've only spoken to Matt a handful of times. Wouldn't it be weird if I just showed up?"

Ridley pursed her lips. "Mara, have you been collecting Matt's mail while he's gone?"

"Yeah, I usually pick it up every other day so it doesn't pile up," Mara said.

"Why didn't he just forward his mail?" Ridley asked.

Kay rolled her eyes. "He probably got the same lecture about security Eli gave me. If you forward your mail, then your name goes on a list somewhere and potential thieves will know your house is empty. Also, anyone observing will notice that you're suddenly not getting any mail."

"Well, that's the perfect excuse for you to stop by. Surely something has come in the mail that's important. Right?"

"Not really, but I can pretend I thought it was." Mara shrugged. "I doubt he'll question Kay about why she's there. He'll just say thank you and to tell everyone hi."

Ridley clapped her hands together decisively, as if the matter was all but settled. "Excellent. If we're lucky, Penny will be there when you see him, so he'll do the polite thing and introduce her. If something's off when Eli meets her, he won't be able to resist checking her out. It's in his nature. When he gets a hunch about something, he can't let it go. He's like a dog with a bone."

"I know," Kay muttered crossly.

"Cheer up. At least you two will have to stay overnight in a hotel," Ridley whispered.

Kay placed a hand over her chest, trying to contain her suddenly rapidly beating heart. "What? Why would that cheer me up?"

Ridley gave her a sarcastic look. "Gee, I wonder. Are you really going to pretend you haven't been panting after my incredibly buff brother-in-law for months now?"

Kay groaned. "Great. I guess that means everyone knows.

I'm sure that means *he* knows. He's probably gotten a good laugh out of it. God, this is so embarrassing."

"Calm down. Eli has no idea. I just like to watch people, so I see things. It's not a big deal. You guys will stay in a hotel and have a nice dinner. All paid for by the record company."

"Why would we stay in a hotel when Eli has a house there? Won't he want to go home?"

"Matt's already staying there. Eli won't drag you back to his house and inconvenience Matt when the hotel is already paid for."

"Ridley, I don't think this is such a good idea." Kay had never been a rule breaker. In general, if there was something that could go wrong when she was taking a chance and bending the rules, it would. Historically, it had never worked out for her. She had a feeling that if she tried to pull the wool over Eli's eyes, he'd wrap her in it until she was bound so tightly she couldn't move. Especially since he didn't seem to like her much anyway.

"Don't worry. I'll take care of everything," Ridley assured her.

Somehow, Kay didn't find that all too comforting.

♥

MATT WATCHED PENNY walk around his bedroom. She picked up the cologne on the dresser and sniffed it. Then she picked up the few items of clothing he'd dropped on the floor and folded them, placing them neatly on top of the dresser.

"This room looks like you. It's definitely a tough-guy room." She glanced back at him with a grin.

"I'm just glad to have you here, in my home. Finally."

"I'm glad I'm here too. I almost didn't come."

"Why did you, Penny? Really? You know I want you. I couldn't deny that even if I wanted to. I'm pretty sure my hard-ons give me away. But I want more than that. So much more. If you don't feel that way about me, then it's probably better that we continue to keep our distance. I can't survive another day of making love only to have you push me out the door as soon as it's over."

"I want to tell you something." Penny stepped away from the dresser and took his hand. She dragged him over to the bed. They sat on the edge, facing each other. After a few moments, she started talking. "Before I met you, I dated a really great guy."

"The suit?" Matt could barely keep himself from growling and beating his chest.

"Yeah. His name was Scott and he was an assistant district attorney. He was smart, handsome, and a genuinely nice guy." Penny dropped his hand and stood. She paced back and forth on the carpet a few times before she stood before him.

"So what happened?" It wasn't like he didn't already know, sort of. However, he wanted to hear it from her. It wasn't enough to know they'd broken up. He needed to know how. He needed to know why. Was it because the other guy had moved on? Or was it Penny's doing?

He hoped it was Penny's doing.

Penny sighed and held up her hands. "I don't know. That was the whole problem. On paper we were perfect together. I might have gone on to marry him except something happened." She turned and looked at him. The look in her eyes was so unbelievably tender that Matt couldn't believe it was directed at him. "I saw *you* again. After that I couldn't even contemplate marrying him. Everything missing in my relationship with Scott was what I felt for you."

Yes. Matt wanted to howl at the moon he was so overjoyed. There wasn't anything in the world a man wanted to hear more than his woman declaring that he gave her what no one else could.

"As soon as we met, I felt that connection I was always hearing about. I wanted to be near you, to talk to you. To kiss you." She blushed a little and sat next to him. "It made me uncomfortable at first since you were coming to me for help. But I looked forward to seeing you week after week. The days you missed treatment were really hard to get through."

"They were for me too, baby. You have been the highlight of my life for the past two months. I want so much more from you than an occasional night of passion. Do you? Or is that enough for you?"

Penny climbed into his lap and held his face between her palms. "I'm so sorry I treated you the way I did. I was just running scared. I do want more from you. I just don't know how much more, and I know that's not fair to you."

"Let me worry about what's fair to me. Just spend a little time with me. By the time I'm done with therapy, you'll know if you want me to stay."

"What if I don't?"

"You'll know." He pulled her closer and held her still so she couldn't look away. "So beautiful." He trailed his fingers up and down her arms and she shivered under his caress.

"I love the way you touch me. You always make me feel so feminine and beautiful. You touch me like I'm delicate, even though I'm not."

"You're not delicate, you're strong, which I find incredibly sexy. But being strong doesn't mean you aren't precious. Because you are, Penny. You are so very precious to me."

She let out a soft pant and gripped the front of his shirt in her hands.

He took that as a directive and pulled his shirt over his head. "That can go."

Her hands raced over his skin greedily. When she skimmed over his stomach and stopped at the waistband of his shorts, it was Matt's turn to hold his breath with anticipation. He lifted his hips so she could unbutton him and then helped her slide them off. He quickly shed everything else while Penny took off her own clothes.

When she leaned over him the next time, her magnificent breasts swung in his face. It was a privilege to cup the heavy weights and take a taut nipple in his mouth. She sighed above him as he gently laved the tip. He loved watching her fall apart, the faces she made, the soft sounds that rose from the back of her throat.

He rose and walked to the bed, kissing and caressing the whole way. By the time they fell atop his sheets, Penny straddled him. She looked into his face as she took him deep inside. Matt gripped her hips as she rocked against him, taking him closer and closer to the edge every time. It wasn't long before he hung suspended on the edge, staring up into Penny's eyes.

They tumbled over together, Penny gasping her pleasure against his mouth.

After a few minutes of cuddling, Matt reluctantly got up to dispose of the condom. Once he got back in bed, he yanked Penny back against his chest.

"This time you aren't running out on me." He held her tightly and rolled, tucking her against his side. Her back was slick with sweat and it gave him a visceral level of satisfaction to know he'd worked her up. After a few minutes, Penny pushed up to sitting. His grip on her waist tightened.

"I'm not running away. Promise." Penny's eyes sparkled as she climbed from the bed. "I just need to wash my makeup off before I fall asleep."

Matt dozed lightly, hearing the distant sounds she made, cabinets opening and shutting, running water, and the squeak of the pipes as she turned the faucet off. The bed dipped under her weight a few minutes later and his eyes popped open.

With one look, he knew he was done for. He'd never thought that by scrubbing off her makeup Penny would reveal the one thing he was powerless to resist.

"What are you staring at?"

She scrunched her nose at him before she leaned over and kissed him lightly. The freckles usually covered by her makeup were a beguiling pattern covering her pert nose.

Freckles. His Penny had freckles.

Yeah, he was done for.

Chapter Fourteen

♥

WHEN PENNY PULLED open the front door of Matt's house the next morning, she'd only been intending to get one of her bags from her car. She wasn't sure who was more surprised, her or the group of people standing on the doorstep.

"Hi, we're here to see Matt Simmons." The guy in the front was tall and well built. He was clean-shaven and wore his dark hair razored extremely close.

Military, Penny thought. As she observed the man standing behind him, she got the same impression.

Penny blinked several times before her brain kicked in. "Oh, yes. He's here." Before she could turn around, the group let out a collective whoop. "Ace!"

She whirled around to see Matt standing directly behind her. To her surprise, he kissed her squarely on the mouth before he reached around her and opened the screen door. "What the hell are you guys doing here?"

The group filed past them and into the house. Penny backed up slightly until she was half-hidden behind Matt. Surreptitiously, she patted the top of her hair down. She was seriously regretting her decision not to put on makeup and comb her hair before leaving the house.

"Penny, these are some of the guys from my old unit. This is Tommy McCann and his wife Danielle. And this is Saul Shepard and his wife Cora. Guys, this is my girlfriend, Penny. She's the physical therapist I told you about."

A warm glow rose to her cheeks as she observed Matt's pride in introducing her.

"So you're the physical therapist?" The guy he'd introduced as Tommy picked her up and spun her around.

"Wow. It's nice to meet you, too!" Penny clutched at his arms when he finally set her on the ground.

"Guys, don't scare her off yet." Matt put a possessive arm around her shoulders.

Saul chuckled. "You can't keep her hidden away forever. We've all been hearing about your miracle worker. Look at you, man. I'd never know you got hurt looking at you now."

Matt led them into the living room. Penny dragged in a few extra chairs from the kitchen.

"So, you're all in the same unit?" Penny asked.

"We used to be. Matt was reassigned last year."

"There are so many stories we can tell you about Ace," Tommy bragged.

"For starters, why do you call him that?"

There was a chorus of voices then.

"Oh you haven't seen his competitive side yet?"

"He always has to be number one."

"I don't care what it is, from shooting to bowling, he has to be the best. If he isn't, he'll practice until the day he can beat you."

Penny laughed along with the others. She'd gotten a small glimpse of his competitiveness in the bedroom. The man was an inexhaustible sex god. He'd been determined to make her feel so much pleasure that her eyes had almost rolled to the back of her head.

"I've seen how hard he works in therapy. He hates to lose."

It was a good thing too, she thought. It was likely the only reason he hadn't given up on her.

Over the next few hours Penny got a chance to see a different side of Matt. He was more serious with his friends than he was with her. It made her wonder if he found it as difficult to let down his guard as she did.

"So how long have you and Ace been dating?" Cora asked. The guys had migrated to the kitchen, leaving Penny, Cora, and Danielle in the living room. Loud trash talking and laughter spilled into the room every few minutes.

"Not very long. It's all still sort of new. Have you been with Saul long?"

"We've been married for five years now, and it's been tough at times. I miss my family back home in Colorado. When he's deployed, I feel like I'm living life in a constant state of limbo. Like I'm sort of stuck in a holding pattern, waiting for him to come home. But at the same time, I've learned that I'm a lot stronger than I thought I was. I can hold down the fort while he's out there doing his job. I love him so much that it's worth it."

"My dad was a captain in the Army. He just retired last year. We moved a lot growing up, so I know how hard it can be. How isolating."

Both Cora and Danielle made soft sounds of agreement.

"If you ever need someone to talk to, feel free to call me or Danielle. Military wives stick together. No one else understands how hard it is. Don't be shy about asking for support if you need it."

Penny sat stunned as the other woman got up to refill her drink. It was stupid, but once again she was being caught off guard because she hadn't thought about the future. She'd come down here impulsively because she couldn't stand the thought of Matt not being a part of her life. But when you were in the military, your life wasn't your own. She knew this from experience. If she and Matt stayed together, she'd have to live it all over again. A military wife. That's what she would be eventually.

The one thing she'd sworn she wouldn't do.

♥

AFTER EVERYONE LEFT, Matt closed the door and walked back to the living room where Penny was curled up on the couch. She'd been extremely quiet the last hour. His friends could be a bit much, so he'd tried to hurry them along. Penny wasn't as extroverted, so he was worried they'd overwhelm her. Or that they'd tell her something he didn't want her to hear. There were certain embarrassing stories that he'd prefer stay buried. Penny finally seemed to see him as a man instead of the bratty kid she used to babysit. He didn't want anything to change her opinion.

She looked up when he entered the room. "Is everyone gone?"

"Yeah. Sorry about that. I didn't know they would be here that long. Shep said they were just passing through."

"That's okay. They were all really nice. So nice that it made me feel bad." Penny hugged her arms close.

He sat on the couch next to her and pulled her into his lap. "Why would you feel bad? I want you to like my friends."

"I feel bad because I'm not like Cora and Danielle. I can't keep a smile on my face as we move from city to city and base to base. I've done it too many times already."

"I know. But, Penny, I'm not asking you to do that."

"You aren't asking me right now, but there's going to come a day when you're reassigned somewhere far away and then I'll be stuck in the same situation. Caring about someone that I can't have. Worrying about you all the time."

Hope burst forth in his chest. Matt could feel that the smile on his face was too big, but he couldn't seem to rein it in. She didn't even realize it, but she'd just sealed her own fate. Now that he knew she cared for him, there was no way he'd let her go. Ever.

"Now that I know you have feelings for me and it's just fear holding you back, I have hope. We can overcome fear. I can't overcome lack of interest."

She elbowed him playfully. "You knew I was interested. I doubt I'm that good of an actress."

"Well, no, you're not. You make this little sound in the back of your throat." He stroked her behind the ear with the tip of his nose and she let out a little murmur.

"Mmm hmm. That's the one."

"Matt! You're always teasing me."

"Trust me, I'm not teasing you, pretty baby. You'll know

when I'm teasing you. I might do this." His hand slid down her front to rest right between her legs. The heel of his hand nestled against her and she let out another soft, arousing sound. "Or this." His fingers pressed through the cotton fabric of her jeans, rubbing the seam against her in a circular pattern.

"Matt, we can't."

He could only assume she'd meant it to come out sounding like a denial, but to his ears, it sounded more like a plea. "Oh, but we can." He laid her back on the couch and tugged on her jeans. After a few wiggles of her hips, they slid easily down her long legs. He used his teeth to pull at her panties and she reared up off the couch. The motion allowed him to pull the cotton down her legs. He tossed them over his shoulder.

She wiggled halfheartedly in his arms. "I need to get on the road."

"I know. I'll be fast." He punctuated the statement with a soft nip to the skin on her inner thigh. She shuddered and bit her lip while he settled himself between her thighs.

He had no intention of going anywhere for a while. At least not until she screamed his name a couple of times.

♥

THE NEXT DAY, Penny patted Matt on the shoulder after they finished a set of exercises. "You've made some amazing progress over the past two months. It won't be long now before you don't need me anymore."

He'd regained full range of motion in his shoulder, and they were now working to increase his strength and flexibility through the use of light weights. Although she knew it hurt his male ego to use the small, brightly colored dumbbells instead of the large weights he'd probably been pumping before, he'd been a good sport through it all. He'd even allowed her to take pictures for the website and had posed comically with the small weights as if he was struggling to lift them.

It wasn't that often she got to see Matt in such a playful mood. It was a heady thing to realize she'd had something to do with that. There were many known scientific benefits to having great sex. Less stress, lower blood pressure, and better sleep were just a few of the more obvious benefits.

It was also a phenomenal mood booster. She'd caught herself humming in the shower that morning, and nothing Charles had said to her today had pissed her off. She simply didn't care.

"Not that I haven't enjoyed this, but I'm anxious to see how much progress I've made. Is it safe for me to do a mock fitness test just to see how I'd do?"

"It should be fine. Do you want to use the gym?"

At his nod, she gathered her clipboard and led him down the hall to the gym.

"I'll start with the sit-ups. Last time I barely passed this part because my shoulder was aching so badly I couldn't concentrate." He sat on one of the thick blue mats and then interlocked his fingers behind his head. He started slowly, lowering and raising his torso carefully.

"How do you feel?" Penny asked.

"Good. I think I can do more than enough to pass."

"No pain?"

"None. It's strange to be able to do this without trying to hide how much it's hurting me." He increased his pace and then stopped a few minutes later. "I can do more than fifty sit-ups and I'm barely winded. This is encouraging. You were right that I needed to give my upper body a rest for a little while. I must have been overtraining because I feel stronger than ever now."

He lay back until he rested on the mat. Then he turned over and got in push-up position. Penny sprang forward, instinctively ready to assist if he needed it. But it seemed like her help was unnecessary because he lowered himself smoothly before coming back up.

He's doing it, she thought. Up and down, he pumped out push-ups to a beat no one else could hear.

He was healed.

Penny felt a pang behind her heart, but she pushed it aside. Her goal with her patients had always been to get them back to where they'd been before. Helping a patient rewind time so they could do the same things they used to was always her ultimate endgame. It shouldn't be any different for Matt just because she cared for him. Despite how hard it would be for her to see him go, his goal was to qualify for the Special Forces. It was his dream and she wanted to help him achieve it.

It appeared she already had. Until he suddenly stopped moving.

"Matt? Are you okay?" Penny moved closer and then sprang forward when his arms gave out and he collapsed to the mat below him.

"I can't do anymore."

"It's okay. You did quite a few. I'm sure with enough time you'll be able to build on what you've done."

"You don't understand. I only have a certain amount of time to qualify." He sat back on his heels. "I was so sure that this was the miracle I needed. I thought that if I worked hard and did everything you said that I'd be strong enough. But I'm not. I'm still not."

He hung his head. Penny's heart ached at the devastated look on his face.

"I'm not going to pass like this." He stood and scrubbed his hands through his hair. "It was all for nothing."

He walked out of the gym without giving her a backward glance.

♥

THAT NIGHT, PENNY arrived at Matt's house and pulled into the drive. She'd waited for him in the gym for ten minutes before she realized he wasn't coming back. It was hard to know how to handle the situation. He probably wanted space, but she wanted him to know she was there if he needed to talk.

His whole existence the past few months had been focused on one goal: passing the Army fitness test. Penny had always been confident that he would get there eventually. However, she hadn't known he was under time constraints. She could help him get better, but there was only so much healing the body could do at one time. After he'd walked out, she'd gone back and reviewed his medical file again, looking for something, anything, she might have missed that could have helped him heal faster. There was nothing.

The stark truth was that he'd sustained a serious injury, one that had been exacerbated greatly by his actions in pulling his friend to safety. She couldn't even imagine the agony he must have endured to somehow keep a grip on his friend's body. In fact, dragging his friend for such a distance was probably what had caused the shoulder dislocation in the first place.

It broke her heart that someone heroic enough to try to save a friend was paying the price by losing his dreams. It just wasn't fair.

She knocked and after a long wait, Matt opened the door. Before he said anything, she opened the screen door and hugged him. He shook in her arms and Penny didn't look at him, afraid that he might be crying. He wouldn't want her to see that.

"I'm not here to talk. You can just go back to whatever you were doing. I just want to be with you. Is that okay?"

He nodded against her hair and shut the door. Penny took his hand and led him back into the living room. His hair was rumpled and when she saw the blankets on the couch, she realized he must have been asleep.

"Go back to your nap. I'll just watch TV."

He stared at her for a long time, then pulled her forward. The soft kiss on her forehead touched her heart.

While Matt settled back in his corner of the couch, Penny dropped her bag and kicked off her shoes. She took the remote he handed her and curled up on the other end of the sofa. She finally settled on a documentary about deep-sea fishing. Before long, her lashes grew heavy and she closed her eyes with a sigh.

"No, Cyrus! You have to help him."

Penny woke with a start. Matt thrashed at the other end of the couch, one of his legs striking her in the side. She sat up and shook his shoulders gently.

"Wake up, Matt. You're having a nightmare." He woke, wild-eyed and breathing hard, one hand clutching his shoulder.

"It's okay. You're at home." She stroked his arm gently. His breathing slowed.

"I was dreaming," he repeated. He flopped back against the cushions of the couch and rubbed his shoulder.

Penny waited until his breathing was normal and he'd lost the manic look in his eyes before asking, "Who's Cyrus?"

Matt froze. His eyes lifted to hers. Her heart ached at the dead look in his eyes. The hand on his shoulder tightened. "He was the friend I couldn't save."

Penny's heart ached anew. "I'm so sorry, Matt."

He met her eyes. "He was a good guy. We were both planning to be Rangers. We had our whole lives mapped out."

"That's why it's so important to you? As a way to honor your friend?" That would be just like Matt. He was the most honorable guy she knew.

"Partly. I had so many plans for the future. When I joined the Army, it was a revelation for me. I'd finally found something I was good at."

Penny's surprise must have shown on her face because he laughed for the first time. Some of the tension left his body. She took the opportunity to sit next to him on the couch and snuggle up under his arm.

"I can't imagine you not being good at everything, Ace," she teased.

"I wasn't always this competitive. In high school I wasn't a great student like you, and I was only an average athlete. I wasn't exceptional in any way. That was something I had to accept a long time ago. I'm not the most talented guy, but there's nothing to stop me from being the hardest worker. That's why I'm so competitive and why I work so hard to master every skill I can. That's my only advantage. My determination. It's the only thing that sets me apart."

Penny stroked his shoulder. His skin was still slightly damp. "It's not the only thing. I know I've given you a hard time about your ego, but truthfully, you're not arrogant at all. You're honorable, Matt Simmons. You care. A lot of people don't. You've gone above and beyond to take care of me, and I know you've always taken care of your sister. I suspect we're not the only ones in your life that you look out for."

She pulled him to her, allowing him to settle his head against her breast.

"That's what sets you apart. Your heart."

Chapter Fifteen

♥

MATT SAT IN the cab of his truck Wednesday afternoon, chewing furiously on a piece of grape-flavored gum. He dropped his head down to the steering wheel. He'd spent all of Tuesday on the couch, eating ice cream and feeling sorry for himself. Penny had come over and stayed with him again that night. She had to be getting tired of him. He was tired of himself.

He'd tried to hype himself up for his appointment. Just because he wasn't going to heal fast enough to be eligible for reenrollment didn't mean he could give up on treatment. He still needed to get better. He'd been sitting here in his truck for the past hour, trying to get up the nerve to go in. To move forward with his life. But despite it all, his mind just kept repeating *It was all for nothing* on an endless loop in his mind.

He wanted to punch something so badly but couldn't, so he squeezed the steering wheel until the leather squeaked beneath his fingers. It was just so hard to accept that all this time and effort wasn't enough to make his dreams come true. Even though he was under time pressure, the truth was he'd had a year to heal. It was a cop-out to blame it on lack of preparation or time. It just wasn't going to happen. Probably ever.

Maybe it was time for him to face it.

When he'd first joined the military, it had been for the usual reasons. It was a way to pay for college and see the world. But as time went on, he'd come to rely on the camaraderie. He hadn't had many opportunities to excel before. Being a soldier had given him an identity. Taught him discipline. The Army had literally made him a man. All he'd ever wanted was to be a part of something bigger than himself. Something important. Joining the Special Forces would have made him a part of an elite team.

But now that he was older, he'd discovered other ways he could belong. He'd learned things and discovered talents he hadn't known he possessed.

The relationships he'd built with his friends were just as strong as blood ties. The Alexanders had become his "team" and the bonds between them were ones that would last a lifetime.

His fingers loosened on the steering wheel as he thought about his friends. They were there for him even if he failed the test. It didn't matter if he was considered a hero by anyone else because he knew they regarded him as one.

Maybe it was time to stop searching for something he already had.

The passenger-side door opened, letting in a burst of cold air. He watched as Penny hopped up into the seat and slammed the door. She looked over at him apologetically.

"I'm sorry. I wanted to give you your privacy, but it's really cold out there."

He rested his head against the steering wheel again and closed his eyes. "It's okay. I had every intention of coming in. It's just that every time I was about to... Well... Anyway, I didn't mean to stand you up."

"I understand." She didn't say anything else, so he opened his eyes a few moments later. Her eyes were closed, too.

He took the opportunity to study her. It wasn't often that he could look at her without being observed. She'd started to let down her guard a bit lately. She'd styled her hair in a loose bun and she was wearing a pair of earrings he'd never seen on her before. Watching her blossom had been a joy. She had so much inside of her to give, and he was honored that she'd begun to share herself with him.

Her eyes opened suddenly, and she jumped when she noticed him looking at her. He laughed softly at her shocked expression. "Hey."

"Hey," she whispered. "I just want to say that I'm really sorry you couldn't heal before your deadline. I know this was really important to you."

"You know, I'm okay. It was my dream to belong to something. To be a part of something meaningful. I'm finally understanding there are many different ways to make your mark on the world and to be a part of something. I've found the sense of family that I was looking for already."

It was comforting to say it out loud. The world wouldn't end if life took him in a different direction than the one he'd planned on. For the first time in days, he felt the tension in his chest loosen.

"I'm really glad for you. Like I said before, it won't be long before you've completed my treatment and you won't even need me anymore."

He glanced over at her, his emotions playing across his rugged features. "I seriously doubt there will ever be a day when I don't need you, Penny."

Her eyes softened in that way that never failed to hit him straight in the heart. "I still can't believe you feel that way about me." She peeked up at him from beneath her lashes.

Did she still not know how he felt about her? It seemed insane that she could have him in the palm of her hand and not know that for her, he was completely undone. Everything about her slayed him. His heart was literally hanging by a thread.

"Believe it, pretty girl. I want to stay here with you after my therapy is over. I've already talked to my friend and he's agreed to rent to me for the rest of the year. I can get a job here. Now that I'm doing so much better, I can work in construction again instead of just taking odd jobs. We can do this. We can see where this goes."

Excitement took over and Matt reached across the seat to take her hand. Life was taking him in a different direction than he'd expected, but he was ready to go with it. Dealing with the events of the past year had taught him a few things. Namely to take what happened to you as an opportunity to learn and grow. Even though he wasn't where he'd wanted to be, it didn't mean he couldn't be happy. Fulfilled.

Grateful.

"All my life, I've been skeptical of things that seem too easy. What if you wake up tomorrow and don't want this anymore? Maybe you should take some time to think about where you want to go from here?" Penny bit her lip and looked down at their hands entwined on the seat between them.

"I already know what I want. I want to start living my life and you're a big part of that, Penny. I don't want to scare you off. I know we're supposed to be taking it slow, but I just want you to know this isn't casual for me. I care about you. And I plan on being in your life for a long time."

"Matt. I don't know what to say."

"I don't want you to say anything. Just think about what you want and how you feel. We have a few weeks left, right?"

At her nod, he continued, "Well, I won't be going back home until then. If you feel the same way, then tell me to stay. Don't say anything now. Just promise me you'll think about it?"

"Okay, I will."

He lifted her hand and kissed her knuckles. Then he opened the door of the truck and hopped down. They walked together back toward the center. "What are you about to do now?"

"I'm sure I have patients." Penny passed a hand over her face. A pang of guilt made him take a closer look. She was exhausted, and he was sure it was partially because of him.

"Isn't it time for you to eat lunch?" Matt glanced at his watch. He'd been keeping her up late at night and then she was working all day. He was overcome with the need to look after her and take care of her.

"It is. I mean, I will in a little bit," she hedged. Her eyes dropped to her shoes.

When she wouldn't look at him, Matt instantly knew something was up. "It was lunch time at noon, wasn't it?

That's how you fit me into your schedule on such short notice. You gave up your lunch hour." Matt cursed as his cell phone went off. "Yeah. ... Oh hey, Kaylee. ... Um, okay. Bye."

Penny followed as he walked to the center. "What's wrong?"

"Nothing. A friend is in the area, so she's bringing me some important mail that I got. I wonder how Mara convinced her to go out of her way just to bring me a letter?"

"Your sister can be very persuasive. I know this from experience."

Matt pinned her with a hard stare. "Oh, I know she can. Believe me, *so can I*."

♥

WHEN KAYLEE FINALLY stopped driving, Eli pulled up behind her blue sedan and hopped out. He wasn't even sure if he turned the car off. He was that pissed.

Pissed.

"What the hell is going on?" Eli watched in disbelief as Kay held up a finger indicating he should wait. She dialed a number on her cell phone and, after a quick conversation, she pushed the door open and got out.

"Sorry, what did you say?"

"I said I've been calling you for the past two hours. You said you had a gig. You didn't say it was over a hundred miles away."

"Does it matter?" Kay didn't look at him as she closed her car door and started walking across the parking lot toward the building.

"Just a little," Eli said through gritted teeth. "It's my job to keep you safe. It would help considerably if I knew where the hell you were going before you decide to take a trip."

"Well, sorry, but I didn't think it would matter. You're supposed to accompany me wherever I go, right?" She tipped up her chin and put her hands on her hips. The motion drew his attention to her breasts again. She was wearing another clingy sweater. Didn't she own any baggy clothes? Or at least something that didn't hug her every inch and make him wonder how her ample curves would feel beneath his hands.

Eli didn't trust himself to speak just then. He was torn between wanting to yank her up on her toes and kiss her until her eyes crossed and wanting to put her over his knee. While he was wrestling with himself internally, Kaylee reached the front doors of the building.

When he read the name of the facility, his blood pressure rose again.

"You have a gig at a physical-therapy center? Really? Just days after I declined to investigate Matt's new girlfriend?"

"This isn't my gig. Relax. Matt got an urgent letter and I'm just here to drop it off since we're in the area anyway. Mara asked me to do it and I didn't mind."

She pushed the door open and let go so quickly it almost slammed into Eli. He followed her, seething. By the time he caught up with her, she was already seated in the waiting room. He sat next to her and pinned her with an accusatory stare.

"You know, I wouldn't have expected this of you. Mara, yes. Raina, definitely. But not you."

She turned toward him, her brown eyes slightly wounded. "How would you know what to expect of me? You don't know me at all. I'm not as innocent as you seem to think."

Before he could respond to that ridiculous statement, she stood again.

"Matt! There you are." Kaylee trotted across the room to where Matt stood next to the blonde she'd seen him with at the party. That must be his physical therapist.

The one Mara was trying to get you to investigate.

He'd refused out of loyalty to Matt. The dude was getting his life together and he needed privacy, not a bunch of nosy friends digging into his business. However, it looked like Mara was going to get her way after all.

He wondered if driving him up the wall was part of her plan or if that was just a side effect. Kaylee was hugging on Matt as if they were old friends who hadn't seen each other in ages. He liked Matt, but if the guy didn't pull his hand a little higher from where it was currently resting on Kay's lower back, he might have to forget they were friends.

"Eli, this is a surprise. I didn't know you were coming."

"I didn't know either."

"It was a spur-of-the-moment trip. I have a gig in D.C. Anyway, so Mara asked me to deliver some mail." Kaylee turned toward the blond woman. "Hi. I hope we're not interrupting the appointment."

"No, it's fine. We just finished, actually."

"Oh, this is my miracle worker, Penny Lewis. Penny, this is Kaylee and Elliott. Kay is a singer with my friend Jackson's record label. Eli is Jackson's older brother."

"We met, actually. At your party." She looked at Matt and the warmth of her smile was enough to give Eli a sunburn.

Mara was good, he had to admit. His instincts were usually pretty good about people when he first met them. He'd been wrong about his sister-in-law Ridley, but he chalked that up to his judgment being clouded. His initial impression had been correct, but he'd been so determined to keep Jackson from being hurt by another woman that he'd been quick to judge her when the evidence had been against her. He hadn't seen the truth until it was almost too late. He'd learned a valuable lesson. Emotions had to be left on the table.

"Well, we'd better go. Kay has to get to her gig." He turned to Kay and watched as she flushed slightly.

"Eli's right. It was great to see you again, Penny. Come on, Eli."

He waved goodbye and followed her back out to the car. "So do you really have a gig or was that just the excuse to come up here?"

She flushed again. "I know it was wrong, but Mara was really worried. I didn't want to say no. Plus, Ridley offered to babysit." She looked up at him entreatingly. "Do you know how long it's been since I've slept more than four or five hours at a stretch?"

Eli rocked back on his heels. "I'm guessing a long time."

"Since before I was pregnant. I'm going to climb into that hotel bed and sleep all night. God, it even sounds like a wet dream."

Eli sucked in a breath at the visual that slammed into his brain. Kay on a white comforter, her ample breasts spilling over the cups of her bra, her back arched as she moaned for him.

"Jesus," he muttered.

Kay clamped a hand over her mouth and shook her head back and forth slowly. "Okay, I didn't mean to say that out loud. Let's just rewind and pretend that didn't happen. Meet you at the hotel."

Eli got in his car and followed her sedan back out to the main road. There wasn't a chance in hell he'd forget that visual any time soon.

♥

A FEW WEEKS later, Penny was reviewing a patient file when she looked up to find Matt standing in her office. Her heart leapt and she tried to tamp down the incredibly cheesy grin taking over her face. Eventually she gave up. It was useless.

She was officially smitten.

It was a struggle to keep her mind on work lately. She couldn't concentrate on anything other than him, she didn't hear anything except the sound of his voice, and if someone asked her what the morning staff meeting was about, she'd have no clue. Falling for him was an exhausting process that had taken over her mind and body.

And there was no longer any use in denying it. She was falling for him. She could only hope for a soft landing.

"What are you doing here? You don't have therapy today."

Despite his announcement that day in his truck, she could tell he'd still been upset the past few weeks. She'd done everything she could to distract him. They'd gone to see an action movie with lots of explosions and had found several new restaurants to try. They'd taken a cooking class one weekend where they'd learned to roll their own pasta. She'd baked him cookies, and they'd eaten them in bed while the chocolate chips were still warm and gooey. They'd enjoyed cleaning each other up with lips and fingers and tongues.

Penny was willing to try anything that could provide an evening of distraction. She was trying to make up for not only his disappointment, but also for the fact that she really wasn't a good girlfriend. Not the kind he deserved.

If Matt didn't re-enlist with the military, then she wouldn't have to deal with him being deployed again. He'd be here with her. He'd be safe.

No, she wasn't a very good girlfriend at all because at one of his lowest moments, she'd felt an indisputable flash of joy. When he'd realized he wouldn't pass the physical fitness test, he'd been devastated and she'd been *happy*.

Nothing could make up for that.

Matt pulled out one of the chairs in front of her desk and sat down. "I missed you. So here I am."

An unexpected swell of emotion made her puff out her breath. He'd missed her. It was a thrill to know she wasn't the only one so affected.

"Guess what I did today?" Matt leaned back in the chair nonchalantly.

"Rearranged my closet?" Penny giggled at his dark look. He teased her constantly about her slightly obsessive-compulsive desire to keep things organized. In her closet, her clothes were grouped by color and type. In the bathroom, she had her skincare products lined up against the counter in the order they were used. It had always bothered her to find things out of place, but she'd lived alone so long she'd never had to worry about whether it was weird.

Now that Matt had left a few things at her place, she'd automatically started arranging his things neatly for him. His boots were kept against the wall in the living room, and she'd even started buying his favorite snack food. It was always funny to see his brand of barbecue potato chips next to her healthy pita squares in the pantry.

"I signed an employment contract with Alexander Security today. I'm officially on the payroll as an employee now. Since we still have a few days of therapy left, I won't get my first assignment until after that."

So many emotions were battling for space in her mind. On

one hand, she was so happy for him that he'd found a job that would utilize all his skills. Then there was the part of her that was worried about what this meant. The end of therapy signaled the return to the real world. Once Matt was working again and they had less time for each other, would the connection they'd found here hold up?

"Congratulations. I know you'll be great." If nothing else, that much was a certainty. She'd never met anyone as determined as Matt. When he wanted something, he went after it, no holds barred.

"I hope so." His brow furrowed as he leaned forward. "Anyway, I stopped at the deli on the way in and got you a sandwich."

"You brought me lunch?" Penny pushed back from her desk and accepted the foil-wrapped sandwich he shoved at her.

"I've seen how you work. You're on your feet for hours at a time, and you go full speed ahead until you drop. You can only help other people if you're in one piece, so yeah, I brought you lunch. It's a steak and cheese."

"That is really sweet, but I don't have time to eat right now. I have to check on Ms. Wright and then I have my next session with Mr. Eisenberg..."

"Georgia?"

Georgia appeared at his elbow, looking altogether too pleased. She didn't even try to hide the fact that she'd been right outside the door, eavesdropping. "Yes, sir?"

"Would you mind checking on Ms. Wright?"

"Of course. I'll do it now." She looked at Penny and raised her eyebrows.

"But Mr. Eisenberg—"

Matt turned back around. "Is a dirty pervert. Who can wait. Now sit your ass down and eat your lunch."

Penny gritted her teeth and stared him down. No one ever talked to her like that. Even when Charles started throwing his weight around, she'd always managed to stand up for herself. She wouldn't be disrespected by anyone, even her boss.

But when Matt crossed his arms and tipped his chin in the direction of the sandwich, she couldn't deny it was kind of *nice* to have someone so invested in her welfare that they'd bully her into taking care of herself. She doubted if Scott had ever noticed when she skipped meals. Not out of malice or anything, but he'd simply never paid that much attention to her.

She peeled back the foil and almost fainted from the delicious aroma. It smelled like heaven. She hadn't realized just how hungry she was until that moment. She looked up to find Matt watching her closely. His eyes softened when he took in her mutinous expression.

"Take a bite. I'm not leaving until you eat that sandwich. You might as well get started, baby."

Penny wasn't used to anyone talking to her this way. It was shocking, in a way, but also gave her a warm feeling to have his entire attention devoted to something as simple as whether or not she was well fed. It felt incredibly possessive. Like something an alpha male would do in the wild for his mate. She had no idea what to do with that kind of emotion coming from Matt.

So she sat her ass down and ate her sandwich.

Chapter Sixteen

♥

MATT COULDN'T BELIEVE the rest of the week had passed so quickly. He'd never wanted to rewind time before but found himself wishing he could now. Ever since he'd declared his feelings, he'd made a conscious effort not to pressure her. They ate together, made love together, and every night he held her against his heart. She fell asleep now to the gentle rap of his heart against her back.

He hadn't said another word about where their relationship was going. There had been no mention of the coming last day of therapy or discussion about what would happen after. No gifts, smooth lines, or promises were needed. He was wooing her without words. His every action proved his intentions. To be there for her.

He could only hope it was enough.

"So, this is your last day. You're going back home tomorrow?" Penny had finished the appointment by running him through some of the same exercises they'd done in the beginning. He could do them all with ease now.

Matt flexed his arm and stood. "Yeah." He didn't bother saying any more than that. They'd talked around the issue long enough. There was nothing else he could say that would convince her what they had was right if she wasn't ready to hear it.

"I've made a list of things that you can do on your own. It might be helpful as you're easing back into your usual work-out routine." She handed him the list and he scanned the items on it quickly. It was some of the same things they'd done together and a few additional moves.

"Thank you, Penny. For this." He held up the list. "For putting up with me. Yeah, just everything."

She looked like she was on the verge of crying, which made him feel like smashing something. Clearly she'd already made her choice. She wouldn't be crying if she was going to ask him to stay.

"It was my pleasure." There was a husky quality to her voice that just about sliced his heart in half. Hurting her had never been his intention. All he wanted was for her to give him a chance, but he had a feeling their relationship was going to be a casualty of timing. If only he'd met her at a different time, when she wasn't fresh from a breakup or he wasn't injured and angry at the world. Maybe there had just been too many obstacles against them all along.

"I haven't said anything all week. I haven't wanted to pressure you. But now we've run out of time and it's the last day. So I guess that gives me my answer, doesn't it?"

"It's not that simple, Matt. If I ask you to stay and this doesn't work out, then you've uprooted your whole life for me. This is still all so new. I can't help but wonder if we'd feel this strongly if we'd met under different circumstances. If I wasn't helping you heal and you weren't lonely and in need of a friend. Maybe it's better if we just date long distance so there isn't as much pressure."

Matt groaned under his breath. "You think I feel this way because I was just lonely and desperate?"

Penny winced. "Okay, that didn't come out at all the way I intended. All I meant was that we met again under stressful circumstances. I'm not sure that's enough to base a major life change on."

"It's about taking a risk. Do you believe I'm worth the chance or not?" Matt shrugged when she didn't answer, even though it felt like his heart was being stomped on. "It's clear I'm a risk you're not ready to take yet."

He didn't want to leave. They had a connection he'd never felt with anyone else. Part of him wished he could have healed a little slower so he'd have more time with her.

Although that wasn't really the problem, was it? He could stay a little longer. For all anyone knew, he could pretend he was still getting therapy and just stay at Eli's house another month. Eli wouldn't care.

But it was about so much more than that. It was time for him to stop feeling like he was on borrowed time. It was time for him to start living life on his own terms again. To take control.

He wanted Penny. He wanted to mix his clothes with hers

and drive her crazy by leaving wet towels in the middle of the bathroom floor. He wanted to bring her food so she didn't forget to eat and hold her close at night so she was never afraid. He could imagine a million ways to spend a million days together.

And every single one would be precious.

"If you want me to stay, you know where I'll be. I'm not leaving until morning." He kissed her on the forehead. Her eyes followed him as he walked to the door.

He hoped this wasn't the last memory he had of her.

♥

BY THE END of the day, Penny still hadn't made a decision. She didn't want Matt to leave, but it was a huge step from hanging out and having fun to moving in together. They'd only been together for a few months.

"Good night, Georgia." She waved absently as she passed the reception desk. Just before she reached the front doors, she turned around. Georgia looked up from her computer and raised her eyebrows.

"Are you okay?"

"You said once that you weren't with James because of what he could do for you. You're with him because he makes you happy. It's just... how did you know beforehand that he would make you happy? How did you know it was worth the risk?"

Georgia smiled gently. "I didn't. No one knows that ahead of time. But I knew if I didn't take the chance and find out that I'd regret it forever."

"Right. Thanks. Good night." Penny stepped out into the parking lot. A second later, the door flew open behind her.

"Penny!" Georgia jogged across the lot to where she stood. "I've tried to stay out of it because this needs to be your decision. I'm sure you can appreciate how hard it's been for me to keep my opinion to myself."

Penny smiled at the thought.

"But just ask yourself if you can stand there and wave goodbye to Matt when he leaves. Can you watch him leave and not feel like your heart is being ripped out?"

Penny imagined what it would be like the following week. Things would go back to the way they'd always been. Ordered. Logical. Safe. No more Italian dinners or smart-ass comments. No one to hold her at night and make fun of her quirks. No one to fight with. No one to laugh with.

She missed him already.

Penny shook her head. "No. I feel like my heart is being ripped out just thinking about it. I don't want him to go. I'm just scared to move too fast. What if one of us gets hurt because we forced it?"

"Don't take this the wrong way, but as your friend I'm telling you to stop being a chickenshit. As for the timing, you could do with forcing it a little."

Penny nodded briskly but the disbelief must have been evident on her face.

Georgia pulled her into a hug. "It's okay to be afraid, Penny. Anything worth having comes with the risk of losing it. But you can't let fear rule your life. Now go."

Penny raced to her car and threw her bag and jacket on the passenger-side seat. Urgency pushed her to get to Matt as soon as possible. It had hurt him to wait for her but he'd done it anyway. She drove out of the lot so fast her tires squealed when she turned onto the main road. Matt had said he was leaving tomorrow, but what if he'd gotten tired of waiting and left early?

Ten minutes later she pulled into the driveway of the house Matt had been using for the past few months. She got out and stood, staring at the single light burning in the window. The rest of the house was dark.

Was that light always on? The driveway was empty and she didn't see Matt's truck parked on the street. Had he already left? Maybe he'd gotten tired of waiting for her and decided to go home early. Maybe it hadn't hurt him to drive away from her.

"Penny? What are you doing just standing out here?"

She looked up. Matt stood silhouetted in the open doorway. His chest was bare and a pair of ripped jeans hung low on his hips. Her heart sped up when she saw him, the way it always did. How could she have hesitated as long as she had? The man was magnificent and he wanted her.

She ran across the grass, skipped the two steps leading to the porch, and launched herself at him. Matt caught her and buried his face in her shoulder.

"I want you to stay." She was trembling so hard she could barely get the words out. When he tried to pull back to look at her face, she just held on tighter. In that moment, she didn't ever want to let go.

"That's my decision. Stay."

♥

A FEW HOURS later, Penny was nude, snuggled up with Matt beneath the covers. The only light was the small lamp burning next to the bed. It was unbelievably intimate to rest quietly with his heart beneath her ear. There was a sense of peace surrounding them both. She couldn't imagine if she'd allowed him to leave.

"I've never been this happy. I'm scared to trust it."

At her words, his arms tightened around her. Their lovemaking this time had been different. There was a tender component to the way he touched her now, like he couldn't believe she was real.

"So you're going to stay here and rent from your friend?" Penny pushed up slightly so she could see his face.

"Yes. I don't think either of us is ready to live together yet. I won't ever pressure you into anything you aren't ready for. All I wanted was for you to give me a chance."

"We're actually going to do this?" Penny grabbed him around the waist and buried her face in his chest. "I feel like I must be dreaming."

"I know you aren't ready to hear this, but I'm in love with you, Penelope. This is no dream. Nothing I've fantasized would come anywhere close to the reality of you."

Overwhelmed, Penny reached up to brush his hair back from his forehead. "Matt... I don't even know what to say to that. I can't believe you really feel that way about me."

He held her face between his hands. "Believe it, pretty girl."

She opened her mouth to speak, but he stopped her with a finger against her lips. "I don't want you to say it back because you feel you have to. I'm waiting for the day when you say it spontaneously just because you mean it."

Penny was sure she was glowing. She kissed him softly. "I'm more than halfway there already."

"I'm not worried. I know it will come in time."

Penny ran a finger over the grooves of his abdominals. Each one stood out in sharp relief under his incredible bronze skin. Just like everything else, they seemed to be too good to be true. It was so tempting to relax into the happily-ever-after. To believe that *this time* things would really work out in the end. But she'd experienced this feeling one time too many. Every time she'd finally started to fit in at school and wasn't just the "new girl." When she'd finally gathered the courage to open up and start making friends.

Every time she found something she didn't want to lose.

Matt tipped up her chin until she couldn't avoid his eyes. His thumb caressed gentle circles on the side of her face. "Stop worrying. This is that unbelievable fairy-tale stuff you didn't believe existed. It may not have been love at first sight, but I definitely felt it when we met again. When I saw you standing in the waiting room that first day, it felt like I'd finally found what *I've* been waiting for."

"What's that?" Penny rested her head against his chest. She absorbed the feeling of being close to his heart. That was where she wanted to always be. For however long she had him.

"Someone who makes me feel alive." Then he flipped her over and showed her exactly what he meant.

Chapter Seventeen

♥

WHISTLING, MATT MOVED around Eli's small kitchen. My kitchen, he mentally corrected himself. Now that he was officially moving in for the duration, he needed to think of the house as his home.

They'd spent the past week working out the details, but he didn't care about any of that right now. It was a beautiful Saturday morning, the woman he loved was still asleep in his bed, and he was healthy.

He'd never felt so blessed.

The coffee maker made a soft spluttering sound as it

percolated, and the scent of bacon was still heavy in the air. Breakfast was his favorite meal of the day and he was anxious to share it with Penny. He'd gotten up early just so he could fix her bacon and eggs before he drove her to see her surprise.

He soft-scrambled a few eggs and then dumped them on a paper plate. Eli didn't have a breakfast tray, so he'd improvised by using a large serving platter instead. A few slices of bacon and a cup of coffee later, he carried it all upstairs and into the master bedroom.

Penny was still asleep facedown, the covers twisted around her legs.

"Wake up, beautiful." He placed the tray gently on the nightstand and then climbed back in bed.

As soon as his head hit the pillow, Penny rolled over and plastered herself against him. He pulled her onto his chest. Then he slapped her on the ass playfully.

"Oh my god, it's so early."

"I know, but I brought you a peace offering. Coffee, two sugars, and scrambled eggs."

Her head popped up. "Did you say coffee?"

They set the tray in bed between them and Penny let out a sigh of delight at the first sip of coffee.

"Are you always going to be this nice? I could get used to this."

"You like that, huh? You'll have to take care of dinner most nights, but I can do breakfast."

"Fair enough. So is there a reason you're so chipper this morning? Because if you're going to wake me at the butt crack of dawn every day then I might have to reconsider this arrangement."

Matt leaned over to steal a kiss. "I wouldn't disturb your precious sleep without a good reason. I have a surprise for you." He glanced at the clock on the nightstand. "We need to get going, actually. Like right now."

"Going? I need to take a shower and put on makeup."

He kissed her on the tip of her nose. "You are gorgeous without makeup. Those freckles get me every time."

She rolled her eyes and put her cup down on the nightstand. "Flattery will not sway me. The last time I went out without makeup, I ended up talking to your friends for an hour with hair that looked like it had been put through a wood chipper. I need to shower."

After rushing through the quickest shower possible, they were dressed and walking out to his truck.

"Okay, turn around."

She eyed the blindfold with trepidation but finally allowed him to wind it gently around her head. There was a good chance she wouldn't figure out what he was up to even if she saw where they were going. However, he thought it added a little mystery to things.

He headed for the highway and then they were on their way. Air rushed through the open windows, bathing them with the moist, cool air of spring. Penny laughed and turned her face into the wind. It was a sound that came from deep in her belly and went straight to Matt's heart. It was a sound of pure joy.

Northern Virginia was not only a center of military activity, it also boasted several private airfields. His buddy Shep had called in a few favors so he could pull this off. He only hoped Penny didn't think he'd gone too far.

He parked and tugged gently on the scarf at the back of Penny's head. Once it was off, she blinked in the light. He could tell when she finally figured out where they were.

"Where are we?" She turned around and stared at the row of small planes behind them.

"We're in Warrenton, Virginia."

"Are we going somewhere?" Penny looked puzzled.

"That's up to you. I have a buddy who flies here. He's taken people up for tandem jumps before."

Her eyes widened. "Tandem *jumps*? You aren't serious."

It was now or never. Matt figured he'd better talk fast before she ran away screaming. "I want to give you something more personal than flowers or chocolates. I don't have a lot of money, and I'm not sophisticated like that other guy." He scowled at the thought.

Penny grabbed his hand and squeezed. "I like you exactly the way you are."

"I know. This is part of who I am. I wanted to share that with you. You told me that you'd always wanted to try skydiving, to know what it felt like to lose control. Well, that's something I understand. After I went through jump school, I loved it so much I took civilian classes so I could skydive whenever I wanted. I wish I could be the one to take you down, but I'm only licensed to skydive alone. I'm not qualified as a skydiving instructor. So I did the next best thing and found you a great divemaster. But it's up to you. We can go home right now or we can take the leap together."

Penny stared at him, fear and longing clear in her wide-eyed expression. She turned in her seat and looked at the planes behind them again. Then she gave a little nod of her head.

"I want to take the leap."

Matt grinned. "Come on. This is going to be fun."

♥

THEY WERE MET on the tarmac by a guy named Carter. He was a friendly, thirty-ish blond guy who looked more suited to surfing than flying a plane. Penny swallowed her nerves. Matt had said this guy was one of the best tandem instructors in the area, and he wouldn't compromise when it came to her safety. That much she knew for sure.

After signing a never-ending stream of paperwork, they joined a class of four other students. For the next hour they learned about parachutes and the safety procedures necessary for a safe skydiving experience. Penny was happy to learn that in addition to a reserve parachute in case the first didn't open, there was also an automated activation device called an AAD that would open the chute below a certain altitude even if the instructor didn't. She let out an audible sigh of relief and felt Matt's chest shaking with silent laughter behind her. She elbowed him and gave him an evil look. In response, he held her closer and kissed her ear.

"I'm only teasing you, love. It's very safe."

"I know." Penny really did know that it was an extremely safe sport when you followed the safety rules, but it still went against human nature to jump out of an airplane. She was happy to have all the automatic safety features available just in case.

After the instructor demonstrated the safety harness they would wear, it was time to get ready for their jumps. "Have you changed your mind yet?" Matt whispered.

"Not yet. Ask me again when we're actually on the plane."

They changed clothes into bright red jumpsuits and adjusted their safety gear. As the instructor checked her harness, she started to feel the first stirrings of real fear. It was fascinating and scary to think she'd be jumping out of an airplane that day!

The ride up in the small prop plane was an event in itself. Penny was used to large aircraft where she could barely tell they were in the air. The floor of the plane vibrated with the drone of the engine and every air pocket they flew through made the plane rock and bump. Once they were above twelve thousand feet in altitude, the first students took their jumps. All the other students in their class had jumped before and one even had his individual license like Matt.

"For safety reasons, I can't jump right after you and Carter, but it won't be much of a delay. Are you ready for this?" Matt had been holding her hand since the plane took off. Penny gave him a bright smile, hoping to reassure him.

"Okay, let's go." Carter led them to the door. They were the only ones left besides Matt and another dive instructor. All the things they'd learned in the safety portion of class ran through Penny's mind on a loop. Once they exited the plane they'd fall at about 125 miles per hour.

"Are you ready?" Matt shouted.

Penny was too terrified to do anything other than nod. She was strapped to her tandem instructor so tightly that she had just enough leeway to look over her shoulder. She couldn't see Carter's eyes through his dark glasses, but when he nodded at her, she experienced a rush of excitement. The adrenaline in her system was so strong she was shaking.

She had a sudden, insane urge to ask Matt to call the whole thing off. To have them turn the plane around and put them back on the ground. Where it was safe.

Then she straightened her spine. She could do this. No more playing it safe. This was the chance to do something she'd always wanted to do, and she wasn't going to run away from it.

She was ready to fly.

"I'm ready. Let's do it," Penny shouted back.

The instructor nudged her toward the door, and they

balanced there for a moment. The sky stretched out below them forever, an endless expanse of blue and white. Penny let out a small squeak. It was incredibly windy and *cold*. So much colder than the weather on the ground. The air slapped at them mercilessly until the instructor pushed off.

Penny opened her mouth to scream, but any sound she made was swallowed in the rush of air. She instinctively closed her eyes but then a second later she forced them open. It was disorienting to feel herself in motion without being able to see where she was going. Plus, she didn't want to miss a thing.

It was a curious feeling, to fall and fall and fall. It was curious and wonderful and terrifying all at the same time. She'd expected it to be frightening, but it wasn't. Not really. It felt like she was gliding.

I've never seen anything so beautiful, she thought as they flew over the wide green landscape. Everything looked so small from this high and the only things that mattered were the wind in her face and the incredible sense of weightlessness.

There was a slight jerk when the parachute deployed.

She glanced up at Carter. They'd learned beforehand that the force of air in free fall was so great that they wouldn't be able to communicate by talking. He gave her a hand motion that meant "legs up." It would be less than a minute before they hit the ground, and she had to be prepared to land properly. She gave him a thumbs-up so he'd know she was okay.

Understatement of the year. She was more than okay. She was in love with a man who made her feel everything she'd thought didn't exist. Tears welled in her eyes, blurring her vision. There were no words to describe how it felt that Matt had arranged this for her. He was always there for her, always looking for ways to help her and make her life better.

"I love you."

She whispered the words as they glided toward the ground. It was cowardly to admit it to the wind when there was no way Matt could hear her, but she needed to let it out somehow. He'd come into her life again by chance and was quickly becoming one of the best parts of it.

She smiled the whole way down to the ground.

♥

WHEN MATT PICKED up the phone to call his sister, it was with a sense of anticipation he hadn't felt in a long time.

"Say congratulations."

"Congratulations?" His sister was obviously not paying close attention. Normally she would have caught on by now that something was up. He'd told Mara to expect him home today. He hadn't wanted to let her know that he might not be coming back in case Penny hadn't given him a chance. He'd be depressed enough on his own. The last thing he needed was all his friends finding out that he'd been rejected.

"Aren't you going to ask what for?"

"What for? Are you okay? You're acting really weird." Mara must have finally sensed something was up because she suddenly said, "Hey, aren't you supposed to be coming home today?"

"My home is no longer in New Haven. I've decided to move up to Northern Virginia so I can be close to Penny."

"Are you serious?"

Matt pulled the phone back from his ear at Mara's high-pitched squeal. But he was laughing when he said, "I take it you approve, then? You don't think I'm moving too fast?"

He'd meant to call her yesterday after he and Penny had

come home from skydiving. But they'd been so hopped up on adrenaline they'd ended up making wild, sweaty love all afternoon. They'd passed out, exhausted, after a few hours.

Mara sobered. "No, I don't think you're moving too fast at all. Life is short and you should do what you want. Matt..." She stopped and he could have sworn he heard her sniffling. "I am truly thrilled for you. You've been living a half-life since you got back and it's not fair. I was worried that I was never going to see my brother again. The real you hasn't been around in a long time, but I saw him when you were here."

Matt coughed, the lump in his chest feeling suspiciously like the precursor to tears. He wouldn't have been able to articulate it as well, but he'd been worried about himself, too. For the first time since his injury, he was hopeful and excited about the future. There were so many things he wanted to do and they all started with Penny.

Everything started with Penny.

"I'm going to be okay now, sis." It was something he felt strongly. No matter what happened, it would be okay if he had Penny at his side. He could get through anything, endure anything, knowing that she was waiting for him at the end of each day.

"I know. I knew that when I saw you with Penny. You were laughing, Matt. I haven't heard you laugh like that in a really long time."

Maybe it was because he was feeling hopeful for the first time in so long that he felt compelled to ask, "Are you happy, sis? I mean about getting married? Because I wouldn't blame you if you wanted to wait a little bit. Take your time. Travel."

"Yeah. That's what it is. I guess I just thought I'd have done more before I settled down."

"Don't let Mom make you feel like you have to rush into

this. It's your wedding. You should deliberately pick a wedding venue that's booked for years to buy some time. Then you and Trent can take some wild vacations to a nudist colony or go blow all your money in Vegas."

"You know what? I think I'll do that."

She sounded lighter than she had at the start of their conversation, so Matt decided to ignore the niggling twin-sense that something still wasn't right.

"Now I just have to figure out what to do with my house. I'm not sure I want to sell it yet." He'd bought it so he could feel like he was building a life, but he'd barely done anything to the place. There was no great sentimental attachment to that particular location. He knew now that building a life was about more than just the things you bought. It was about who you shared things with. Eli's place was more of a home to him than his own house was. When he closed his eyes in this house, he could smell Penny's scent and imagine her laughter bouncing off the walls. They'd already made some pretty great memories here.

"Rent it out. I'm sure we can find someone who'd rent from you until you decide to sell. Plus, since I'm here I could keep an eye on it for you. Make sure they take care of the place."

"That's a great idea."

"I'm full of great ideas. Such as you and Penny. That was *my* idea, you know. I'm totally taking the credit for matchmaking." She let out a happy sigh. "You're so lucky you have an awesome sister who bugs you and makes sure you go to your appointments."

Matt couldn't agree more.

Chapter Eighteen

♥

"TEN MINUTES, KAY."

She looked up when Matt stuck his head into the dressing room. Anxiety had become a constant companion for Kaylee the past few weeks. Now that Jackson had announced the group would go their separate ways after the summer, there had been an undeniable thread of tension present at each of their gigs.

In the past, that would have made Kay anxious, but it barely fazed her now. No, what had her on the edge of her seat was the tension between her and Elliott.

Thank God for Matt, she thought.

He'd been shadowing her the past week, and it had given her a break from Eli's terse company. Matt had seemed gruff when she first met him, but she'd soon learned he had a quick wit and a ready smile. He didn't mind when she took a little longer getting ready than the other girls. Eli always tried to rush her along, which annoyed her to no end. She couldn't skip steps in the makeup department like her friend Sasha or the other girls. They were all thin and beautiful. She was, well, she was just herself.

Now Matt stood staring at her outfit with a shocked expression. "New costume?"

"Too much? I knew these things were too tight!" Kay turned back to the mirror, tugging at the clingy spandex.

"No. No, you look great," Matt assured her. "I was just surprised since you usually don't wear bright colors."

Kay appreciated his tact. She usually didn't wear clothes that were this sexy. A tickle in her belly made her wonder what Eli would think when he saw it. Then she shook it off. Ever since they'd spent the night in the hotel together, nothing had been the same. She wasn't sure if it had been Ridley's intention to force them into the same room, but when they'd arrived at the hotel the desk clerk had only shown one room under their reservation.

Kay rubbed her stomach. She still wanted to barf sometimes when she thought of the horrified look on Eli's face. You'd think sharing a room with her was a fate worse than death.

He'd been a gentleman and offered her the bed, but she hadn't been able to sleep a wink all night. How could she when he was sleeping on a cot a few feet away? The next morning, they'd gotten on the road early, neither of them anxious to extend their stay any longer than necessary. Ever since then, Eli had been a bear.

"Have you seen Eli?" She tried to sound like she didn't really care, but she could tell by the gentle look on Matt's face that she hadn't succeeded.

"He's screening everyone coming into the backstage area. I know you guys have a big interview tonight, so he's been keeping security tight."

"He's being unreasonable."

Matt just smiled. "He takes your safety seriously and so do I." The walkie-talkie on his belt crackled. He stiffened and pulled it off. "I have to go. I'll see you after the show. Good luck."

"Thanks." Kay turned back to the mirror and tried to suck in another inch. Jackson seemed really confident that taking each of them solo was the right way to go, but Kaylee wasn't so sure. Singing solos in front of the choir was a whole different thing. No one could make fun of you when you were singing for Jesus. That would just be wrong, and as her mother liked to say, "you'd go straight to hell." Although her mother thought pretty much everything would send you straight to hell.

Either way, she knew she had the voice. She was confident in her talent, but pop stars needed a certain look.

She didn't have that.

This was the final show that she'd have the other girls on stage with her. It was a really scary thought. The only one she was close to was Sasha. She knew the other girls, Mandy and Christina, didn't really like her much. But at least when they were on stage there was someone to cover for her if she forgot a lyric. The crowd wasn't just looking at her.

After this, she'd be on her own.

♥

MATT HELD UP his walkie-talkie, listening to Eli's update. The first few weeks of his employment had taken a bit of adjustment. To Matt's surprise, there were few hard and fast rules governing who could be a bodyguard. Most states just required you to go through a short training program and be licensed by the state, so he'd spent a week training in D.C.

It was almost laughable to be required to take an entry-level firearms course since he was an expert marksman. He was used to shooting everything from a 9mm to an M-16. However, it had allowed him another week of being close to Penny, so he didn't care. It was so natural to go to sleep with her each night.

It made him wonder if he would have been able to walk away from her even if she hadn't come to him. Likely, he would have gone crazy the first week without her and come back, begging her to reconsider. He had to laugh at himself. He'd teased his friends about being whipped by their women and now he was in the same boat.

He'd been assigned to a security detail for a senator last week. This was his first week working in southern Virginia. He called her every night and they talked for hours, often falling asleep with his cell phone still in his hand.

"Everything okay?" Tank appeared at his elbow. His eyes darted around. Matt had instantly liked the ex-Army captain. He'd been helping Eli on the Divine group's detail for a few months now, so he'd been helpful in bringing Matt up to speed on their case. All the guys on Eli's team had been welcoming so far. They treated him like he'd been there all along.

He had a new team now.

"Yeah, Eli was just telling me everyone else is in place,"

Matt answered.

Tank nodded. "The show is about to start. The girls decided to add an extra song to the set. I'm not sure why," he added under his breath.

Matt understood the other man's disgruntlement. That would mean a slightly longer show. If they were supposed to be on the alert for someone after Kaylee, wouldn't it make more sense to cut the show short?

"I don't get it either, but I trust Eli. If they want to do an extra song, I guess a few more minutes won't make much difference in the long run."

They did another lap of the backstage area, meeting back at the side entrance.

Eli looked up when Matt approached. "The girls are on in five minutes. After the show, we'll leave through the back entrance."

Kaylee stood in the center of the group of girls. Her head was bowed and she looked like she was praying. Spending time with her over the last few days, he'd been humbled by her talent. The first time he'd attended a practice session for Divine, he hadn't expected the sounds that had come out of her mouth. She'd blasted out a particularly high note and Matt's jaw had dropped. Eli had let out his deep grumble-laugh.

"I'm guessing you've never heard her sing before?" he'd commented.

Matt had just shaken his head and continued watching in awe.

Despite her amazing talent, Kay was one of the sweetest, most humble people he'd ever met. No matter how long their practices ran or what she was asked to do, she always wore a smile.

"Okay, you two guard the separate stage entrances. I'm staying here by the dressing room."

Tank and Matt spread out, following Eli's orders. Matt took the left-side stage entrance. A few minutes later, the girls filed past him and out onto the stage. There was a roar from the crowd. He smiled. It was interesting to see the entertainment industry from this side of the stage. Few people knew how much hard work went into the performances they enjoyed. He wasn't distracted by the show because he'd seen it many times as they'd rehearsed in the days leading up to the event. It was to be their final group event before each of the girls started working on their solo projects.

Matt sensed movement behind him, so he turned. A young man who looked about early twenties with dark, spiked hair walked toward the stage entrance.

"Clearance pass?" he called. The guy stopped, then turned slowly.

"Sure. Here's my pass." He handed it to Matt. It was a green pass, which meant he had backstage access. Eli scrutinized the list of backstage passes that were issued and he'd personally manned the door to allow people into the backstage area. So he would have known if the guy was legit.

"Thanks, man. If you're here to meet the members of Divine, you might want to wait in the Press area." Matt pointed to a cordoned-off lounge with refreshments. The girls would give several interviews tonight, the most important to *Entertainment Weekly.*

"I'll do that. How long until the show is over?" The man's eyes darted around when Matt turned back to him.

"About an hour. What press outlet are you with again?"

"The local paper, the *Virginia Chronicle.*"

"Okay, well, there's coffee and donuts and stuff over there.

If you need to leave and come back, you'll have to go through security again."

The guy nodded and wandered away, aiming one last glance at the dressing-room door. Matt watched as he ambled over to the press area and sat down. A few minutes later, he glanced around, freezing when he noticed Matt observing him.

Matt pulled his walkie-talkie from his belt. "Eli? Are the girls scheduled to do an interview with the local paper, too?"

Static crackled over the line as Eli responded. "That was yesterday. The only interview they're doing tonight is for *Entertainment Weekly.*"

Matt turned back to the press area. It was empty. "Shit. We have a problem. There was a guy poking around backstage who looked a little off to me. He claimed he was from the *Virginia Chronicle* and had a green pass."

"Where is he now?"

He could tell by the sound of Eli's voice that he was running. Probably on his way to where he was.

"He's gone now. There's only two ways he could have gone."

"I know," Eli interrupted. "I'm heading to the back entrance now to see if I can cut him off."

Tank interrupted them then. "Should I hold position?"

"Everyone stand fast," Eli stated. "If this is the guy sending the letters, we can't let him leave."

He moved to the side of the stage area and scanned the platform. The club had its own security so if there was a problem in the crowd, they'd handle it. His concern was making sure no one got onstage near the girls. Several people were pointing to the ceiling. Matt looked up and then raised his walkie-talkie.

"He's in the rafters. I repeat, he's in the rafters above the stage area."

"I'm on my way now," Eli replied.

"I'll get the girls." A scream from the audience rang out. Matt's blood chilled. The guy had jumped from the rafters to a speaker on the side of the stage.

Matt strode out onto the stage and grabbed Kaylee, ignoring her gasp. The girls had been facing the crowd, so they hadn't even realized what was happening behind them.

He pushed her toward the exit, causing her to stumble into Sasha. The other girl stopped singing mid-lyric and turned to glare at Kaylee. "What is going on?" Sasha cried.

"Security breach. You need to leave the stage now." The other girls ran over and he herded them toward the other side of the stage where Tank was waiting. "Go!"

"Look out!" Tank's surprised face gave him a split second of warning, so he moved to the side. The arm that came slashing down had a knife with a three-inch-long blade in it. Another fist crashed into his cheek.

Tank ran out and jumped in front of the girls. Matt shoved the guy and then kicked him in the kneecap. The man fell to one knee with an anguished cry. Then he swiped at Matt's legs.

Matt jumped back and landed on his ass. He got to his feet and pulled his weapon.

"Stay right where you are."

The other man chuckled, the sound incongruous with the position he found himself in. "It's about time you got here," he rasped.

Matt figured the guy was delirious until he heard the click of a chamber near his ear. Instinctively, he rolled the other direction and ducked behind one of the large speakers. He peeked around the side, then pulled back abruptly. A bullet whizzed over his head and took a chunk out of one of the stage backdrops. Great, there were two of them.

"Come out, come out, wherever you are," a voice taunted.

Matt fired blindly to the ceiling, hoping the noise would scare them. There was a shout and a thud to his left. It sounded like the men falling to the stage as they dove for cover. He couldn't actually shoot toward the crowd because there were still people in the club.

It was time to assess his options. He pulled out his phone and sent Eli a quick text, letting him know his location and how many assailants there were. He could likely hold them off for a while since he had a lot of ammunition on him. But sooner or later, they were going to lose patience and rush him. At that point it was just a matter of who shot who first.

You're also assuming there are only two of these guys.

Matt sent up a silent prayer that Eli wasn't busy holding off any other attackers. Tank had been with the girls, so he could only assume they were safe.

Another shot whizzed over his head.

"Come on, Eli," he whispered.

♥

WHEN THE FIRST scream rang out, Mara thought it was just the usual crowd noise. Ridley had asked her to come because she wanted to support Kaylee. Mara didn't know her that well, but Kay seemed like a real sweetheart and she'd been a sport about helping Mara spy on Penny and Matt that day. She'd heard that Eli hadn't been too happy about how that had gone down.

Mara shivered. She couldn't imagine having Eli mad at you. He was always friendly when he saw her and she was grateful to him for giving Matt a job, but he kind of scared her a little. There was something about the way he stared at you without blinking.

"I don't know how Kaylee deals with this all the time," Mara remarked over the sound of the crowd.

"Well, it's not always this rowdy," Ridley yelled back. "But Kay was really nervous about performing today. Things have been tense. The other girls don't want the group to break up."

"Why are they breaking up, anyway?"

"Because Jackson thinks Kay will do better on her own. She's really the one carrying the group." Suddenly Ridley stopped talking and grabbed Mara's arm. "Oh my god. What the hell is he doing?" She started pulling Mara backward.

"Where are we going?"

When someone else screamed, Mara clutched Ridley's arm. She wasn't much of a concert-goer, so she wasn't sure what was normal. It was actually kind of strange that she didn't enjoy them more. She loved parties and concerts were like parties on steroids.

But this was just a little too much for her senses to handle.

"I've learned a few things lately. When something weird starts going down, you don't hang around to watch. There's a guy who just jumped onstage from the ceiling."

Mara tried to look over her shoulder as they pushed through the crowd. Matt had come out onstage and was dragging Kaylee to the other side. Then she saw the man come up behind him.

"Matt, look out!" She knew it was useless, there was no way he could hear her over the crowd. But she had to warn him.

"Wait! We have to go back. That man is attacking Matt." She fought against her friend's hold, but Ridley tightened her grip and pulled her through the crowd. Mara saw Matt fighting the man and then suddenly they both fell to the ground.

"Ridley, please wait," she sobbed. The sound of gunshots rang out and the people started screaming and pushing. Tears streamed over her cheeks as she struggled. Ridley wrapped her arms around her and forced her toward the exit.

"Eli and the others are trained to deal with this. We aren't. Your brother would never forgive you if you got hurt trying to help him when he doesn't need help."

Once they were out of the main stage area, they ran past the bar toward the exits. Just as they pushed outside into the cool night air, Mara heard sirens.

"See, help is on the way. Let's go across the street so we aren't in the way."

She followed Ridley to the parking lot across the street where they promptly sat on the curb to catch their breath. Mara pulled out her phone and dialed Penny. Her fingers shook so badly that she could barely bring up the number. All she could see was Matt falling.

"What are you doing?" Ridley asked. They watched as several police cars and a fire engine pulled up outside the theater.

"I have to let Penny know what's going on. Those guys were attacking Matt. What if he's hurt? She'll need time to get here." Mara broke down into tears and Ridley pulled her into a hug.

"It's all going to be okay. I know it is." But she didn't sound any more confident than Mara felt. She'd seen Matt go down, too.

And they hadn't seen him get back up.

Chapter Nineteen

♥

PENNY HATED DOING patient reviews. There were a stack of case files on her desk that she needed to get through, and she'd only done one all evening.

One. Freaking. Review.

She sighed. If she was being honest, it wasn't really the case file reviews making her miserable. She hated everything right now. Matt had only been gone for a week and it felt like an eternity. She hadn't been sleeping well at all, despite the fact that they stayed up all night talking on the phone like teenagers.

She loved him and she was going to tell him. There was no time frame for loving someone. He made her happy. When she envisioned her future, she couldn't imagine it without Matt.

That was love.

Her cell phone rang and she grabbed at it eagerly. When she saw the number, she stopped. It was Mara.

"Hello?"

"Penny!" Mara's voice was a cross between a scream and a cry.

Penny stood, the papers on her desk slipping off and scattering to the floor. "Mara? Are you okay?"

A soft sob came over the line. "We're at the club where Divine is playing their last show. I don't know what happened." She dissolved into tears again. Everything she said after that was lost in a jumble of tearful sounds.

"Wait, Mara, slow down. Who's hurt? Are you hurt?"

"No," she wailed. "It's Matt."

Penny stopped breathing. "What happened to Matt? Where is he?"

"I don't know. I don't know what's happening. I saw him onstage and there was this man and I saw him fall."

Penny gripped the phone and pressed it closer to her ear, trying to hear. Mara was incomprehensible at this point. There was a loud shuffling sound and then an unfamiliar voice was on the line. "Hello, Penny?"

"Yes, I'm here. Who is this?" Penny plugged her other ear with her finger so she could hear.

"It's Ridley Alexander. We met briefly at Mara and Matt's birthday party. I'm so sorry I have to tell you this over the phone, but something happened at the show. There was a guy who jumped on stage and went after the singers. Some crazed fan, I guess. Mara says she saw Matt get pushed down and didn't see him get back up. We heard gunshots after that, but we couldn't see who was shooting."

Penny heard a soft moaning sound and didn't realize at first that it came from her. She held a hand over her mouth. Matt was facing some lunatic and she had no idea whether he was safe or not. Her every nightmare come to life.

"The police are inside now, but I don't know what's happening," Ridley continued. "Eli knew we were at the show, so he'd contact us if everything was fine. He hasn't been in touch, so I'm not sure what's going on. Mara wanted you to know what was happening so you'd have time to drive down here. Just in case."

Penny understood what the other woman was really saying. Just in case Matt didn't get back up. Just in case he was dead.

"Thank you. I'm coming now."

"Okay, we'll text you if we hear anything in the meantime."

They hung up and Penny dropped down into her desk chair. She stared, unseeing, at the piles of paper on the floor.

Matt had called her last night, like usual. He'd told her all about guarding Kaylee and what a nice, humble girl she was. He'd actually laughed at how it didn't seem right to be getting paid to hang out with his friends. He'd sounded so happy that it had temporarily made her feel better about the separation. It sucked not seeing him every night, but at least he was enjoying himself. He'd found a career that fit him well and gave him the sense of teamwork he'd been looking for. She'd been happy for him.

Briefly, Penny thought about how many years he'd spent in the military and how she'd thought he'd be so much safer in the civilian world. She'd assumed the military was the only danger to their relationship. To her perfect future. By avoiding risk and keeping everything in her life in perfect order, she'd fooled herself into thinking she could control things. That she could ensure she'd never have to feel as helpless and out of control as she had as a teenager.

How had she not learned by now that fate had a way of getting you where it wanted you no matter what you did? Her glee, no matter how momentary, that he hadn't qualified to stay in the military had brought this down on them. She'd been smug in her triumph and this was the payback. She covered her eyes with her hands.

Fate was such a miserable, catty bitch.

♥

A FEW MINUTES after she'd hung up with Ridley, the door to her office opened.

"Penelope?" Charles stood in the doorway uncertainly.

"I don't have time to talk right now, Charles. I need to go." His appearance jerked her from her shocked stupor, and she realized she'd just been sitting in her chair, staring into space. Her man was in trouble and there were one hundred and fifty miles separating them.

She swept all the papers on her desk into a pile. She'd have to ask Georgia to rearrange things since she didn't know how long she'd be gone. It would depend on how badly Matt was injured. Mara hadn't been sure of exactly what she'd seen.

"Go where?" Charles watched as she pulled off her lab coat and threw it over the back of her chair.

"I'm having a personal emergency. I need to take a few days."

"You just took vacation."

Penny grasped her head between her hands and pressed hard against her temples. She wasn't sure if it was possible to physically hold in rage, but she was trying. If Charles didn't get out of her way, she was liable to turn green and come bursting out of her clothes.

"No, Charles. I used my vacation time to attend to a pro bono patient. That's not a vacation. A vacation is lying on a beach somewhere, sipping mai tais and checking out cute cabana boys. I was doing my job on my personal vacation time. Something I should not have to do."

He took a step back when she pointed at him, her finger almost jabbing him in the chest. His face turned a mottled shade of red as he watched her racing around the room, ignoring him.

"Well, yes, but it still counts as vacation time. I don't think you have enough hours left to take more time now," he stammered.

"That may be the case, but my boyfriend was injured while on the job. I need to be there."

Charles stood up to his full height. "Look, Penny—I'm not heartless, but you can't just run off."

Penny pulled her handbag from her desk and slammed the drawer. "Watch me."

"Now wait a minute!"

Penny whirled around. "I have busted my ass for this place since the day I was hired. It's never enough. I'm doing too much or too little. I'm getting too much attention and the center isn't getting enough. Or was it really that *you* weren't getting enough? Well, you're finally going to get what you've been angling for since the beginning. I quit. You get to be the star of the show now. Good luck with that. Trust me, it's not what it's cracked up to be."

She burst into tears. "Now get the hell out of my office."

Charles watched her uncertainly until she screamed "Get

out!" Then he ran out the door.

A few seconds later Georgia pushed the door open. "I saw the snake go slithering off. What happened?" When she saw Penny standing in the middle of the room crying, she shoved the door all the way open and ran to her side.

"What happened? Penny? Are you okay?"

"I should have listened to you. You tried to tell me love is simple. I made it complicated and now he'll never know how I felt."

"He knows, Penny. I'm sure he knows." Georgia held her and rubbed a hand up and down her back. The gentle touch broke down the last of Penny's emotional defenses.

She collapsed into her friend's arms. "It's not enough."

After Georgia calmed her down enough that she could drive, her friend walked her out to the parking lot to her car. She'd promised to call as soon as she had any news. The thought made her look at her phone again. Mara would call if she got any word on Matt. She hadn't, so that meant he really was injured. If Mara had seen him walk out of the club alive, she would have let her know.

She didn't bother going home to get any clothes. If Matt was hurt, she wasn't taking any chances on getting there in time. If she drove fast enough, she could make the trip in about two hours.

As she raced over the darkened highways, she kept her eyes on the road ahead and tried not to speculate about what was happening. But it was pretty much impossible not to worry. Matt was supposed to be safe. Safety was an illusion and she'd fallen for it. She'd been so stupid to think that him getting out of the military meant they got to have a happy ending.

After an hour of driving, her phone rang. She snatched it off the seat. "Mara? Is he okay?"

"Eli sent us a message that they're all alive but not out of danger. There's a standoff situation in the building. He was separated from Matt, so we still don't know exactly what happened. But the good news is that Matt is alive."

Relief streamed through Penny. Her hands shook on the steering wheel. "Thank God. I'm on my way. Since it's so late, there isn't much traffic. I should be there in about an hour."

"Okay. We're at the Alexander farm. We decided to all wait together. I'll send you the directions. It's actually closer to you."

"Great. I'll see you soon."

"Penny?" Mara's voice sounded so small. She'd never heard her sound like that. Even as a little girl, Mara had always been vivacious and confident.

"I'm really glad you're coming. Matt has never been happier than when he's been with you. I feel like you're my sister already."

Penny's eyes welled with tears. The road before her blurred slightly. "Thank you."

"Okay, see you soon."

A minute after they hung up, Mara texted the directions. Penny looked down at her speedometer and pressed harder on the gas until the needle inched closer to eighty-five miles per hour. Luckily the speed limit on most of the rural highways between northern and southern Virginia was seventy miles per hour, so she hadn't been pulled over for speeding. She might be pushing it if she went any faster, but she was willing to take the chance.

Matt had gone through training classes and refresher courses and she'd been shocked to see the amount of weaponry he'd been issued. Apparently Elliott Alexander considered his private security force to be a sort of army. Matt had cases of weapons and he'd taken a mini-arsenal with him when he'd packed to leave for this assignment. She knew he was trained and excellent at his job, so she had to believe that whatever was going on, he could handle it.

"Just hold on, Matt. Whatever happens, just hold on."

♥

WHEN THINGS SUDDENLY went quiet, Matt peeked around the corner of his hiding place. He likely wasn't going to get another opportunity, so he dashed from his spot behind the speaker and raced for the stage exit. He plastered himself against the wall before glancing around the corner.

It was clear.

Tank had sent a message that he had the girls blockaded in their dressing room, so Matt dashed down the hallway. He scratched at the door three times, keeping his eyes on the empty hallway behind him. There were three scratches from the other side and then the door opened. He didn't move, allowing Tank to see it was him and he was alone.

Finally, the door opened all the way and he stepped inside. Kaylee let out a soft cry when she saw him. "Matt! I thought they'd gotten you."

He smiled at her because he could tell she needed to see it. "It'll take more than that to knock me out. I'm just glad you're all okay."

He turned back to Tank. "Where's Eli?"

Tank made a frustrated sound. "He was here with us and then he left. He was talking to the police and decided to use himself as bait to draw the guys out. He hasn't contacted me since."

Matt cursed. "Well, whatever he did worked. The guys were

right on me and then suddenly they were gone."

They glanced behind them to where the girls sat in a huddle, talking quietly amongst themselves. Kay saw him looking and sent him a tremulous smile. He couldn't let her down. She trusted them to keep her safe.

"Procedure is clear. In situations like this, we're to stay with the client." Eli had drilled that into his head. As much as Matt wanted to charge out there and look for his friend, he knew he needed to stay. Even if the guys came back and started shooting, he and Tank could keep the room secure. They had plenty of weapons between the two of them, and the other man was an excellent shot. Almost as good as Matt.

"Let's secure the room." The door had a flimsy lock, so he swiped all the crap off one of the girl's dressing tables and used the furniture to block the door.

"There are no windows, which means no one can get in, but it also means we can't get the girls out if there are explosives," Matt whispered.

"What are we going to do?" Sasha cried. The other girls looked at them expectantly. Matt decided to keep it simple.

"We haven't gotten the all clear yet from Eli. So until we do, we're going to stay put."

Chapter Twenty

♥

PENNY ARRIVED AT the Alexander-Bennett Co-op after the most tension-filled two hours of her life. She'd spent the entire drive thinking about the last time she'd spoken to Matt. Wondering if she'd ever get to speak to him again.

If she'd ever get to tell him she loved him.

Eli had sent one message letting them know the guys were all okay but still stuck in the building and working with the police to hold off the two suspects. The relief they'd all experienced at hearing that was short-lived when they saw a news report speculating that there were explosives in the building. Penny had no idea what to think after that.

There were so many things they didn't know. But Eli had promised to send another update as soon as he could.

The time spent waiting for Eli to check in again seemed interminable. Especially since Penny wasn't sure he would. He was trying to catch killers. Calling them with updates had to be low on the priority list.

But Mrs. Alexander seemed confident that he would call, so she could only assume they had some kind of agreement. Matt had said that Eli had been running his company for almost a decade now, so surely this sort of situation had occurred before. She would have to trust that they'd have news soon. Otherwise she was liable to break down and weep like a baby.

Trent, Mara, Jackson, and Ridley stood across the room with their heads bowed. She could hear the soft murmur of their voices as they prayed. It was soothing even though she couldn't hear the words. The patriarch of the family stood in the corner, one hand on the mantel of the fireplace. Penny noticed with sadness that one finger was stroking the picture on the end. She could only assume it was a picture of Elliott.

Julia Alexander walked into the living room. She'd excused herself to have privacy while she called some relatives. Julia was a petite woman. Her head only came to Penny's shoulder. Her age had to be about the same as Penny's own parents, but her light brown skin was remarkably free of lines.

"Would you like to join the prayer circle, honey?"

Warmth settled over Penny as Julia stood next to her and placed a hand on her shoulder. With her soft, soothing voice and gentle smile, Julia instantly made Penny feel like she belonged there with the rest of the family. She could understand why Matt regarded this woman as a surrogate mother.

"I'm not very religious. I probably shouldn't."

Julia motioned for Penny to move over. "Why don't I sit with you? I could use a little company."

They sat and watched in companionable silence as the others prayed. Surprisingly, Penny found herself calmed just by watching.

"I wish I could believe," she whispered.

Julia reached over and patted her arm. "Have you ever hoped for something that you weren't sure would happen?"

"Of course. All the time."

"Praying is an expression of hope. Even if you aren't religious, we can all have hope for the things we want. For the people we love."

Penny bit her lip and the tears she'd been holding back spilled down her cheeks. "It's not just that I'm not religious. I feel like I made this happen." At Julia's surprised look, she explained. "It sounds so stupid, I know it does, but it's true."

When Julia pulled her down against her shoulder in a soft hug, Penny didn't resist. She could see Mara and the others watching from across the room and was even more ashamed. It was Mara's brother who was in danger and even she was keeping it together.

"You didn't cause this, child. Things happen. Things we have no control over."

Penny looked up through her tears. "When Matt realized he couldn't pass the fitness test to reenroll in the Army, I was happy. He was devastated and all I could think about was myself. Isn't that awful? Now he's hurt in a civilian job. It's like fate is trying to teach me a lesson."

"You think fate is punishing you?"

Mark ambled over and silently set a box of tissues on the side table next to his wife. Julia smiled up at him, then handed one to Penny.

"I told you it sounded stupid." Penny tried to mop up her face, then blew her nose with an undignified honk.

"It's not stupid. But it's also not true."

"How do you know?" Penny asked softly.

Julia squeezed her shoulder. "Because if being happy that Matt was out of the military brought on the wrath of the universe, we'd all be affected. I was happy, too."

Penny looked up in surprise.

"You thought you were the only one? I think we were all happy. We love him for serving his country and doing it so well. Matt has the heart of a warrior, but he's served his time honorably. Now I believe it's time for him to be at home."

"I felt so guilty. He was so upset when he realized he wasn't going to pass. Being in the Special Forces was his dream."

"I understand, but thoughts don't make bad things happen," Julia continued. "Because let me tell you something, honey. If that was the case, there's some folks who'd be dead as a doornail!"

Shocked, Penny laughed. It felt wrong at first, then it rolled through her. The hysterical giggles finally stopped and she sighed. She was so tired.

"I never told him how I felt. I was worried that we were moving too fast, that if I felt too much too soon, it wouldn't be real. Do you know how stupid that seems now?"

"I feel like I can speak here because I've known Matt since he was a teenager coming home with Jackson. He used to show up with Trent, Nick, and Jackson on the weekends, looking like a lost boy." She looked over to where Trent and Jackson stood. "I adored my lost boys like they were my own. I used to send them all back to the dorm with cookies and clean clothes. So, I've known Matt a long time, and I saw the way that boy looked at you. He loves you. And unless I'm blind, you looked at him the same way."

"I do love him," Penny admitted. "I wish it hadn't taken me so long to see it."

"It takes as long as it takes." Julia patted her hand. "Now, let's take a moment to hope for him."

♥

THE SOUND OF gunshots had Tank and Matt on their feet. They glanced at each other while the girls huddled closer together, and he could hear one of them crying softly.

"He would want us to stay here," Tank stated. It was clear the other guy didn't like it any more than he did.

"I can go outside the door. Technically, I wouldn't be leaving the client."

Tank glanced back at the girls. "*Do it.* I don't like not knowing what's going on. Those guys could be building a bomb in the hallway. I feel like we're sitting ducks if we stay here."

Matt moved the dressing table from in front of the door. Tank stood to the side, his gun at the ready. Matt eased the door open to peer into the hallway.

"I don't see anything," he muttered in a low voice.

They opened the door wider. Matt stuck his hand out. Nothing happened. So he stepped out into the hallway. Something slammed into his side. He pushed it off and swung around. The man who'd tried to stab him earlier looked just as surprised to see him. He must have been running from something else.

Before the guy could react, Matt punched him in the face. He dropped like a stone. Matt took his weapon and unloaded it, tossing the gun to the side.

"Nice one." Tank grabbed the guy by the shirt and dragged him in the room where he handcuffed him and pushed him against the far wall. The girls looked horrified to have the guy in the same room with them, but it was necessary. They couldn't chance leaving him outside where his partner could possibly find and free him.

"Okay, I'm going back out. Maybe the other one will show up."

"Or maybe I'll show up." Eli appeared in the doorway. Both Matt and Tank were so startled they drew their weapons, then immediately lowered them.

"Sorry, boss." Tank went back to securing the suspect. He tied something around his feet so he couldn't move even if he woke up.

Eli came farther into the room and closed the door. When he saw the man hog-tied in the corner, he immediately pulled out his phone. "My men caught one suspect. We have him detained. I'll wait for further instructions." Eli listened for a moment, then hung up.

"They're sending a SWAT team in. They want us to stay put until—" Shots splintered the door behind them, then started coming through the wall. It was obvious the dressing room wasn't solidly constructed because bullets were tearing through the drywall like it was tissue paper.

"Get down! Get down!"

Eli threw himself on top of Kaylee and took her to the ground. They all covered their heads as more shots exploded through the wall. When it finally went silent, they all drew their weapons.

"Girls, get in the bathroom," Eli ordered.

Kay jumped up and ran for the bathroom, the other girls

close on her heels. The door closed behind them. Matt, Eli, and Tank spread out in the room. If the guy crashed in, there was no way he'd be able to hit all of them. A second later, the door exploded inward.

"Drop your weapon," Eli warned.

"Or we will shoot," Matt added.

Matt watched as the guy swung toward him. His eyes were crazed as he realized he was outnumbered. "It wasn't supposed to be like this."

"What do you want from her? Why are you stalking her?" Eli asked. The guy swung back toward him. He was panicking, Matt observed. Having them talk at him from two sides was confusing him, dividing his attention.

"Nothing. He said this would be an easy job. He didn't say anything about bodyguards."

"Who? Who said it would be an easy job?" Eli's face was twisted into a mask of rage. He'd been working for months trying to uncover the identity of Kaylee's stalker. So far it had just been threatening letters, but it seemed the guy had graduated his efforts. He was no longer trying to get close to her. He was trying to kill her. He wanted it badly enough to hire out.

"*Who said it would be an easy job?*" Eli demanded.

Matt edged closer, using the guy's distraction to put himself between the line of fire and the bathroom where the girls were hidden. The guy whipped his head toward Matt and fear flashed across his face when he saw how close he was.

"I know what you're trying to do. You tricked me!" He raised his gun and a sudden pain stabbed into Matt's side.

There was an explosion of gunfire as Matt, Eli, and Tank all discharged their weapons at the same time. When he lowered his weapon, the suspect lay on the ground, blood already pooling beneath him.

A throbbing pain in his side brought Matt's attention back to himself. He looked down at the hole in his shirt. "The bastard shot me."

That was going to hurt in a minute, he thought dimly.

♥

PENNY HADN'T THOUGHT there was anything worse than being on the outskirts of Matt's friends and family as they'd prayed. But being included in their circle, hearing the stories of how loyal he was and what a great friend and brother he was just reminded her of all the experiences they hadn't had yet.

It also made her think about him actively. The purpose of a prayer session was to remember him and focus their energy on him, but Penny couldn't do that. She couldn't think about him without wondering where he was right then. Was he in danger? In pain?

Alive?

There were so many questions and too few answers. The only thing that gave her comfort was closing her eyes and pretending she was somewhere else. It hurt too much to consider the possible scenarios.

"They're okay. Oh, thank god." Julia held her cell phone aloft. "Eli just sent me a message. They're all right. The standoff is over. Matt is fine. They're all fine. They'll be home soon."

There was a collective sigh of relief. Mara let out a squeal and hugged Trent. Jackson and Ridley got pulled into the hug somehow. Penny didn't know them well enough to get in the middle of the love-fest, but Julia came over and hugged her anyway.

Now that they knew everyone was okay, the tension in the room lifted. Someone found a deck of cards and Mark dealt a game. Penny was so tired her eyes kept closing against her will and then popping open whenever someone spoke to her. She wasn't sure how much time had passed before Mara squealed again.

"Matt! Oh my god!"

Penny's head shot up from where she'd been resting on the couch. Matt and Elliott stood in the doorway, looking at them. Elliott had a bandage on his arm and Matt's right cheek sported a bruise that was already swelling.

Mara got up from where she was sitting on the floor and flew across the room. She stopped right before she ran into Matt and then hugged him gingerly.

"Hey, there. It's okay." Matt patted his sister's shoulder awkwardly. His eyes searched the room until they met Penny's. Everything she'd been holding inside the past few hours twisted around inside her in a jumble. Matt and Elliott made the rounds, getting hugs from everyone in the room. Julia fussed over them, then excused herself to the kitchen to get them something to drink. As she passed, Penny saw her wipe tears from her eyes.

Matt sat next to her on the couch. Penny leaned against his side and he sucked in a sharp breath.

"Oh no, you're hurt." She reached for his shirt. He covered her hands with his.

"Bruised ribs. They're not broken. I'm okay."

He put his arm around her and she leaned over, careful not to put any pressure on his side.

"I'm so not okay. I was really worried about you," Penny admitted.

"I'm so sorry, baby. That was a tough situation, and I'm grateful to be back here with you. Thoughts of you were all that kept me sane." Matt stood and Penny followed. "I think it's time to go home and get some rest."

Mara gave him another careful hug. Then promptly dissolved into tears again. Trent led her out with a gentle hand at her elbow.

After another round of hugs, Matt turned back to Penny. "You ready to go, baby?"

She nodded. "Yeah. Let's go home."

♥

PENNY HELD THE door open for Matt, aching for him when she saw how slowly he was moving. He had to be in serious pain, but he didn't utter a word of complaint. She was trying to hold it together for him. Getting hysterical wouldn't help him, so she just followed him to the bedroom quietly.

When he took off his shirt, she couldn't hold in her cry. There was a fist-sized bruise on his ribs that was almost black.

"That's where he shot me. If I hadn't been wearing Kevlar, I'd be dead right now."

"It didn't stop it completely though. I always thought those vests made you invincible or something."

He shook his head. "No, unfortunately not. As you can see, all that force still leaves its mark. It feels like being punched by a superhero."

He climbed into bed and settled himself on his back with a loud groan. Penny crawled in on the other side of the bed. "I'm so glad you're all right. I love you so much. All I could think all day was that I might not get the chance to tell you."

There was no reply, so Penny looked over at his side of the

bed. He was fast asleep, breathing through his mouth. He normally didn't snore, but he was making sounds like a freight train.

The most overwhelming sense of love came over her. The sight of him, sleeping safe and sound in his own bed, was the best thing she'd ever seen. She propped herself up on her arm and just watched him. There was nothing in particular she was looking at, she was just grateful for the chance to look at him.

She would never take it for granted again.

Ten minutes later, Matt woke with a jolt. When he saw that she was awake, he grimaced and tried to sit up. He paled and sagged back against the pillow. "Penny? What are you doing still awake? You have to drive back home tomorrow, don't you?" He tried to push her back down to the pillow. "Go to sleep, woman!"

Penny giggled. "I am home, you crazy man. I'm exactly where I'm supposed to be."

He watched her curiously. "I got shot tonight so I'm not firing on all cylinders, but I don't get it."

"I had this idea that military life represented danger and civilian life was safe. But the truth is they both have their challenges. There's no easy route guaranteed to end in happiness. Any day could be your last, no matter how safe you think you are. I was so worried about doing things the right way. Now I'm just grateful we get to do them at all. I love you, Matt. I'll love you all my life."

He raised a hand and brushed it against the back of her cheek. "I love you, too. So much. I really wish I could hug you right now, but I'm not sure I can move."

Penny laughed softly and leaned over to kiss him. "Well, I'll come to you then." His lips opened under hers and she breathed in his scent. "Oh yeah, and I quit my job." At his surprised look, she laughed out loud and kissed him again.

It turned out that home was knowing Matt was coming back to her, wherever she was. Home was having the right to brush his dark hair off his brow and to kiss the stress line that always formed on his forehead.

He wasn't a fairy-tale prince, but he was the only man she'd ever wanted to come home to. The only man who had ever mattered.

He's the man I'm meant for.

Chapter Twenty-One

♥

A few weeks later.

MATT HELD OPEN the door to Jackson's patio and waited as a stream of children raced by. There were Jackson's two boys, their cousins Annabelle and Isabelle, and then a few more he wasn't sure he'd seen before. Jackson came out of the kitchen, holding a tray of cookies.

"Is it my imagination or did some of these kids come out of thin air?"

Jackson shrugged. "You know how Mom is, she invites the

whole church. It's my house and I have no idea who's here either." He offered the tray to Matt.

"Did Ridley make these?" Matt snagged one off the tray and took a bite. They were still warm.

"Raina made them. She's due in two weeks, so she claims she's not worrying about nutrition for the baby anymore. Apparently the baby is technically done at thirty-seven weeks, so she's decided she's just going to eat whatever she craves from here on out."

Matt took another bite of his cookie. It was a masterpiece of chocolate and sugar. "Makes sense to me."

Jackson took the platter outside and Matt followed. Eli already had the music pumping. Mara waved at him from where she stood at the buffet table. Trent had his arms around her and was whispering something in her ear.

"Hey, Matt. When did you get here?"

Matt turned and accepted a handshake from Jackson's oldest brother, Bennett. "I just got here. How's it going?"

"I'm great. Actually, I have a message for you. Kaylee asked me to keep a lookout for you and tell you that she and Penny are upstairs and they'll be down in a minute."

"Oh, okay. Thanks." Matt wasn't surprised the two women were huddled somewhere. Over the past few weeks, they'd gotten to know each other really well since he'd been guarding Kaylee. Penny accompanied him most of the time, and they spent time talking and playing with Kaylee's baby girl, Hope.

"I'll just go say hello to your parents while I wait," Matt said.

Bennett nodded and walked toward the buffet table. Matt walked across the yard to where Julia and Mark sat in picnic chairs under the shade of an old elm tree. They sat with hands entwined, watching their children and grandchildren.

He stopped next to them. "Do you mind if I sit?"

Julia beamed up at him. "Of course not, honey. Pull up a chair and join us." They were both tanned a deeper brown than usual and looked like they'd just been on vacation.

Matt dragged over a metal folding chair and sat down.

"We would be out there mingling, but you know, it's not as easy for us to do that now. The heat wears on me. Getting old is hell," Mark grumbled.

Matt laughed along with them. He turned and looked at the party, trying to see it from their eyes. What was it like knowing you'd built a family forged with love so strong it could support this many generations? A love so strong it could carry the weight of children who weren't even your own?

He looked over to find Julia watching him with knowing eyes. "Penny mentioned you were going to that counselor she recommended. I'm proud of you."

"I am, too." Matt held a hand over his heart. He'd been talking about Cyrus more lately. Not just about how he'd died but about how he'd lived. It helped to think of the things his friend had accomplished in his life and the joy he'd brought to his family. It helped to realize that his friend's death didn't define him. He could remember the good times now.

"Are you all right, Matt? Truly?" Julia put a hand on his arm.

He glanced at her. She had those eyes that could see straight through him when he lied, just like Penny. So he didn't even bother trying.

"I will be. I have a job I love and friends who believe in me. I just wish I could be as brave as they all think I am. The truth is I'm terrified."

"If you weren't scared, you'd be either foolish or ignorant. You think bravery means never being scared? It's easy to do things that don't scare you. To be afraid of something but willing to do it anyway... Well, that's *true* bravery."

She ruffled his hair. Matt's heart warmed at the easy affection. He looked up to see Penny standing across the yard. When their eyes met, everything inside him came alive.

"I want to say something to the two of you. But I'm not exactly sure how I want to say this. I'm not good with words."

"Take your time, son. The words will come out as they're meant to," Mark drawled.

"Well, that's a good place to start, I guess. You just called me son." He stopped, the meaning of the word settling around him. "You've always called me that. More importantly, you've always treated me like one."

Mark watched him, his brown eyes wise. "That's how we've always thought of you. You and your sister. Trent, too. You were great friends to our sons and you've grown into fine people we're proud to know."

Julia cupped his face gently. "I used to help you with your dirty laundry just like my own boys, didn't I?"

"Yeah, you did. Both of you were always happy to see us. I just wanted to tell you how much I've appreciated that over the years. My parents love us, but they don't *enjoy* us. Not the way you and Mr. Alexander enjoy being with your kids. I'm honored to be a part of your family."

Julia's eyes glittered and she sniffled. "See, now you've gone and made me cry." She reached out and he fell into the hug she offered, soaking up all the love.

"Now, go on and dance with your lady. It makes me smile to see all you young people out there dancing. Even if I can't understand anything these songs are about."

Matt walked toward Penny, leaving the Alexanders arguing about the merits of modern music versus "real" music. He still had a smile on his face when he reached Penny's side.

"Hello, Sergeant."

He grinned the way he always did when she called him that.

"Hello, my love." He pulled her against him. They moved to their own beat, dancing much slower than everyone else around them. Matt held her against his heart, secure in their love, secure in the knowledge that they were meant to be together.

The diamond ring he'd bought last week felt like a stone in his shorts pocket. *Not yet.* He wanted to wait for the perfect moment. Penny deserved a perfect proposal. They were going to live happily ever after. He glanced back at Mark and Julia, who were watching them from the shade.

Thanks to them, he knew exactly what happily ever after should look like.

♥

PENNY SWAYED IN Matt's arms, watching everyone dance around them. It didn't matter that they were slow dancing to a pop song or that it was so hot it felt like a layer of the Underworld. All that mattered was that she was in Matt's arms. It was like floating in a dream.

Not that the past month had been all smooth sailing. Charles had called several times with pleas for her to come back. Penny had been touched until Georgia told her several of the athletes had threatened to go elsewhere if she wasn't treating them. Charles had freaked out at the potential loss of some of their most lucrative clients.

It made her feel good to know her work had enough of an impact to cause people to threaten to leave the center. But after a lot of discussion with Matt, she'd decided not to go back. She'd spent the last few years of her life working herself into the ground. If the events of the past month had taught her anything, it was not to take her life for granted. She only had one chance to do this right.

Matt looked down into her eyes and her heart skipped a beat. She only had one chance to be with him, and she was not going to let anything interfere with that.

At Julia's suggestion, she'd applied for jobs at several hospitals in surrounding cities as well as New Haven General. Penny knew her résumé was strong and she'd get an offer soon. Until then, she'd been enjoying the chance to get to know Matt's family and friends.

Mara was a regular visitor to their house, and they'd become as close as sisters. Since Matt was guarding Kaylee, she'd also spent a lot of time with her. It was the first time since her teenage years that she'd allowed herself to open up completely and let people in. It was a novel experience.

She'd also been in close contact with Georgia, who was planning a summer trip with her family to New Haven's beach so they could spend some time together. Her heart was a little rusty, but with regular use, she expected to be a great friend again.

"Oh my god."

The shocked cry came from Raina. Penny lifted her head. Matt glanced at her and then they both trotted over to where Raina stood with Nick and Ridley. She was holding her arms out to the side and looking down at her feet in terror.

"What happened?" Penny asked breathlessly, but as soon as the words left her mouth she saw the answer. There was a large wet stain on Raina's leggings running all the way down her leg.

Matt followed her gaze and his hand tightened around Penny's waist. "Whoa."

Nick looked down too. "Raina?"

"My water just broke," Raina commented needlessly.

By this time, everyone was clustered around them, and Eli had cut the music.

"Okay, it's all going to be okay. We're having a baby. We're ready for this." Nick pulled out his car keys and started running across the lawn. Everyone watched him in confusion.

"Nick!" Matt shouted. His friend skidded to a halt and glanced back. "I think you forgot something." He pointed at Raina.

Nick's skin took on an ashen hue. "Aw, hell. Sorry, baby." He doubled back and took Raina's arm gently.

A tall, light-skinned man stepped out of the crowd. "Raina, take deep breaths. Are you having contractions?"

Raina shook her head. "Well, I've been having those weird things where my stomach gets all tight for the last hour. But those aren't real contractions. They're just the fake ones, right?"

"Braxton Hicks. Yes, those are very common leading up to the birth. But in some cases, what feels like Braxton Hicks can be real contractions. Which is definitely the case since your water broke. We need to get you to the hospital. Who's your doctor?"

"Dr. Waters," Nick answered.

"I'll call her and let her know you're on your way in." He pulled out a cell phone and started dialing.

"Who is that?" Penny whispered to Matt.

"That's one of their cousins. Grant, I think."

"I can't believe we're having our baby." Raina grabbed Nick's hand. She looked up at him with pure, naked love on her face. "Our baby girl is anxious to get here."

"She wants to join the party, that's all," Julia added. "Now let's get you to the car." Julia took charge in her efficient way, taking Raina's other arm and helping her forward. "I'll swing by the house and pick up your overnight bag so that Ridley doesn't have to do it. I'm sure you want your sister with you."

"I do. Ri? Where's Ridley?" Raina looked back at Ridley, who was following her slow steps.

Ridley looked like she was struggling to contain her own emotions as she followed behind them. "I'm right here, Ray. I'll be there with you the whole time," she promised.

Suddenly Raina stopped. "Can someone call our father? He should know. I mean, I think he'd want to know."

Matt stepped forward. "I can do it. What's his name?"

"William Ranier-Ridley," Nick responded.

"No problem. I'll get his information from Sam." He looked at Raina. "Don't worry about anything. I can't wait to meet the newest Alexander."

Raina nodded shakily. She had to stop moving when another contraction hit. It was extremely hard to watch. It appeared to pain Nick as much as it did her, Penny observed. He paled while watching her struggle to catch her breath.

"It's okay, Nick." Raina started her slow steps forward again. "At our last appointment the doctor said everything looked great."

"It's too soon. We had a birth plan. We're supposed to have a relaxing, natural birth with a midwife," Nick babbled.

Raina cried out again and leaned heavily against her husband. She put a shaky hand on her belly and grabbed Nick with the other. "Screw the birth plan. We have to get to the hospital. This hurts!"

♥

THE ENTIRE ALEXANDER family had taken over the

waiting area in the maternity wing of New Haven General Hospital. Matt perched on the edge of a chair next to Penny.

Julia had gone into the delivery room along with Nick and Ridley. Everyone else passed the time talking and speculating on how Nick was doing.

After an hour Elliott arrived. "Hey, am I too late?"

Bennett moved over so Eli could sit down. "No news yet. Last we heard Raina wasn't dilated enough yet, and Nick was driving the nurses crazy."

They all chuckled. Half the group already had bets on how long Nick would last in the delivery room before passing out. The other half was betting on Raina cussing him out during a contraction and tossing him out. Matt was undecided.

Eli turned to Jackson. "I packed clothes for the boys and drove them to Miss Bessie's house. They're helping her make cupcakes."

"Thank you." Jackson looked relieved.

Over the next six hours, they entertained each other with stories about Raina's pregnancy, Jackson left and came back with donuts, and Penny even fell asleep sitting on Matt's lap. After what felt like an eternity, Matt looked up to see Nick standing at the edge of the group. He looked sweaty and exhausted. Julia stood at his elbow beaming.

"She's here. Our baby girl is six pounds and nine ounces. They're moving Raina to a private room while the baby's getting her tests done," Nick said.

Matt held out a hand to his friend. "Congratulations, man. I can't believe you're a father now."

Nick looked dazed. "I can't believe it, either. She's absolutely perfect."

Bennett pulled Nick into a hug while Jackson and Eli slapped him on the back.

"Do you guys want to see her?" Nick shook his head. "What am I saying? Stupid question. Let's see if the nurses have finished their tests and put her in her crib yet."

They followed Nick down a hallway to the long glass window of the nursery.

"There she is." Nick's pride was all over his face as he pointed through the glass.

A nurse waved at him and then came to stand next to the glass, holding the tiniest baby Matt had ever seen. She was pale-skinned with a shock of jet-black hair that seemed determined to escape the pink cap on her head. Although she was swaddled in a white blanket, one fist peeked out of the top like she was struggling to escape. She looked like she was going to be a handful.

"She's so beautiful," Penny said. She looked up at Matt with eyes full of longing.

"I agree." They hadn't talked about kids yet, but after this, he was willing to bet they would be. He glanced over at Trent and Mara. Mara had her face so close to the glass he wouldn't be surprised if she left a noseprint. He had a feeling there would be a lot of baby talk for them both when they got home.

It was going to be an interesting night.

He turned to Nick. "She's beautiful. She's going to be a knockout. You'd better invest in some guns now." They all laughed. Behind the glass the baby squirmed in the nurse's arms as she set her down gently in her bassinet.

When Nick pulled back, he was beaming. "Her name is Jada. Since both our mothers' names start with the letter J, we decided to keep that going. Her middle name is May since she didn't wait for June and came early. So, she's Jada May Alexander."

"I like it. Sweet, simple, and strong," Penny commented.

"Thanks. I need to go check on Raina." They watched as Nick jogged back down the hall toward the patient rooms.

"He looks so happy," Penny observed. "It's all such an adventure. They're going to raise her and watch her grow. I bet he'll be a great dad, too."

Matt reached in his pocket and pulled out the ring box he'd shoved in his pocket that morning. He'd been planning to propose to her after the party, once dark had fallen and he had a canopy of stars as a backdrop.

Nothing ever went according to plan, and he was perfectly okay with that.

"It is an adventure. I want that with you and everything else, too. I want Christmases and birthdays, fights and frustrations, joys and sorrows. I want to take that adventure with you."

Penny's eyes landed on the black box and she covered her mouth with her hand. "Matt? Oh my god." Her eyes sparkled with tears. "Are you always going to surprise me?"

"I hope so. For the next fifty years at least. After that, things might get a little routine. I can't make any promises. But it's up to you. We can go on like we have been or you can take the leap with me."

Penny shook her head. "You crazy man. Haven't you learned by now?" She threw her arms around his neck and kissed him amid the catcalls of his friends. When they finally broke apart, she pushed his hair back from his forehead tenderly.

"I'll always choose to leap with you."

The End

Keep reading for an excerpt from
Book 4, *All I Need is You*

Chapter One

♥

KAYLEE WILHELM STOOD at the window and
watched the white, cottony flakes fall from the sky, blanketing
the lawn of her childhood home. When she was a child she
used to love the snow, running around and trying to catch the
crystalline fluff in her mouth. It had felt like magic, like
stardust on her tongue. Now that she was an adult, all she
could think of was pollution and acid rain, of the inevitable
mess, of shoveling and clearing off her car. There was no
doubt about it.

Being a grown-up sucked sometimes.

Not that she'd had a choice. She unhooked her daughter

from her car seat. Kay hadn't had the luxury of adjusting to adulthood. She'd been dropkicked into it with no safety net.

"And I wouldn't change a thing," she whispered and kissed her daughter on the nose. She stood, settling the baby on her hip.

"Did you bring her teething ring?" Her mom, Henrietta, pawed through the diaper bag, her usual pinched look in full force. Kaylee felt her good mood start to dissipate.

"Yes."

"What about her blankie?"

Kay bit her lip to suppress a huff of impatience. She'd been raised to be a good girl. To speak with care, to help those less fortunate, and above all else to respect her parents.

It was just really hard to do sometimes when no matter how great Kay was feeling, her mother had the ability to bring her down in sixty seconds or less. Especially when her mother was always impeccably groomed and Kaylee felt like such a mess.

Even now, just spending a quiet evening at home, her mother's black hair was styled in precise curls that formed a halo around her face. Her smooth brown skin bore few lines, and her makeup was perfect. Kaylee pulled her lip balm from the back pocket of her jeans and applied a thin layer, hoping the slight bit of color would keep her from looking like a twelve-year-old. She rarely wore makeup, and it usually didn't bother her.

Except when she was around her mom.

With laser precision, Henrietta's eyes narrowed and focused on Kaylee's bare face. Before she could comment, Kay answered her earlier question. "Yes, I brought her purple blankie and an extra one just in case she throws up on it again."

Her daughter, Hope, squirmed in her arms. Ever since the baby had discovered she could move around by holding on to the furniture, she didn't like to be held anymore.

"Oh, she wants to come to me. You want to come to Grandma, don't you? Yes, you do."

Her mom plucked the baby from her arms and carried her off toward the kitchen. "We're going to feed you. I know you're hungry."

"Actually, I already fed her." Kay sighed when her mom didn't slow down or even acknowledge that she'd heard her. As usual, her mom was going to do whatever she wanted. After all, what did she know? She was just Hope's mother.

No big deal.

Kay looked around the living room. She'd grown up in this house, given her first performances on the shaggy brown rug in front of the fireplace, and brought her first boyfriend here to meet her parents. The familiar sight of the pictures over the mantel and the knitted blanket on the back of the sofa should have been comforting. Instead, it felt like she couldn't breathe in here sometimes.

"Don't let her get to you, pumpkin. You know how your mother is."

Kay turned at her father's voice. With his jet-black hair shot through with streaks of silver, Leeland Wilhelm was a striking man. To Kay, he was the most handsome man alive. He'd always been her champion and her protector. Even now when he didn't agree with the way she was living her life as a single mom trying to break into the music business, he was always in her corner.

Always on her side.

"Thanks, Daddy. I won't." She gave him a quick hug and then walked down the hallway and into the kitchen. Hope was already strapped into her high chair and eating a cup of yogurt. Half of it was on her cheeks and the other half was on the front of her bib. She gave Kaylee a big, toothy grin when she saw her.

"I'll be back around ten to pick up Hope. I'm sorry it's so late. I've just got a lot of catching up to do."

Her mom waved her apology off with an impatient flick of her wrist. "It's always something. They want you to sing it again, sing it differently, sing it better. They're never satisfied."

Kay swallowed her usual protests. She was tired of defending her profession to her mom. Especially since she should have understood. Her mom had been a jazz singer before getting married and had recorded a few albums.

"Okay, I'll see you then."

Kay kissed Hope on the top of her head and then left, her steps quickening as she approached the front door. There were days when it was harder than others to leave. Days when her mom made her feel guilty for having to work so late or days when Hope cried and clung to her. Those were the worst. Even though she knew intellectually that Hope was fine as soon as she left, it was still hard to leave when her baby girl was crying.

There were some days it was all she could do to get out while she could.

♥

FOR NOT THE first time in the past few months, Elliott Alexander wondered if he was getting old. He was great at his job and that hadn't changed. But being the muscle had never been this exhausting.

"The senator has asked me to convey that he will answer

questions at a short news conference after the hearing."

He ignored the riot of questions thrown out by reporters and blocked them from following his current client, Senator Ross Evans, up the courtroom steps. A particularly nasty reporter who'd been dogging their steps for days stopped short just before bumping into his chest.

Shame.

He wouldn't have minded knocking that little twerp to the ground.

The senator hadn't been sure about hiring a firm headed up by a former bouncer, but due to his connections from his younger brother his firm had an impeccable record when it came to protecting celebrities. Alexander Security Incorporated had started out providing protection for boy bands, but after his move to Washington D. C., they'd branched out to protecting the celebrities of the nation's capital: senators, congressmen, and influential businessmen.

"Hey, boss, I've got a message for you."

Eli turned to face one of his newest employees, Tank Marshall. He'd hired the young gun straight from the military. That was how Eli got most of his guys. They were tough, disciplined, and determined. Exactly what he needed.

"What is it?" He kept his eyes on his client as he responded. The senator was spearheading a controversial new bill about immigration. He'd contracted ASI because he expected threats against his life. He wasn't wrong. They'd intercepted several messages in the senator's mail that indicated he was a target.

Now they just had to keep him safe.

"Carly's been trying to get in touch with you. She has some stuff that needs your signature, and she also said you got a package."

Eli's brow furrowed. This was exactly what he'd been trying to avoid. Sleeping with an employee was the worst cliché in the book and for good reason. It was messy. It was complicated. And when it was over, it was awkward. His assistant had seemed fine with their no-strings-attached arrangement. Until she suddenly wasn't. Now he was ducking his own business affairs just to avoid dealing with her.

"Right. I'll take care of it. Thanks."

"Oh yeah, she said it had something to do with a prior case. K. Wilhelm."

Everything in Eli seized up in that instant. "Wait, which case?"

Tank backed up a step, which wasn't surprising if Eli's face looked half as tight as it felt. He tried to smooth his features into something resembling calm as Tank fumbled in his pockets. He finally pulled out a scrap of paper and offered it to Eli, who squinted to decipher the other man's crappy handwriting.

Package from K. Wilhelm. Received over the weekend. Already checked by security.

He looked up to see Senator Evans was entering the courthouse. He'd assigned a team of guys to shadow him, but he'd wanted to be personally involved in this case. Pushing papers behind a desk didn't suit him. The more he threw himself into work, the less he could obsess over how jacked up his life had become. He still remembered the soft, open expression on Kay's face when she'd realized they were standing under the mistletoe last Christmas. Kissing her was a luxury he shouldn't have allowed himself.

Especially since he'd had to witness the devastation on her face a short time later once she realized he wasn't coming back.

"Wasn't she one of the girls in the singing group? I was on that job last year. Do you need me to check on it?"

Eli shook his head and motioned for Tank to follow the senator. Even though her case had been closed, he didn't need anyone to check on Kaylee.

He always knew exactly where she was.

♥

KAYLEE ADJUSTED THE microphone and nodded to Jackson, who was behind the glass in the control room.

"Whenever you're ready." Jackson's voice came through the headphones, a crisp whisper directly into her ear. His production assistant, Michael MacCrane, gave her the thumbs-up.

It was still a little weird to sing by herself. She'd grown up singing in the church choir and had performed with her friends for years. But it was only recently that she'd started singing solo. It was exhilarating and wonderful. It was also incredibly scary.

There weren't many things she was good at. Kay considered herself a good cook and great mother. But there was only one area of her life where she never entertained insecurity. One thing she knew she could do better than just about anyone else, without question.

Sing.

Kay knew she had the voice. It was all the rest she was worried about. She wasn't fashionable and she wasn't thin. These were things that shouldn't have mattered but did. People expected their pop stars to be glamorous. Kaylee wasn't glamorous.

But she knew what it was like to hope for something more. That was what her songs were about. It had taken months and her best friend Sasha threatening to do it herself before Kay had worked up the nerve to show Jackson any of her music. The songs she'd written were personal and it wasn't easy to open them up to criticism. But Sasha was right. Kay didn't want to record other people's songs. If she didn't put herself out there, she'd never know if she had what it took. More importantly, she wouldn't have an album that felt like it was truly hers.

The glass door to the recording booth opened and Jackson entered. He crossed the room and stood next to her for a few moments before speaking.

"Kay, we don't have to do this song if you're not ready. We're actually a little ahead of schedule, so if you need to just take a day, it's cool."

"No, I really want to record this today. It's just the first time I've sung it in front of anyone."

"It's a great song. The title, "Don't Stay So Far From Me"—I'm assuming it's personal?"

She couldn't look at him as she nodded. Sharing her voice was like breathing. It was as natural as talking and walking. She'd been doing it her whole life. But her songs had never been public before. She'd always written in the seclusion of her room, keeping her songs as a private record of her innermost thoughts and feelings. Sharing them now, even with people she liked and respected, was difficult.

"It gets easier, you know. Putting your heart on paper. I originally told Ridley I loved her through a song I'd written. I'm not even sure I knew what I was saying myself when I wrote it."

"She loves you just as much." Kay smiled thinking of

Jackson's wife, a sweet girl who'd become a close friend over the past year.

Jackson inclined his head. "He cares about you, too. I can tell."

Kay pasted a smile on her face but didn't comment. She couldn't talk about Eli with him. It was his brother. Of course he would assume the best.

On New Year's Eve, after having a few too many glasses of champagne, she'd made a list of things she wanted to change in her life. Her relationships with her parents were at the top of the list. Next was being brave enough to show Jackson some of the songs she'd written. She'd already accomplished that one. Jackson had done so much for her by giving her a chance and helping her at every stage of recording this album. She wouldn't badmouth his brother to him.

The last one was to open herself up to the possibility of love. Eli had kissed her on Christmas Day, and just like every other time she remembered it, her body flooded with heat. She shivered thinking about his strong arms around her. For one shining moment, she'd thought he wanted her.

But then he'd left and gone back to his house in Northern Virginia the next day. There were very few things he could have done that would have pushed his point home more clearly than that. Throwing herself at him had only embarrassed them both. She had been caught up in a fairy tale for the past year. Elliott Alexander wasn't interested in her. He never would be.

It was time to move on.

She looked out to the control room. Mac watched with sympathetic eyes. Did she really look that bad? Like a scared little girl afraid of what everyone would think? But she *was* scared. Scared that people would make fun of her, and worse, that no one would even care enough to do that and she'd just fade back into obscurity.

But fear hadn't gotten her anything so far. Maybe it was time to try bravery on for size.

"No, I'm good. Let's do this."

Jackson started to protest, but something he saw in her eyes must have convinced him she was ready. He left the room and took a seat behind the recording console again. He put his own headphones back on and then gave Kay the thumbs-up.

When the music playback started, Kay closed her eyes and pushed all the negative thoughts away. As she sang the familiar lyrics, all the rest of it ceased to matter. It had been really difficult to sing such personal music at first, but now it was easier than she could have ever expected. This song reflected her experiences and her pain. Singing about it was second nature at this point.

She sang throughout the first verse and then added a few new riffs to the chorus they'd already recorded. Every time she sang, it got easier to be in front of an audience. To be the one that everyone was looking at.

"That was amazing." Jackson's voice came through her headphones again and Kaylee smiled gratefully. He motioned for her to come in the control room, so she took off her headphones and walked through the glass doors separating them.

"Come here, I want you to hear this." Jackson moved over so she could sit next to him. He hit a few keys and playback started. Kay nodded her head to the beat as the familiar music came over the sound system.

"What you just did in there..." Jackson ran his hands through his hair. "We're about ninety percent of the way there with this track. I don't know how you do that. It's almost too easy."

Kay's smile felt like it would stretch around her head it was so big. "So we can finish the song tonight?"

Mac nudged her affectionately. "We can probably finish two songs tonight if you keep singing the way you have been."

Kay hopped up and headed back to the recording studio. "I'm ready if you are."

It was time she learned to focus on the things in her life that were real. She might not be in love, but she had something almost as good.

Music.

Chapter Two

♥

THE NEXT AFTERNOON, Eli waited until the last client left the boardroom before he yanked his tie loose. He'd spent the morning in back-to-back meetings. Welcoming new clients was important work but tedious, and he was more than happy to get it over with.

"Please tell me I don't have anything else scheduled?"

His assistant, Carly, glanced over at him with a sympathetic smile. "No, that was the last one. I don't know why you don't let George handle the new clients. He's the vice president of the company. Why do you bother hiring executives if you won't let them do anything?"

Eli scowled. "What's wrong with having a personal touch? I like the clients to know that every contract will have my personal attention."

Carly harrumphed. "There's a fine line between a personal touch and being a control freak. Anyway, I'm sorry I had to schedule all the new clients on the same day. It's just so hard to get you in the office."

Which was his fault. If he hadn't been avoiding her, he would have been in the office more lately. "Yeah, I know. That's my fault." He rubbed his temples.

"Are you okay? You don't look so good."

"Just a headache."

She eyed him suspiciously. "Is this your way of saying you won't be in the office this afternoon?"

"Yeah. But why don't you just bring me anything I need to sign? I'll be staying in Springfield tonight," he added before she could pout.

Just as he'd expected, her expression brightened. "Really? Okay, I'll get everything together and bring it over. You go ahead home and take some medicine. Maybe a cold compress will help." She brushed a hand against his cheek before gathering the folders containing the new clients' contracts.

Once she was gone, Eli walked back through the maze of cubicles to his office on the west side of the building. Even though he was here at least once a week, most of the employees didn't see him often. He was greeted with a chorus of "Hello, Mr. Alexander" and "Good morning, sir."

He nodded hello to everyone he passed but sped up so no one would try to talk to him. It was still a bit surreal to think that he was leading this diverse group of people. He'd started the company in the midst of personal crisis. It had been a lifeline when he was drowning. Carly probably thought it was an excuse, but he did like to look over every case personally. It was his way of saying thank you. His way of giving back to the company that had saved him.

He grabbed a client file he'd left on his desk and then walked to the elevators. Another pang shot him right between the eyes and he grimaced. It was going to take more than a few aspirin to get rid of this headache, especially since he was sure Carly was going to bring him more paperwork to look over later.

He stabbed the Down button several times impatiently. The woman waiting there gave him a sideways glance and moved over slightly. He sighed.

Now he was scaring his employees.

After a long day, Eli was always happy to go home, but never more so than the days he spent at headquarters handling administrative work. Although home was a relative term for him as he rarely spent the night in the same location more than two days in a row.

His company maintained several houses and condos in the Washington D.C. area, which they used to keep clients safe. He usually crashed at one of them or in his office. However, he had to admit to harboring a particular affection for the little house he kept in the suburbs. It was the only one he didn't allow clients to use.

He guessed that made it as close to a home as he'd had in the past decade.

He rode the elevator down to the first parking level and managed to avoid seeing anyone on the way. He threw the client file on the passenger seat of his truck and then pulled out of the garage and onto the bustling streets of Fairfax.

Today what he needed was a beer and some peace and quiet. Carly kept the different houses stocked with the basics, so he figured he could take a load off and maybe order in. When his cell phone rang as soon as he pulled up to his Springfield house, he figured the second part of the equation would have to wait.

"Hi, Mom. How are things going back home?" Eli locked his truck with the remote on his keychain as he walked up to the house and opened the door.

"Oh, I'm just fine, honey. I saw the news. It looks like you have your hands full."

"I do, but you don't need to worry. People are riled up right now. But once congress has voted on the bill, things will slow down some. Tensions are always high this time of year." He kicked the door shut behind him and flipped the deadbolt.

She sighed, the sound coming over the phone and directly into his ear. "I know you've always had things well in hand; I just get worried about you, that's all. You work too much."

"I like working—you know that. Besides, I'll be home in a few weeks anyway."

"Good. I can't wait to spoil you a little bit. It'll be nice to have you back home. Things haven't been the same since you left." She fell silent on the other end of the phone.

"Is everything all right? Is Dad still having those chest pains?" Eli tensed, waiting for her answer. His mother had mentioned his father having chest pains on his last call and the thought of it had never been far from his mind.

His father had always been larger-than-life. This was the man who'd taught him how to ride his bike and given him the facts about the birds and the bees. The thought of anything happening to his dad made him feel ice-cold all over. Mark Alexander represented everything that held his family together.

If there was something wrong, he wanted to know about it.

"No, it's nothing like that. We just miss you. I'm getting sentimental in my old age, that's all."

"You don't look any older than you did when we were kids, and you know it," he said, relieved when she laughed. He hated to hear her sound so depressed. His mom had always been the cheerful sort. It went against the natural order of things for her to sound so down.

"I just wish you were here already," Julia continued. "I've been worried about you. Working so hard, sleeping so little. I know you want to succeed and I'm so proud of you. But I also want more for you than just work. You're letting life pass you by, and I think it's time you face things head-on."

Eli gripped the edge of his cell phone as her words sank in. "There's nothing to face. I just need a vacation, that's all."

"Maybe you can lie to yourself but not to your mother. I don't know what sent you running all those years ago, but whatever it was cost me too. It made me lose my son. I think it's time I got him back."

An unexpected rush of emotion stole his voice, thickening his throat like he'd just swallowed a giant fist. He pushed back his shirtsleeve and stared at the tattoo he hated with a passion, a small number seven surrounded by several concentric circles.

In the beginning there was rarely a day that went by when he didn't think about the things he'd done. His monumental mistakes. Then gradually he'd been able to go days, then weeks, and then finally months without flashbacks. He'd finally stopped looking over his shoulder every few steps, finally trusted someone else enough to invite them into his home.

His mother had no idea what he'd really been doing while he was "traveling the world." Worse, she had no idea that something he'd witnessed happening to her had been the catalyst to send him into his personal hell in the first place.

"Elliott Alexander, are you listening to me?"

"Yes, ma'am," he answered automatically. He had to get this under control. His mother sounded worried, and when she was worried, she got crazy ideas like coming to visit him. He adored his mother, but he couldn't have her here while he was in this mood.

"I'm doing fine, Mom. Seriously, I'll be home next week. Time will fly and before you know it, I'll be back under your feet again."

She sighed and Eli knew he might have avoided the lecture for now, but she'd ambush him with it later.

♥

KAY UNWRAPPED HER sandwich and took a bite as she opened her e-mail. She glanced around to make sure Nick was still ensconced in his office before pulling up the photo Ridley had sent her from Christmas. It was a picture of her and Eli, standing under the mistletoe. It must have been taken right after he'd kissed her. The look on his face was a mixture of lust and longing.

If Ridley hadn't sent her the picture, she'd never have believed he could look like that.

After his abrupt departure following their kiss, she'd been through a gamut of emotions: hurt, embarrassment, despair, and finally anger.

She'd been *pissed*.

But ever since seeing the photo, her emotions had been in a blender. Everything around her was the same, but it was like viewing the world through tinted glass. Things took on new meaning through the lens of possibility.

The positive of the situation was the anger had finally pushed her to start making changes. She'd resolved to finally stand up to her mother, to share her music, and finally to get out more and start dating again. But if there was even a *chance* that Eli might want her, it made everything else fade into the background.

Her cell phone buzzed against the desk, making a clattering sound as it bumped around on the hard surface. Kay dropped her sandwich in her haste to pick it up.

"Oh, shoot."

"What happened?" Her best friend, Sasha, sounded like she had a mouthful as well. She called Kaylee on her lunch break most days, so she probably did.

"I just dropped my sandwich. It landed mainly on my lunch bag though, so I think it's okay."

A soft harrumph came over the line. "As long as it didn't hit the floor, it's fair game as far as I'm concerned. Food is too expensive to waste these days."

Kay picked up her sandwich and shoved the turkey back between the bread. "You're right about that. I'm not sure how I'm going to afford to feed Hope when she's older and starts eating more."

"I wish I lived closer. We could cook for each other. That's what my sisters and I do. Brenna is making lasagna tonight and she's going to bring half of it to me."

Kay would kill for someone to make her half of anything. Especially lasagna. She'd learned to cook at her mom's side, so she at least didn't have to spend a lot of money on prepackaged food. She bought in bulk and always froze her leftovers so there was no waste, but it was still a lot of time and energy to cook everything from scratch.

"You're not *that* far. Although I suppose driving over the bridge just to carry food back and forth is probably asking a lot."

"Are you kidding? I'll fight traffic if it means I don't have to eat my own cooking every day. Your macaroni and cheese has ruined me for life."

"At least I got you off that yucky boxed stuff."

"Whatever. Anyway, I was calling to see if you wanted to hang out tonight. I was supposed to be going on a date, but he canceled. Remember that new guy I'm dating? I think I told you about Devin?"

Her friend had a tendency to collect boyfriends just like she collected snow globes. It was possible Sasha had mentioned him and Kaylee had just forgotten.

"Yeah, I think you told me about him. How're things going?"

"Okay, he's just the commitment-phobic type, I can tell. But God, he's hot."

"I hope this one doesn't look like a felon. That last guy you introduced me to was a little scary."

"Yeah, he was." Sasha was silent for a moment and all Kay could hear was the soft crunch as she bit into something. "Speaking of tall, dark, and scary, have you heard when Eli's coming home?"

Kay's appetite immediately diminished. "No. Ridley said he hasn't told them a date. So I guess he's in no hurry."

"Sorry, sweetie. I know you were hoping—"

"I'm not hoping for anything. Because that would be stupid. As a matter of fact, I think us hanging out tonight is a great idea. Why don't you bring a movie or something and we can veg out after Hope's asleep?"

"That works for me. I'm getting off early today anyway. We've been working way too hard and I need a mental-health day. Basically, I need a *get-me-out-of-here-before-I-bitchslap-somebody* day."

"Isn't that pretty much your normal state of being over there? You can come by here and pick up my spare key if you want."

Since she didn't know any of her neighbors, Kay had decided to leave a spare key at the office. She spent most of her time at work or at the studio, so if she lost her main set of keys, it was easiest to have the spare somewhere she could easily get to it.

She pulled open the third drawer on her desk and shoved a few highlighter markers and a random receipt to the side. When her hand hit the key immediately, she leaned down and peered closer. She'd always put the key all the way in the back. She shrugged and pulled it out. It must have shifted around due to all the junk she kept in that drawer.

"Okay, I'll do that. I'll stop by the store and get some popcorn, too. That low-fat kind you buy is gross," Sasha added.

"Whatever."

Kay's smile faded as her eyes were drawn back to the picture still open on her computer. It was tempting to get caught up in the fantasy of what could have been. This was how she'd always lived her life, caught up in the clouds and high on the possibilities. She'd always played by the rules, done the safe thing. The predictable thing. She looked down at her sandwich. She even ate the same thing every day for lunch.

But she wasn't an impressionable young girl anymore. She was an independent woman. A mother. And the time for believing in fairy tales was gone. She clicked the *x* in the upper-right-hand corner of the picture to close it.

And dumped the last of her sandwich in the trashcan.

♥

THE DOORBELL RANG and Eli jumped. "Mom, I have to go. I'll call you soon. Love you."

"I love you too, my darling. I hope you know how much."

Eli pocketed his cell phone as he walked from the kitchen to the entryway. A faint shadow hovered behind the glass in the brand-new front door he'd just had installed. Part of his preparation for moving back home was selling his current place. He'd made a lot of upgrades to the house over the past few months, including new carpet upstairs, wood floors on the entire main level, and energy-efficient windows. Now that he saw the place looking so good, he wondered why he hadn't done the improvements years ago. It seemed strange that he was doing all this work and wouldn't even get to enjoy the results.

He tapped the screen of the iPad installed next to the front door and, with just the push of a button, brought up the camera feed for the front door. All you could see when you looked out the peephole was the front stoop, so his cameras showed a panoramic view of the entire front of the house, including the areas to the sides of the door where an assailant could hide.

Carly stood on the doorstep, carrying a box and several shopping bags. Eli suppressed a groan. He hadn't thought she'd be there that fast. Apparently, they had different definitions of the word "later." He took a deep breath and then opened the door.

"There you are! I was trying to call you on the way to ask if you wanted me to bring you lunch." Carly pushed past him and strutted toward the kitchen. Eli followed and watched as she set the box and several letters on his kitchen counter. She dropped the shopping bags at her feet. "Having an assistant is useless if you don't answer my calls."

Eli held out his hand until she put the letters in his palm. "I was on the phone with my mom."

Carly grabbed his wrist before he could pull his arm back. "You wouldn't have answered anyway. You never do. I don't understand why you're being like this. We're good together." She came around the side of the counter and slipped under his arm. When their chests brushed together, she let out a soft sigh. "We're *really* good together. Not just anyone can give you what you need."

Her brown eyes were luminous as she gazed up at him hopefully. He let his eyes flow over her, the long dark hair, the sun-kissed skin courtesy of her Trinidadian ancestry. She was exotically beautiful and didn't have an inhibited bone in her body. He had no doubt she would do anything he asked of her. *Anything.* But the thing he needed most wasn't something she could give him.

Because as beautiful as she was, hers wasn't the face he pictured when he closed his eyes at night.

Eli pried her hand off his arm, squeezing until she loosened her grip. Her lashes fluttered and she looked up at him flirtatiously. "Mmm, yes. You always make it hurt so good."

He dropped her arm and stepped back. "I'll sign this stuff and bring it back later."

She pursed her lips in a well-practiced pout. "Fine. But I need those contracts signed before the end of the day. They're already late."

"Late. End of the day. Got it." He followed behind her as she walked out.

She stepped onto the porch and then swiveled on the heel of one of her extremely high, red-as-blood stilettos. "You can't avoid me forever. Some things are inevitable. You and I, we're the same. We need the same things. So whatever's going on with you, fix it." She pulled the collar of her jacket up and then strutted down the stairs to where her car was parked in the driveway.

Eli closed the door behind her and flipped the deadbolt. Carly had no idea how good he was at avoidance. If she was waiting on him to give in, he could only hope she wasn't holding her breath.

After a hot shower and several aspirin, Eli returned to the stack of mail on his counter. The first was a solicitation for money from his alma mater. He put that in the *Keep* pile since he usually tried to make a contribution several times a year. Next, he opened the smallest box. He pulled out the Wartenberg wheel and grinned.

He could imagine there was probably some confusion in the mailroom when they'd opened this one. He normally liked to buy his toys directly from a discreet shop in Georgetown, but he'd wanted to replace this quickly. Carly had broken the last one. Deliberately, he was quite sure.

Eli tucked the box under his arm and walked back to his room. It was the only area in the house that he'd taken the time to decorate. With deep plush carpet and midnight-blue walls, it was a sensual haven. He'd chosen white curtains to lighten it up slightly, but everything else in the room was a deep jewel tone. The color palette reflected his personality, he thought. Nothing was too bright or showy. It was a room for introspection and meditation. He looked up at the mirrors installed over the bed. And sex.

Hair-pulling, backbreaking, mind-numbing sex.

He crossed to the closet and pulled it open. "Hello, beautiful." Everything he needed to torment a woman into mindless pleasure lined the walls. He eyed the first row of vibrators—small ones, big ones, and waterproof ones.

Yes, he could do a lot of damage with those.

The second row held his instruments. Nipple clamps, feather dusters, clothespins, and zip ties lined the shelves. He pulled out his replacement Wartenberg wheel and placed it carefully on the shelf.

He couldn't imagine not wanting to make a woman beg or not wanting to control each and every aspect of her response. Watching that moment, when a woman looked at him with absolute and complete trust, it was better than a drug. He needed to feel that instant when they gave themselves over to his inevitable possession. Without it, sex was mechanical. An act between two bodies as opposed to the union of two people.

Sensation play was something he'd gotten into by accident. He hadn't been looking for a "lifestyle," but he'd happened to date a woman who was heavily into BDSM. To Elliott's surprise, his natural tendencies in the bedroom were apparently hard to find and in high demand. For him, it was just a natural part of his personality.

For women like Carly, it was a highly sought-out characteristic. Eli sighed and threw the empty box on his bed. His one night of stupidity had already complicated his life immensely. Women were such emotional creatures, something Eli feared and respected at the same time.

It had been obvious for a long time that Carly was willing to "assist" in more ways than one. She'd intercepted one of his packages he'd accidentally had shipped to the office. The order had been for a new flogger, a sweet brown cowhide that was only available online. He'd intended to ship it directly to the Springfield house but had inadvertently put in the billing address, which was to his office. He'd told Carly to intercept the package and bring it directly to him. She'd caught the mailroom worker just as he was cutting into the packaging.

As soon as she brought it to him, he'd known she'd looked inside.

"You shouldn't have gone there." He blew out a breath and flopped down on his bed. His reflection stared balefully back at him. A late night when she'd stopped by to bring him his cleaning had turned into ordering dinner and then ordering her onto her knees.

He'd avoided female company for years and then had only allowed himself quick, impersonal encounters in clubs and hotel rooms. To allow her to come here and enter his personal space had been a mistake.

One he would pay for again and again.

Chapter Three

♥

THE SOUND OF the doorbell ringing was like nails on a chalkboard. Eli pulled out his phone and brought up the camera feed for the front door. Carly stood on the front step, holding a brown paper bag. He groaned and rolled over. Allowing her to come here again had been a mistake. She needed a firm hand, and any sense of softness on his side simply gave her hope of more.

No doubt she'd concocted some excuse for why she'd needed to come back. A document he'd forgotten to sign or something she'd conveniently left behind.

He stalked down the hall and to the front door. When he yanked it open, the smile on her face faded. "What are you doing back here?"

She looked down at the bag she held and then back up at him. "I forgot something. Since I had to come back anyway, I brought you dinner."

Eli accepted the bag. "Thank you, but you really shouldn't have." Guilt assailed him. She'd done something nice, and he'd bitten her head off.

"It was no trouble." Carly pushed past him and walked toward the kitchen.

He followed reluctantly. "You still shouldn't have." Eli held her gaze until he was sure she got the message.

Her shoulders drooped slightly before she picked up the purple gloves on the edge of the counter. "I really did forget something. See?"

While she yanked the gloves on angrily, Eli's gaze settled on a box at her feet.

"What's in the box?"

She glared at him and then picked it up and placed it on the counter. "I don't know. This is one of the boxes I left here earlier. You didn't open it?"

"I didn't see it."

"The mail room said it was some kind of present. Something personal from a former client."

Eli pulled the box toward him. Kaylee's name was on the upper corner of the label. His heart sped up a little at the sight. Why would she send him a gift? The only people who ever sent him gifts were his family members, and they wouldn't bother to mail it. They'd just wait until he came home and hand it to him. The last time he'd seen Kay had been at Christmas. He'd given her a present, just a necklace with her daughter's birthstone. He'd done it because he wanted to see her bright brown eyes light up. He hadn't done it to make her feel obligated to give him something in return.

He yanked at the tape on the box. Even though he'd long ago made the decision to have his mail checked at headquarters before he opened it personally, they still tried to give him some illusion of privacy by closing his envelopes and packages back partially and securing them with tape.

Inside the box there was an unsealed, padded envelope. He tipped it over and something slid out, weighty in his palm. Frowning, Eli turned it over, examining the ceramic cat figurine with interest. Why would she send him a knickknack? He wasn't the type of guy who collected shit. He glanced around at the barren decor of his house. Anyone who knew him—hell, anyone who'd ever met him—knew that dainty breakables weren't his style.

"So, this former client? Is she a little old lady or something?" Carly eyed the cat figurine with interest. "I think my grandma had one like that."

Eli ignored her and picked up the envelope included. It wasn't sealed and contained a single sheet of computer paper.

I wonder if she even noticed it was missing.

His blood chilled. Something in his face must have alerted Carly because she took the letter away from him and scanned it.

"When was this sent?" he barked.

Carly fumbled with the packaging. "It was postmarked a week ago but I only got it from the mailroom a few days ago."

Eli tucked the figurine back into the padded envelope and closed it. He wished now that he hadn't opened it with his bare hands but doubted it made much of a difference in the end.

The types who were crazy enough to send threatening letters were rarely crazy enough to leave fingerprints. He tucked the box under his arm and grabbed his coat off the back of the kitchen chair.

"Wait, Eli! Where are you going?" Carly trotted behind him as he walked to the front door. She stepped out onto the porch and waited as he locked the door behind him.

He didn't look back as he got into his truck and started the ignition.

"Cancel all my appointments next week."

♥

KAY WALKED BACK into the control room to a hearty round of applause. Jackson had called that afternoon and asked if she was available to record that night because one of his other artists had canceled. At first she'd said no because she didn't want to be one of those girls who constantly bailed on her girlfriends. However, when she told Sasha, her friend hadn't minded at all and decided instead to meet her at the studio. Now she was clapping and whooping the loudest.

"As many times as I've heard you sing, you can still bring tears to my eyes." Sasha swiped her cheeks with the back of her hand. Her long, glittery nails sparkled under the studio lights.

Her friend loved making a statement, which was obvious from the bold manicures she got every other week to the daring clothes she wore. Today her entire outfit was made of some kind of lime-green shredded fabric that hugged her hourglass figure perfectly. The color looked good against her cocoa complexion. With her hair elaborately braided and twisted up into a high ponytail, she looked like an Egyptian princess in a club dress.

Kay grinned as Sasha enfolded her in a hug. They'd just finished recording the first power ballad on the album, and Kay was quite sure she'd nailed it. Mac and Jackson both seemed really pleased with her, so she could only hope that meant they liked her songwriting. She'd been afraid they were only saying they did to spare her feelings.

"Thank you. I'm starting to get really excited about this. I mean, I was excited before, but it's different now. Having my songs out there."

She shook her head, not sure how to express what she was trying to say. Luckily Jackson seemed to get it.

"It's because these songs are yours. They represent you. It's great to have people love your singing, but it's better to have them love your style. To have them love *you*."

"Yes. That's it exactly."

Mac sat back in his chair, appraising her openly. "I have to say, I didn't know you had it in you, Kay. You're not singing like a church girl anymore."

Kay was about to respond when the outer door leading to the general office opened and Matt Simmons, her former bodyguard, strode in. His eyes swept over all the electronics in the room with a cursory glance before stopping on Kaylee.

"You're here. Good. I've been trying to find you for the past hour."

Kay jumped up, unconsciously responding to the urgency in his voice. "What's wrong? Are you all right?" She clapped a hand over her stomach. "Is it Hope? Did something happen?" She could hear her own voice rising with hysteria until Matt came forward and put a hand on her shoulder.

"She's fine." Matt squeezed her arm. "It's nothing to do with her. I just need to show you something.

Kaylee let out the breath she was holding. "Okay."

"Have you ever seen this before?" He held up his cell phone. There was a picture of a small ceramic figurine displayed.

"Yeah. I have a similar one." Kay leaned closer. It was hard to tell from just a picture, but the figurine looked almost identical to the one she had.

"That's what I thought. Uh, are you done for the day?" Matt glanced at the others uncertainly.

"Not really. Why?" Kay asked.

"Because we need to go. Now."

Even though it had been months since Matt was assigned as her bodyguard, some part of Kay still responded to his authority because she immediately turned and gathered her things. It had taken her a while to get used to someone shadowing her every move, but she'd gone along with it because it was for her own protection.

"Whoa, what's going on? Is she in danger again?" Jackson directed the question to Matt even as he stood and helped Kaylee with her coat.

Matt hesitated and the two men seemed to be having some sort of silent conversation. Kay rolled her eyes. This was exactly how things had been last summer, except then it had been Eli and Matt making decisions for her, treating her like she was a little girl who couldn't handle knowing the truth.

"Just tell me, Matt. What's going on?"

Matt finally looked at her directly. "I don't have that many details. Eli just called and said I had to find you."

"Well, I'm fine. I've been at the studio for the past two hours and Sasha and I are going back to my apartment now."

Matt looked uncomfortable. "Uh, I'm supposed to bring you to the Alexanders' place and stay with you until he gets here."

Sasha appeared at Matt's side. "*Gets here.* Eli's coming back?"

At Matt's nod, Sasha turned to Kay, her eyes gleaming. "I don't mind if you take a rain check on our movie date. You should go, make sure everything's okay."

Kay narrowed her eyes at her friend. "I'm sure it won't take that long. You could come with me."

Sasha made a show of looking at the clock hanging on the wall behind her. "It's already so late. I'm sure you'll need time to get all this sorted out. I'll just call you later. Or tomorrow. In case you get home late tonight."

Kay grabbed her handbag. "I'm sure I won't be out that long." Although it would please her friend immensely if she was. Sasha had never agreed with her decision to give up on Elliott. If her friend had her way, Kay would have followed him to Northern Virginia and cornered him with an offer he couldn't refuse.

"A girl can always hope," Sasha whispered.

Kay pasted a smile on her face and zipped up her coat. "I guess we'd better go, then." She turned to Jackson and Mac. "Sorry to run out on you. Hopefully we can finish tomorrow."

"Whenever. Like I said, we're ahead of schedule." Jackson exchanged another one of those silent looks with Matt. "I think I'll come with you guys if you don't mind."

"I can close up, Jack." Mac offered her a sympathetic smile.

"Thanks, man. I'll see you tomorrow." Jackson retrieved his own coat and followed them out into the freezing night air.

He waved at them before getting into his sedan. Sasha gave Kaylee another quick hug. "Call me tomorrow with details. Hopefully something juicy."

"I doubt there will be anything good to report." She waited, Matt at her side while her friend unlocked her little economy car and got inside. Then she followed Matt over to his truck. He unlocked it with the remote on his keychain and she threw her stuff on the floor of the cab before hoisting herself up into the seat.

"So, are you going to tell me what's really going on now?"

Matt glanced over at her. His eyes were so dark she could barely make out the color in the dim interior of the vehicle, but she couldn't miss his smirk. "You thought I was joking before? When have you ever known boss man to be forthcoming with details?"

Kay couldn't argue with that. Eli Alexander didn't like unnecessary questions and rarely bothered with explanations at all. She was probably lucky he'd told Matt anything at all instead of just ordering him to drag her by her hair back to his parents' house.

"Hold on, I think this is him now." Matt pulled out his phone and turned on the speakerphone. "Eli, I'm here with Kay now."

"Good. I don't want to get into specifics over the phone, but I need to ask her a few questions."

"Okay, what do you need to know?" Kay asked.

"Are you dating anyone? Specifically, anyone with access to your apartment."

Kay flushed. Matt kept his eyes on the road, but there was no way she was imagining the sudden tension in the car. It had to be as awkward for him as it was for her.

"No. I've been too busy recording and working. The only men I see on a regular basis are your brothers and my dad."

Eli grunted on the other end of the line. "What about Hope's father? He hasn't come around recently has he?"

"No. That would require him to acknowledge her existence. Something he doesn't really want to do."

"Have you noticed anyone hanging around? Seen anyone who doesn't look right near the studio or anything?"

Kay exchanged a glance with Matt. He looked as worried as she felt. "Not that I've noticed. Am I in danger? I thought the guy who sent those letters was in prison."

"He is." Eli paused. "I just received something in the mail that makes me think we might have gotten the wrong guy."

♥

KAYLEE SAT UP to accept the cup of warm cocoa Julia Alexander pressed into her hands. She'd already been wrapped in a warm blanket and given a plate of cookies to munch on. If Eli didn't get here soon, she was going to be delirious and in a sugar coma from all the mothering.

"Thank you so much, Mrs. Alexander. You really didn't need to go to so much trouble."

"Please, call me Julia. You're practically family." Julia fussed around her, adjusting the blanket and tidying the items on the side table.

Kay observed her over the top of the mug, wondering what it was about the woman that put everyone instantly at ease. It wasn't so much that Julia looked different from her own mother, it was that she *felt* different. She exuded a warmth that suggested she would always have a hug and a smile ready for anyone who needed them. Julia Alexander accepted people as they were. She wasn't looking for imperfections in the people she met or searching for things to criticize.

"Thank you, Mrs.... Miss Julia," she stammered. It was nearly impossible for her to call an older person by their first name. She'd never been allowed to growing up so now she found, it just felt wrong.

"Such a sweet girl. I can tell you were raised right. I still can't call Mark's mother by her first name, either. Now, you just drink your cocoa and relax. Hopefully Eli will be here soon." She patted Kay's knee and then walked back to the kitchen.

Matt stood by the window, his shoulders tense as he peered out the window into the night. It was disconcerting to see him so on edge. He wasn't exactly a happy-go-lucky kind of guy, but once she'd gotten to know him, she'd discovered he had a quick wit and a surprisingly similar sense of humor. Usually, he entertained her with stories about his other jobs and the changes his girlfriend, Penny, was making to his house. So it was even weirder that he'd been so closed off and tense since picking her up.

"It's getting late. Can't Eli just meet us at my place? I'm really tired."

Matt's lips thinned before he glanced down at his cell phone again. "Eli is almost here. I think he wanted to talk to you first."

"Okay." There wasn't much else to say, so she sat back into the plush cushions of the couch and sipped her cocoa. Someone walked by and she looked up to see the lanky frame of Eli's older brother, Bennett. He was completely absorbed with reading something on his tablet and almost bumped into the doorframe. He did a double take when he saw Kay on the couch and glanced around as if unsure where he was.

"Oh, hello. I didn't know we had guests." He exchanged a handshake with Matt and then sat on the edge of the couch next to Kay. "How have you been?" He pushed up his glasses but didn't look directly at her.

The palest of the Alexander brothers, with his long slender body and hazel eyes, Bennett always seemed as though he'd accidentally wandered into the wrong family. Conversations with him were usually slightly strange, but Kay had come to enjoy their random interactions. He seemed interested in what she had to say no matter how inconsequential.

"I've been great. I was recording some new songs with Jackson tonight. But apparently Eli needs to talk to me, so here I am."

Bennett's brow crinkled as he considered her words. "That's strange. Why wouldn't he just call you? Or drive to the studio so he didn't have to interrupt your work?"

She glanced over at Matt again. "I'm not exactly sure."

Bennett crossed his arms. "If Elliott asked Matthew to bring you here, he must be concerned about your safety. I was doing some research but I think I'll stick around for a while and keep you company."

"Okay, thanks. That would be nice. Why don't you tell me about your research?"

Bennett sat back and placed the tablet in his lap. "Oh, this? I'm just looking into recent legislation regarding GMOs. That's—"

"Genetically modified organisms, right?"

Bennett smiled then, a genuine smile, and looked at her directly for the first time. "Yes, that's right. There's a lot of controversy surrounding their use and for good reason. However, I'm working on developing several vegetables that can grow under adverse conditions."

"You are? Geez, all I did today was sing a few love songs."

Bennett flushed. Even the tops of his ears turned pink. "The arts are a science unto themselves. We need things that make us happy just like we need food."

While Kay agreed, she was still a little flustered. He was so smart it was kind of scary. "Tell me more about the vegetables you're working on."

"Well, I've identified a few key crops that would benefit the most. Soy, corn, and wheat to start. Imagine what it could mean for people around the world to have food that grows even through periodic drought or extreme heat. We could end hunger. Or at least make a dent in it."

Kay tried to follow the conversation, but after too many phrases like *easy propagation*, *mediated transformation*, and *plant genome*, she gave up on understanding. Either way, it was a joy to see Bennett so passionate about something.

And it was definitely better than wondering exactly when Eli would walk through the door.

Chapter Four

♥

NORMALLY ELI WOULD have ignored his cell phone while driving, but if there was a chance it was Matt calling, he didn't want to risk missing it.

"This is Eli."

"Hey man, it's Matt. I've got Kay and we're at your parents' house."

Eli let out a breath he hadn't realized he'd been holding. A million and one things had gone through his mind when he'd gotten that figurine. Mainly that this nut job had been in Kay's apartment. Could in fact be in her apartment at that very moment. All he'd cared about was making sure she was safe. He'd spent the last half hour worrying they'd be assaulted or run off the road before Matt could get them to his parents' house.

"How is she doing?"

"She's fine. Just a little annoyed that I interrupted her recording session. I know you wanted to talk to her yourself, but she keeps asking what's going on. What should I tell her?"

Now that he knew they'd reached his parents' house safely, he could take a step back and think. Who could have sent the figurine and more importantly, why? When she'd first started receiving threatening letters the previous year, they'd gone through her life with a fine-tooth comb. He'd scrutinized her family and friends, her acquaintances and coworkers. Anyone she came into contact with on a regular basis had been suspect. Everyone had checked out with the exception of the man who'd eventually been arrested. So Eli was forced to face an uncomfortable truth.

He must have missed something.

"Tell her I'll be there soon." He hung up and focused on the road. As he passed the familiar streets leading to his parents' farm, a sense of calm stole over him. By the time he pulled into the long drive leading to the ranch-style home, some of the stress he'd been carrying for the past few hours melted away. He parked behind Matt's truck and got out.

His father, Mark Alexander, poked his head out of the garage. "There you are. You made good time."

"There wasn't much traffic since it's so late." Eli averted his eyes. Even without traffic, he'd still arrived a half an hour faster than usual. He'd made excellent time because he'd been speeding most of the way. He doubted if his evasiveness fooled his father. Mark Alexander always saw way more than Eli would have liked him to.

"That's a nice girl in there. Is she in danger?"

Trust his dad to get right to the heart of things.

"I'm not sure yet. But I plan on protecting her until I know for sure."

Mark nodded and clapped him on the shoulder. "I wouldn't have expected anything less." Then he ambled back into the garage, no doubt to tinker with his old truck or one of the tractors.

Eli jumped over the few steps to the front of the house and then opened the door with his key. Light, warmth and the sweet scent of his mother's baking hit him all at once. Kay sat snuggled on the couch under a blanket next to his older brother, and Eli's eyes immediately homed in on her. When she saw him, she clutched the mug she was holding closer to her chest like a shield.

Bennett stood then and nodded at Kay. "Well, I'd better get going. It was nice to see you again, Kaylee."

He shook hands with his older brother absently before his attention was drawn back to Kay. She looked like a bundle of softness from the nubby texture of her soft blue sweater to the jumble of kinky curls she'd piled on top of her head in a bun. Her brown eyes sparkled as she took a small sip from her cup.

Eli yanked at the buttons of his coat and snatched off the knit hat protecting his bald head from the cold and wind. Kay watched him over the rim of her cup but didn't speak as he drew closer.

"We need to talk."

Matt stepped forward then and Eli realized he hadn't even greeted him. He stuck out his hand. "Thanks for getting to her so quickly."

Matt returned the handshake and glanced over at Kay. "I'm just glad she came easily. I thought she was going to deck me when I interrupted her studio time."

"I thought about it," Kay muttered behind her mug. "Am I in danger? What's going on?"

Eli retrieved the envelope he'd tucked in the inner pocket of his coat. He sat on the edge of the couch tentatively. "Does this look familiar to you?" He opened it and the cat figurine slid out and into his palm.

"Hey! I have one just like that." She reached out to touch it and then her gaze settled on Eli. "I have one exactly like that. What's going on?"

He held out the note next. "Someone sent this to me at ASI headquarters. It had to be checked by my mail department before I opened it, so I didn't see it right away. It was sent last week."

Matt leaned over and, after reading the note, shared a look with Eli. He then picked up the figurine and turned it upside down, peering into the tiny hole at the bottom. "He's taunting us. Showing off that we failed to catch him last time."

Eli agreed. They didn't have anything concrete that linked the two yet, but in his gut, he knew this was the same guy.

What did he miss last summer that could have kept her safe? They'd been so sure they had the right guy. The dumb ass had already had a warrant out for a drug charge, so he'd been picked up and was serving time. Could he have gotten someone else to pick up where he left off harassing Kay? But what would be the point if he was already in jail? He had to know that the police would immediately know it was him and give him more time. It didn't make sense.

Kay's safety hinged on something that was completely illogical.

"This note is sending a pretty direct message. He's right under our noses and he wants us to know it."

Kay read the note, her lips moving slightly as her eyes scanned the page. "I don't understand. What does this all mean?"

"It means we might have made a mistake last summer." Eli took the figurine from her trembling fingers.

"It means you aren't safe."

♥

KAYLEE FOLLOWED RIDLEY into the kitchen, conscious of Eli's gaze on her back.

"I figured you could use a break," Ridley whispered as they sat at the small dining table in the kitchen.

"Thanks. A little space is much appreciated right about now." It had only been a few weeks since she'd last seen Eli at Christmas. So why was her traitorous body reacting like he was just coming home from war? Kay accepted another cup of steaming hot cocoa from Mara, who sat on her left. "Did Matt call you?" she asked the pretty brunette.

They'd spent a lot of time hanging out when Matt had been her bodyguard last summer. With her curvy figure, long dark curls, and sultry bedroom eyes, it would have been easy to hate Mara if she wasn't such fun. It was hard to believe she and Matt were related sometimes since their personalities were such polar opposites. She wouldn't have guessed that those two could have even come out of the same family, much less be twins.

"He did. He's worried about you. We all are." Mara took

a sip of her own tea. "How are you holding up?"

Kay shrugged. "Okay so far. I'm just not sure why this is happening. I'm nobody. The album I did with Divine had lackluster sales, and I haven't released any music since. If it's true that the police arrested the wrong guy last summer, why would he suddenly start stalking me again now? It doesn't make any sense."

Mara regarded her over the rim of her mug. "Maybe this isn't a stalker. Well, not a random one. Maybe it's someone you've dated who is mad that you've moved on."

"That's just it. I haven't moved on. The only things I do are go to work, take care of Hope, and record music. Other than Nick's clients, I don't come into contact with many people."

"Well, that doesn't sound like much fun." Mara glanced over Kay's shoulder. Her eyes narrowed and then sparkled with a mischievous gleam. "You know what you need? You need a man. Penny told me what you guys talked about at Christmas. About how you're going to let us fix you up on a blind date."

Kay thought back to all the things they'd discussed on Christmas Day. Once she'd realized that Eli had left his own family celebration just to avoid her, she'd tearfully confided in the other girls. They'd rallied around her, supporting her decision to move on and start dating after the holidays. But she didn't remember agreeing to any setups. She *hated* blind dates.

"But I never said—" Kay's mouth dropped open as Mara kicked her under the table. "Ow," she whispered.

Mara typed something quickly on her cell phone and pushed it across the table. Raina, Ridley, and Kay all leaned forward to read what it said.

- - - *Eli is outside the door listening.*

"What?" Kay exclaimed. Then she crossed her arms. Pretending to set her up on a date to make Eli jealous was ridiculous. And childish. And unlikely to work since he couldn't seem to care any less about what she was doing.

Mara shot her an exasperated look. "So, who's up for a little matchmaking?"

Raina raised her hand. "I know someone who's perfect. He used to be a model but now he's an actor—"

"No models or actors," Kay interrupted. Just the thought of it made her feel squeamish. Blind dates were awkward enough. She definitely didn't want to deal with a guy who was prettier than she was.

"Oooo-kay then," Raina drawled. "What about bodybuilders? Who doesn't like a strong guy with lots of muscles, right?"

Kay had been pretty sure this was a bad idea from the beginning but she was especially sure of it now. A bodybuilder? Was Raina serious? She looked down at her own body, comfortably ensconced in her favorite pair of worn jeans and a soft sweater. She liked how she looked. Most of the time. But she had no illusions that a guy who spent most of his time in the gym would share her love of elastic waistbands.

"Um, I'm not sure if that would be such a good idea. I'm not that athletic."

Mara waved away her concerns. "That's okay. You shouldn't have to pretend to be something you're not. I'm not athletic either. We'll just find you a guy who appreciates other things. You've got a great rack. And plenty of guys are breast men."

Kay almost choked on her cocoa just as there was a soft *oomph* outside the door as if something had just knocked into the wall.

Mara tittered behind her hand. Kay dabbed at the spots on the front of her sweater with a napkin and glanced behind her at the doorway nervously. She wasn't so sure baiting Eli like this was the way to go.

"What about T.J.?" Ridley piped up, mentioning an R&B singer that Jackson had recently signed to his label.

Kay shook her head. "I'm not dating another singer from the label. If it doesn't work out, it would be weird."

"Actually, he's perfect because he's only in town for a month or so to record his album. Then he's going back to L.A. because he has a condo there," Ridley said.

Kay looked around at the other girls, sure she was missing something. "Why would I date someone who'll be gone in a few weeks? What's the point?"

Mara hugged her. "Aw, you're so sweet and innocent. It's almost a shame that we're corrupting you."

Ridley finally took pity on her. "What Mara is trying to say is that sometimes you date guys just for the fun of it. Not because you plan on being together forever."

Mara pursed her lips. "Actually, I was trying to say she should date him because I heard he is *huge*. Like barely able to walk straight while carrying that—"

The door to the kitchen burst open. They all jumped, including Kay. Eli stood in the doorway for a moment before he crossed the kitchen to stand behind her chair. His fingers curled over the top of the wood so hard it creaked. Kay gulped when his eyes landed on her.

"We need to go now. I want to get to your place and make sure it's safe for the night."

Eli regarded his sisters-in-law with a scowl before turning his dark look to Mara. Kay shrank back into her seat, but Mara just grinned.

"Oh hi, Eli. Lovely to see you," she chirped.

"Um hmm," was all Eli said in reply.

♥

"WE NEED TO get to your place." Eli ignored Mara and the other girls' knowing looks. He didn't doubt for a minute that they knew he'd overhead their conversation. Their amused grins told him that.

As far as he was concerned, he'd shown some serious restraint so far. They were trying to set Kay up with some big-dicked player who'd probably use and abuse her. What the hell were they thinking? He was shutting that down.

Immediately.

Kay raised her eyebrows. "We?"

"I'm not letting you go there alone."

"I figured I wouldn't be going home alone, but isn't Matt coming with me?"

"No."

She made no move to stand up, so he pulled her chair out. It made a loud screeching sound as it dragged over the tile floor. Kay jumped up and gave him a dirty look before marching back into the family room. The other girls abandoned their drinks on the table to follow. Their expressions were a little too bloodthirsty in Eli's opinion. He had no intention of being the sacrifice.

Matt stood near the door, talking to Jackson. He looked up when they entered. "Hey, are you guys getting ready to leave?"

Kay turned toward him with what looked to be desperation. "You're not coming with me?"

Matt glanced at Eli before responding. "I was just assigned

to a new client. I've been working with him all week. It would be unprofessional to yank me off his job and then force him to reacclimate to someone else. I thought Eli explained everything."

A strange sense of satisfaction came over Eli as he watched Kay's face. She was stuck with him and apparently didn't like it. He knew he'd hurt her. Their kiss at Christmas should have never happened. But he was the best man for this job. He hadn't protected her well enough last summer, obviously, or this dickwad wouldn't still be out there toying with her. This was his chance to make it right.

Eli wasn't going to leave her safety up to some new associate who might screw it up. Even if he hadn't gotten the right guy before, he'd kept her safe. They'd kept her security low-key since last summer, but it had been there. She didn't go anywhere without letting someone know and her cell phone and car were constantly being tracked. She also had a state-of-the-art security system at her apartment so she was safe while she slept.

"Is there a problem, Kay?"

She wouldn't meet his eyes. To his surprise, it was Mara who answered.

"It's no biggie. She's just nervous about her date."

Eli gritted his teeth at the reminder of the conversation in the kitchen. He was careful to keep his face neutral when he replied. "Her date? What date?"

"We're setting Kay up on a blind date. She's looking for Mr. Right. Or Mr. Right Now. Whatever. Either way, I know we can find the perfect guy for her."

"I'm sure Eli doesn't care about that." Kay grabbed her coat and slid her arms into it. "I'm sure he has a lot of important stuff to do running his company. In fact, maybe it would be better if Tank or one of the other guys stayed with me for a while."

"You don't want me on your case, Kay?" Eli tucked his hands in the pockets of his jeans, the better to enjoy watching her squirm as she tried to figure out how to respond.

"It's not that." Kay made several indistinct gestures while pointing at him. "It's just that, I don't know…"

"You're kind of scary," Mara supplied.

"Mara! I think Mara meant to say you're a little intense sometimes."

"And you'll scare her date away," Mara finished.

Kay dropped her head into her hand. Eli bit his lip to hold in a laugh. Damn if she wasn't cute when she was embarrassed.

"I've been in this business a long time. We're trained to be inconspicuous."

Kay sent him a disbelieving look as she grabbed her handbag. "So you won't interfere in any way?"

Eli made a motion as if he was crossing his heart. "You won't even know I'm there."

♥

KAYLEE SHOVED THE books on her night table in the drawer. Her eyes swept over the rest of the room frantically. Hopefully she hadn't left anything embarrassing lying around. She wasn't used to having guys at her apartment. Especially not men like Elliott.

Big, masculine men that she fantasized about every night.

The hair on the back of her neck stood up and she didn't have to look to know that he was standing in the doorway.

Her apartment wasn't that big, but it suddenly seemed exponentially smaller with Eli sucking up all her oxygen.

"Tank finished his assessment before we got here. We're all clear." Eli stepped in and looked around. "Where do you normally keep the figurine?"

Kay pointed to the top of her dresser. Eli walked over and looked down at her collection. He touched one and the sight of his thick fingers stroking the delicate china shouldn't have seemed erotic at all. But the image of this big, strong man handling tiny breakables with such care struck her as incredibly tender. Would that be how he treated a woman in bed? Like she was delicate, precious?

Or would he push her hard, demand things she didn't know how to give? Warmth spread to her face just thinking about it.

Not that you'll ever find out.

"There's an empty space here. He didn't even bother to push the others closer together to conceal what he took."

Kay hated to even think of it. Someone had been in her apartment, touching her things. Had he been here while she was home alone? While she was with her daughter?

While they were sleeping?

She shivered and grabbed the duffel bag she kept underneath her bed. Her favorite nightshirt was on top of the comforter, so she shoved that in the bag. Then she pulled open the drawers in her nightstand and added a big handful of underwear and bras. She didn't even look at how much she was taking, just grabbed blindly. Who cared, really, what she wore? All she cared about was getting out of here. Would she ever be able to relax in this room again without wondering if someone was watching?

She crossed to the dresser where Eli stood and yanked

open the last drawer. In went several pairs of jeans, then she yanked open another drawer and added a big armful of sweaters.

"Kay, what are you doing?"

"Packing. I just want to get out of here."

She struggled with the zipper on the bag, almost breaking a nail on the metal teeth. Her breath came in harsh pants until little black spots danced in front of her eyes.

"Kay, calm down. Just hold on."

She struggled against his hold, but he held her securely in his grip, her back to his front. His arms wrapped around her, keeping her from moving but not holding her so tight as to cause pain. Eventually Kay stopped fighting and allowed her head to fall back against Eli's chest.

"Hey, hey. It's all right. Just calm down." He rubbed her arms gently, soothing her.

Kay finally stopped wrestling with him and allowed him to hold her. She closed her eyes and took a deep breath. It was a foolish moment of weakness, but for just a second, she soaked up the comfort and warmth of being in his arms.

"We're safe here. You've got a great security system. I already had Tank check it out and it hasn't been tampered with. I don't know how this guy got your figurine, but he didn't break in to do it."

Tears welled up, but she squeezed her eyes closed, swallowing back the sudden flood of emotion. There was no time for nonsense or feeling sorry for herself.

"Why would someone do this, Eli?"

"I don't know, angel." He spoke in a hush, the words flowing over her in a soft puff of breath.

His features tightened, and for the second time in recent memory, she allowed herself to soak up the masculine presence that was Elliott Alexander: the smooth dark skin, the high cheekbones, the long straight blade of his nose, and the sinfully full lips. It was a harsh face, not quite as elegantly hewn as his brothers' faces, but one that she vastly preferred. It looked like safety.

It looked like strength.

"I'm okay now. I promise I won't freak out on you again." She stood reluctantly. As wonderful as it felt to be held in his arms, there was only so much she could take before she lost all sense of propriety and threw herself at him again. She already knew he wasn't interested. When you kissed a guy and he responded by leaving town, that was plenty clear enough.

"It's okay to be freaked out, Kay. As long as you know that I won't let anything happen to you."

Kay nodded and dropped the duffel bag on her bed. She didn't have enough room to put him up in style, but at the very least she could rustle up some extra pillows and a blanket for him.

"I'm sorry I don't have a guest room. Or an air mattress."

Eli gave her one of his trademark *are you kidding* looks. "I'm not supposed to be on vacation, Kay. The couch is fine. Now, what about Hope?"

Kay gasped. Shame flooded her face. She'd told her mom that she'd pick up Hope by eight o'clock and she was already twenty minutes late. She pulled out her cell phone and hit the first speed dial.

Eli walked away to give her some privacy. Luckily, her father answered, so she was able to explain things with a minimum of fuss. As expected, her parents were thrilled to keep Hope overnight.

When she turned, Eli was watching her with an inscrutable expression. Unsure what to make of his sudden change in demeanor, Kay pushed past him and pulled open the door to the linen closet in the hallway. Several towels fell out and hit her in the face.

"Don't worry about that now." Eli took the towels from her arms and shoved them in the closet. "We need to talk first."

"About what?"

"Everything. Clearly I missed something when I was digging into your life last year. It's time to rectify that."

"But nothing has changed. I don't do anything interesting. So what's there to talk about?"

Eli stopped and nailed her with an intense look. "I need to know who you've been with since last summer." He moved closer and Kay inhaled, immediately assaulted by his unique scent—warm and rich and disarming. She looked up at him, her senses swirling from the intoxicating blend of reactions that only Eli could cause.

"We need to talk about your lovers."

***All I Need is You* is available now

The Alexanders

AVAILABLE IN PRINT

Book 1 - *One More Day* ~ Jackson + Ridley
(contains Book 0.5 - *Teasing Trent: the prequel*)

Book 2 - *The Things I Do for You* ~ Nick + Raina

Book 3 - *He's the Man* ~ Matt + Penny

Book 4 - *All I Need is You* ~ Eli + Kay
(contains Book 3.5 - *Christmas with The Alexanders*)

Book 5 - *Say You Will* ~ Trent + Mara

FUTURE BOOKS

Book 6 - *Just One Thing* ~ Bennett + Katie

Blue-Collar Billionaires

  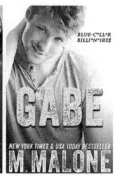

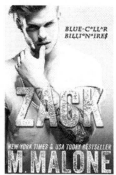 

ABOUT THE AUTHOR

New York Times & USA TODAY Bestselling author M. Malone lives in the Washington, D.C. metro area with her three favorite guys: her husband and their two sons. She likes dramatic opera music, staid old men wearing suspenders, claw-foot bathtubs and unexpected surprises.

The thing she likes best is getting to make up stuff for a living.

www.MMaloneBooks.com
Facebook /MinxMalone
Twitter @MinxMalone

Made in the USA
Middletown, DE
08 April 2016